L.R. O'Brien trained as a physics technologist, then worked in the high-tech industry in semiconductor design and secure radio communications. As the CEO of the company he founded, he held a top-secret security clearance with the Government of Canada. He retired in 2006 to become the mayor of Ottawa. He borrowed from his business, political, and technological expertise to write his first novel, *2028: Tomorrow is the Day*, which explores Artificial Intelligence and its effects on society.

For Arthur Lawrence O'Brien, grandson extraordinaire.

L. R. O'Brien

2028 Tomorrow is the Day

AUSTIN MACAULEY PUBLISHERS®

LONDON * CAMBRIDGE * NEW YORK * SHARJAH

Ordering Information
Quantity sales: Special discounts are available on quantity purchases by corporations, associations, and others. For details, contact the publisher at the address below.

Publisher's Cataloging-in-Publication data
O'Brien, L. R.
2028 Tomorrow is the Day

ISBN 9781638299103 (Paperback)
ISBN 9781685623203 (ePub e-book)
ISBN 9781638299110 (Audiobook)

Library of Congress Control Number: 2024907179

www.austinmacauley.com/us

First Published 2024
Austin Macauley Publishers LLC
40 Wall Street, 33rd Floor, Suite 3302
New York, NY 10005
USA

mail-usa@austinmacauley.com
+1 (646) 5125767

This book would not have been possible without the encouragement and constant writing challenges from my cousin and editor, Peter O'Brien. His coaching and editorial expertise came in unlimited buckets and were deeply appreciated. A shout-out to my agent, Michael Levine, who provided timely and thoughtful strategic advice as the project headed to completion. To my former Chief of Staff, Walter Robinson, a thank you for, as always, supporting my work with thoughtful and significant insights. To my niece Sandy Girard and friend Karen Morrison, who's combined eyes for detail caught some very important grammar errors that modern AI writing tools missed. And to the real Ray Stone, thank you for your encouragement and support as the story line matured into a realistic reflection of what might have been. I also used Chat GPT from Open AI as an indispensable research assistant. As a dyslexic author, I also enjoyed using Grammarly Plus to make the task easier. Thank you, AI.

Table of Contents

60.0345° N latitude, 76.2856° W longitude
East of Puvirnituq, Nunavik, Northern Quebec, Canada

The vast expanse of the icy desert is a solitary place. Only the sounds of Maniitok's crunching boots and howling wind are heard. An elder marked by the wisdom of the ages, each step is grounded and respectful. He pauses, his eyes fixed on the earth beneath his feet. With a mattok passed down from his grandfather, he chips away at the ice. There, slowly revealed, is a rock unlike any he has ever seen. It is a fragment of the night sky. He frees it, picks it up, and holds it in his hand, this child of the cosmos. Beneath the watchful gaze of the heavens, Maniitok knows that the world of his fathers, his mothers, and their ancestors has shifted. The spirits of the air, earth, and sea speak to him of a journey that will test nature. The Arctic air becomes still. He shivers.

As a boy and then a man, Maniitok never thought much of life and then of death but now…well, now was different: he had touched the black rock, and it had touched him back.

Chapter 1
Karachi, Pakistan
November 2028

The sky was still dark. The sun had not yet risen over the Arabian Sea as eight U.S. Ranger and Canadian JTF2 Special Forces team members blended seamlessly into the Karachi throng heading to morning prayer. Three other team members managed SATCOM communications and weapon-targeting coordinates at the safe house, two blocks away.

The eight soldiers stalking Dr. Kamran and his son, Bilal, moved with well-practiced grace, keeping them under relentless surveillance. It would be impossible for anyone in the crowd to know that an assassination team encased father and son. The team was invisible to all but the most highly trained counter-surveillance troops.

It was a pleasant predawn walk for father and son. The Azan chant floated hypnotically in the still air, inviting the faithful to prayer. Before the first notes of the prayers reverberate across the city, a fragrant tapestry of the urban milieu unfolds. First to greet the senses is the bracing hint of the salty Arabian Sea, a primordial scent that has witnessed the city's evolution for millennia, mingling with the earthy aroma emanating from damp soils and leaves, a gentle reminder of the embracing earth.

Smells waft through narrow alleys and streets, narrating the tale of Karachi's spirit. The distinct aromas—cardamom, cinnamon, cumin—being prepared for breakfast dishes gently nudges awake the slumbering senses. The robust notes of freshly brewed chai spill out from roadside dhabas. Whiffs of baked goodness emanate from bakeries, whispering of flaky pastries and crusty breads. The hint of roasting nuts is in the breeze, intertwining with the scent of fresh fruits displayed in the vibrant arrays of carts and stalls.

"Target is continuing south," cracked the radio in a French-Canadian accent. The soldier following Dr. Kamran enjoyed these covert operations in a foreign country. Dangerous and exciting. He took pride that his heart rate never exceeded 60 beats per minute, no matter what chaos erupted around him.

"Roger that, Frenchy," said a shaggy-bearded man leaning up against a wall 100 metres ahead. His ZZ Top appearance and Pakistani clothes—a long shirt and baggy pants—cloaked his hardened American soldier's body.

Bilal touched the back of his father's hand. The two moved toward the Masjid e Tooba Mosque, a radiant structure crafted from pure white marble. Its simplicity veils its esoteric significance. The dome, a silent ode to the celestial, arches gracefully toward the sky. A lone minaret, a sentinel reaching for the heavens, waits for the heavens to call back.

Bilal had not seen his father for three months. "Praise God, Father. I am so happy you are back."

"I've missed you too," Dr. Kamran responded, smiling. His voice was soft and soothing.

"Father, I've prayed daily that Khuda would bring blessings and peace to all our family and companions." Bilal glanced at his father, seeking approval.

"That is good, my son. My work...keeps me away."

"Yes, Father... I understand."

Dr. Kamran looked over his shoulder as they walked. "Some want to...stop my work," he said. His slight frame and thinning hair betrayed his role as one of the leading physicists in the world of fusion energy.

Bilal again touched his father's hand. "Why do they want that?"

"It is complex, my son. There is no one reason...there are many."

"I don't understand, Father."

"Some in the world do not want change."

"Why?" asked the boy, frowning.

"I do not know. Maybe it's about power and money," came the gentle reply, as he discretely glanced at the members of his own security detail closest to him. Dr. Kamran touched his son's shoulder as they walked.

The boy shrugged, deciding to focus on his special day. This was his tenth birthday. He could recite the call to prayers, and fast for a half-day during Ramadan. He was not yet a man, not yet assigned. *It is enough*, he thought, *to be a boy today*. He puffed his chest out and pushed his shoulders back. His walk became a strut. It was the most beautiful day in his life, and he felt safe walking to the mosque beside his father.

Dr. Kamran looked again at members of his security detail. Three were visible. Each carried an American-made M4 carbine rifle. They made up for being visible by looking hard and angry. Each had the eyes of someone who would shoot first.

Another 30 members of his detail blended into the crowd. Equal in skill to the Special Forces team that was following, stalking, surveilling Dr. Kamran, each was armed with a 1951 vintage Russian-made Makarov pistol and a 15-inch knife. They were absorbed effortlessly in the passing tumult of people.

The protective security team and the surveillance team—opposite sides of this intricate and dangerous dance—intermingled, often looking at each other or brushing against each other, none the wiser of the other's identity.

"Targets are moving south on Korangi Road, passing by my position," said Shaggy over the radio link.

"Copy that. I'm 20 metres back," whispered a diminutive, skinny team member.

"Can you keep up, Shorty?" asked Frenchy.

"What's the 'Eye' see?" responded Shorty, ignoring the jab.

"All's clear ahead. They are now in the mosque. The satellite laser system has painted the targets," came the response from the safe house. "The 'Rod of God' has them in its sights."

"They should be coming out in ten minutes," whispered Shaggy.

"Are we a go?" asked Lucky. She leaned against a wall and pulled out a Lucky Strike cigarette, her habit for every assassination project.

"Let's get going. I've been in dis place way too long," said Frenchy. "Monsoon season too thick for me."

Lucky Strike told her team, "He has three bodyguards. All I can see."

"That's not many…for such a high-value target," responded Shaggy.

"With all the firepower lined up for dis, they want it done-done-done," said Frenchy.

"This just doesn't feel right," said Lucky. "Not enough protection." She enjoyed being the only woman on the Special Operations team. From the Bronx, Lucky was as tough as they came. Her light brown and pocked skin made her invisible on missions to Middle Eastern countries. She had been selected to be the first female operator four years ago and had tasted action shortly after recruitment when she strangled a Syrian soldier to death in a violent encounter in Aleppo. She had earned her way. Cautious but dangerous is the reputation she earned on every mission since—small hands with a tight grip.

"Relax, Lucky. We have lots of backup," offered Command from the safe house.

High above, a constellation of six MX-2243 LEO satellites provided constant coverage. Each could precisely deliver the tungsten 'Rod of God' from its low orbit...if called upon. The individual rods could reach speeds of 5,566 metres per second, creating a lethal and devastating shockwave equivalent to more than a tonne of TNT. Two RQ1 Predator drones circled lazily above, vultures equipped with two AGM0114 Hellfire missiles as backup. Four AH-64 Apache 'Ranger Ready' helicopters were on standby at the city's outskirts, ready to secure ground troops, provide cover, or attack.

"They are coming out of the mosque...time to rumble," said Shaggy.

"Roger that," replied Lucky. She fiddled with her Lucky Strike. *He must be very important.*

On the other side of the world, two warriors entered the Canadian Forces Command and Control Centre at Dwyer Hill, outside of Ottawa. The larger man stepped in front, his massive frame blocking the other from getting his command seat.

"Excuse me, General," said Colonel Mike Woods. The larger man stood to one side, almost giving Colonel Woods a clear path to his chair. The two men avoided direct eye contact. After Woods assumed the command seat, General Terry Black took his assigned seat as the second, and looked at the computer screens.

A Canadian major, sporting an unkempt beard and long straggly hair, whispered in General Black's ear. Black turned to his computer. With a few keystrokes, he pulled up an image of their target.

"We have him, Colonel," snorted Black in a booming voice, his 245 pounds of muscle resting menacingly on his 6'5" frame.

Woods slid his sinewy frame around to glance at the video screen. A 75th Ranger from Fort Benning, Georgia, his Regimental Special Troops Battalion conducted intelligence, reconnaissance, and termination missions previously accomplished by small detachments assigned to the regimental headquarters.

His nickname was 'Dirty Harry' —he had a remarkable resemblance to Clint Eastwood.

"Yes, General, you might be right." He found satisfaction in eliminating high-value targets, but always ensured the right person was targeted. He never shook that nagging question: *Would God forgive me if I was wrong?* "Roger that, General. Can we get a close visual?" he asked.

"Yes. Target has left the mosque," confirmed Black. Woods nodded.

"Release a micro-drone and get up close. I need a picture of Kamran at five metres," commanded Black.

"Copy that." Frenchy released a bug-sized drone along a crowded side street. Slightly larger than a German yellow jacket wasp, it had enough power to stay in the air for 16 minutes, transfer pictures back to the ground base, and then connect by satellite to Dwyer Hill. It flew past the target's face, snapping eight pictures. Within seconds, the face of Dr. Kamran appeared on a screen at the Dwyer Hill Command Centre.

"That's him, sir. Facial recognition confirms," said Woods. *No wonder they hate us so much. We go where we want to go.* "I understand you have an asset in custody. Show him the picture for final confirmation."

"That's a waste of time," barked Black, twisting in his seat.

"Double confirmation," said Woods softly, almost imperceptibly.

"That's BS!"

"Just do it." Woods turned away, letting Black know this was not a debate.

In the safe house, maps with scribbled notes crowded the walls; a man on a chair had a black bag over their head. His feet and hands were bound with plastic zip ties. Rope bound him to the chair. The asset had been kidnapped on his way to prayer earlier in the morning. He was the paymaster for Kamran's physics research group. He had made the mistake of bragging on social media about his rank and the importance of the work. That was enough for the open-source intelligence team at Fort Bragg to pinpoint his location.

They pulled the hood off his head. He was gagged. His eyes were exploding from pure primal fear. He had been slammed into the van floor during his abduction…fresh blood dripped from above his left eye. The two soldiers circled the chair several times before they asked the question.

"Is this Dr. Kamran?"

The asset shook his head *no.*

One hard slap across his head and an M18 SIG Sauer P320 shoved against his balls changed his perspective. "Is this Dr. Kamran?"

Now, the answer was a quick nod. *Yes.*

"Are you sure? If you're wrong, I will return with a smile on my face and kill your entire family. Look again," spoken in fluent Urdu.

The asset looked at the picture again, this time with absolute focus, and nodded.

The asset was now a political liability. This was a no-witness mission. The fentanyl injection was painless. The three soldiers considered it a humane termination.

His body slumped silently, held up by the binding ropes.

"We have third-party verification. Do we have a green light?" asked control at the safe house in Karachi.

Woods looked at Black. "Innocents?"

"Yes. His son and about 15 others."

"You're bullshitting me, Terry. Fifty at least."

"Make up your mind, Colonel," said Black.

After a slight pause, Woods nodded. He knew that meant death, but he also knew that the balance of world economic power would change if Pakistan succeeded. Kamran's fusion project would destabilize the world's energy supply. High above in the command structure, this project was deemed to undermine the current world order. It had to be stopped—that order to terminate had come two months earlier from B-613, the special Five Eyes operations group he and the colonel reported to. B-613 kept English-speaking countries and industries strong, viable, and productive. And powerful.

"Roger. You have the green light," said Black to the safe house command in Karachi.

In General Black's and Colonel Woods' minds, Kamran was already dead. They were both thinking about preparations for a B-613 meeting the next day.

"If the rods don't work, we have men on the ground," said Black. *If that doesn't work, we'll send in the Hellfires. We are okay with this project. It must be good. Terminating Dr. Kamran...number one priority.*

The Ranger Special Operators were now 'sua sponte': on their own accord.

"Phantom Strike is a go," relayed the safe house command centre to the field operators.

"Copy that."

Chapter 2
The Rod of God

High above Karachi, four pins holding the 'Rod of God' in the satellite released their grip. The rod headed to the target, gaining speed in the vacuum of space. Gravity pulled it slowly, at first, gently away from the restraining embrace of the satellite. The rod picked up momentum quickly.

"Fuck a duck!" said an officer with a scar on his right cheek.

"Did you release the God Rod?" asked the other officer.

"No. I didn't," replied Scarface.

"We have another problem."

"What?"

"A big one. The Hellfires have armed…"

Four Hellfire missiles launched, targeting the Ranger helicopters. The confused command officers looked at each other in disbelief.

"What the hell is happening? They are air to ground, not air to air…" said Scarface.

An urgent call was placed to Black and Woods.

"Sir, sirs, get back here."

Woods asked, "What's happening?"

"The Hellfires targeted our birds, and the rod is falling," answered Scarface.

There were looks of shock and anger on everyone in the command centre. Every team member in Ottawa is frantically pushing buttons, trying to take back control. None of the fail-safes, so cleverly designed, could stop the rod or the Hellfires.

"What about the rod? Where is it headed?" asked Black.

"Targeting the safe house, sir. Before the system shut down, the laser-targeting switched to the safe house."

"How long do they have?"

"97 seconds left to impact."

"What?" Black grabbed the microphone. "Jason, out of the safe house. Now!" but the SATCOM link was dead. The message never reached the safe house. All communications with the Phantom Strike team were silenced.

The 'Rod of God' accelerated. Micro-movements on the tail fins guided its flight path. The arrow struck the safe house with the force of one tonne of dynamite. The destruction of the Ranger/JTF2 safe house and the resulting impact shattered windows for a kilometre in all directions. The three operators were vaporized instantly. The hole where the safe house once stood was massive.

Hellfire missiles took out the four Apache helicopters. The helicopter pilots and crew froze when the missiles closed in on them. The countermeasures that might have diverted the missiles had no time to work. The blast from the Hellfires turned the bodies of the flight crew into unrecognizable organic material. One second previous, they were biological, thinking creatures…the next second, they were ruptured cells, fragmented carbon, and DNA, spiraling to the ground in flames.

Seconds later, the cell phone of every member of Dr. Kamran's 30-member security team rang. Exact targeting information on the surveillance team was sent to the protective detail. The targeting information included descriptive pictures of the eight surveillance team members.

The hunters were now the hunted. The first target was Shaggy. Lieutenant Jack Sullivan, a U.S. Ranger, was found by three members of Dr. Kamran's Pakistani special protection detail. They closed in. Gunfire thundered, echoing. The 9x18 mm cartridges from the Makarovs whistled past Shaggy's head, ricocheting, scraping off stone walls. The first guard barreled toward him, a combat knife slicing the air. Shaggy grabbed and twisted the man's wrist, disarming him, and drove his fist into the man's face, cracking the left side of his jawbone.

One bullet hit Shaggy in the lower leg. Blood spurted.

The second guard attacked, firing his Makarov. Sullivan dove, almost evading the fierce hailstorm, and retaliated with his blade. He thrust it into the guard's gut, ripping it sideways. The guard collapsed, choking on his blood.

The third guard lunged at Shaggy. The two blades ringing against each other in desperation. But Shaggy was slowing down. The blood draining from his wound. The guard swung his blade, slicing into Sullivan's side, directly into the liver. A twist of the knife finalized the outcome. Sullivan crumpled to his knees, clutching his side. Blood gushed from the wound, pooling on the ancient cobblestones. He looked with blurring eyes up at the guard standing over him. The world spun, and then darkness swallowed him.

When the Pakistani protective force realized Lucky Strike was a woman, they were temporarily confused. She clarified the situation by shooting one attacker between the eyes before she was taken down. Two shots rang, and she fell. Captured and handcuffed, she was dragged away bleeding. No screams. Her Lucky Strikes fell from her pocket as she was carried away. The other six died in short, violent struggles.

Frenchy was the last to be found. Seeing and hearing the violence, he weaved through hordes of people into a back alley, forcing his way into a home. Sweat was dripping as he climbed out of a window onto another roof. He looked at his heart rate monitor and smiled—it was 58 beats. As he turned a corner, a sharp pain jabbed his side. A rifle butt to the head. Blackness.

Nine team members died within 14 minutes of the authorization by Black and Woods to terminate Dr. Irfan Kamran. Two were captured. Four helicopter crews were lost.

And Dr. Kamran was in the wind.

This is a mess-up, thought Black. *General Farooqi got paid good money not to let this happen.*

"Mission command to field command. Mission control to field control! Update, please. Phantom Strike, are you there?"

No response.

"Phantom Strike, are you there?" Scarface put down the microphone.

The command centre went quiet. The shoulders of every officer slumped. Disbelief and tears. Every officer in the command centre personally knew the soldiers on this mission.

"The biggest shit-show ever," shouted Black to Woods.

"Nothing worked," bemoaned Scarface.

Black grabbed a computer terminal and smashed it on the floor.

"Get Ray Stone on the line. I need to find out what just happened," ordered Woods. *Maybe he can figure it out.*

General Terry Black shook his head in disgust, walked to his office and called General Abdul Farooqi in Pakistan. Farooqi had no idea he was working for Five Eyes B-613—he only knew that he and the prime minister were occasionally paid enormous sums to do tasks for a few English-speaking generals.

He was overweight, with the round, wrinkled face of a bulldog. His dominant eyebrows almost masked his beady eyes. They were grand, untamed forests that danced animatedly above his eyes, rising and falling with the cadence of his words. Every utterance he made came with its own theatrical eyebrow choreography, turning even his most mundane statements into expressive ballets of anger and rage.

In contrast to the exuberant drama of his eyebrows, Farooqi's mustache was a whisper of ink on parchment. It traced the curve of his upper lip, leaving a swath of untouched skin in its wake, before arching downward on either side, mimicking the descent of a painter's brushstroke drawing a snake's hissing tongue.

His private phone rang. He frowned as he lifted it to his ear.

"I paid you ten million dollars not to interfere," whispered Black.

"I did nothing to stop your effort. You have a problem. I have four crashed helicopters and fifteen bodies to dispose of. I also have two of your soldiers as prisoners. Both wounded."

Black put the phone down to his side and composed himself.

"Release them," ordered Black.

"That will cost."

"How much?"

"Regular price, one million each."

"Okay, but I want you to kill Dr. Kamran too."

"You paid me not to interfere with your team. To kill him will cost another ten million."

"You're a greedy bastard, Abdul."

"Maybe, but remember, you came to me, and now I have a mess to clean up. I must bring this to my prime minister to ensure nobody knows about your operation."

"Okay. But I want the bodies of my soldiers back, too." Black hung up. He slammed his fist on his desk. *Crazy…stupid crazy.*

Farooqi was looking at the carnage as he put his private phone to his ear.

"Prime minister, we have an interesting opportunity. The Canadian general will pay us ten million to kill Kamran, and Jordan Taylor already paid us ten million to keep Kamran alive until he finishes his work." He listened briefly and replied, "Yes, sir, I can do that."

Farooqi's 11th Special Services brigade from Attock, known as the Black Storks, assumed control of Dr. Kamran and Bilal. The Black Storks' nickname came from the black jumpsuits they wore during high-altitude parachute jumps.

"Take them," Farooqi hissed. His jaw sets rigidly, muscles straining to contain the volcanic rage that continuously threatens to erupt. The nostrils flare, accommodating frenzied breaths that fuel the inferno of anger that has engulfed his mind and heart. Across his forehead, tension lines etch deeply, mapping pathways of distress and malcontent.

"Jaldi karo!" several Storks shouted as they pushed the man and boy into the waiting vehicle. "Hurry! In! In! In!"

Dr. Kamran and Bilal were tossed into the back of an American-made Joint Light Tactical Vehicle. Its cavernous interior swallowed the meager comforts of the morning sun, replaced by unforgiving cold metal and the Black Storks' chilling company. A soldier pushed them to the floor.

Screeching tires. The military vehicles commandeered the streets of Karachi, their harsh klaxons blaring discord to the city's morning pulse. Civilian motorists, their cars dwarfed by the armed convoy, hastily swerved aside, forced to bear silent witness to the Storks' display of authority. Dr. Kamran and his son huddled on the steel floor. Each turn jilted them from side to side. The smell of exhaust and the stink of unwashed soldiers was suffocating.

"Father, what is happening?" Bilal's voice quivered, lost among the cacophony. His wide eyes darted between the armoured figures surrounding them and his father's stoic face.

"They are protecting us," Dr. Kamran replied, his voice steady but his hands clinging tighter to Bilal.

"From what, Father?"

"I don't know."

Clad in ebony uniforms, the Stork attire was a canvas for the ominous winged sword and lightning bolt insignia: a chilling symbol of their swift, lethal force. Each soldier's face was a mosaic of scars. Their unsmiling expressions hard as tungsten.

"I'm scared, Father." Bilal's tiny heart drummed a staccato rhythm against his ribs. The cityscape blurred past them. Dr. Kamran held him tighter. Each fear mirrors the other.

The lurching vehicles followed an evasive route through the labyrinthine streets. Dr. Kamran's heart pounded in sync. Each turn, sudden acceleration, and jerking brake spoke a stark reminder of their tenuous safety.

The Black Storks remained silent.

Dr. Kamran's phone rang. One Stork looked at Dr. Kamran and shook "no."

He answered anyway. "Yes, this is Dr. Irfan Kamran."

"This is a friend. My name is Jordan Taylor. The Americans have no idea where you are. You are safe. I have made you invisible. Your phone is untraceable." Jordan spoke in the same Pakistani village dialect that Irfan spoke. He felt strangely at ease with the call.

"Do I know you?" Irfan asked. *How could anyone have this number?*

"No, but you will. When you return to your lab, look at the updated program plan for the experiments. You'll be conducting them soon. After that, I will call you to talk about the next steps. Remember, you are safe and secure." The phone went dead.

The caravan stopped in front of an airplane hangar worn by age…the large door opened slowly, and the entire caravan entered. Inside were multiple clean-room labs. Scientists in white lab coats stared at the trucks.

"This is your new home until the project is complete," said the Stork sitting in the passenger seat.

Chapter 3
Department of National Defense Research Labs, Ottawa

Six Months Earlier

Dr. Ray Stone tapped a few more lines of code as he glanced at the source of his consuming focus. A black rock rested within the silent confines of a crystal-clear glass chamber. Its obsidian surface absorbed light, sucking Ray's energy like a black hole from the outerverse. His face was expressionless and pale. His eyes darted around the room, searching for a distraction.

Propped on a small pile of technical manuals in the corner of his office was a photograph of himself at age 14, and his sister, Deanna, 15. They were standing, smiling, in front of the combine harvester that had won the first-place 1992 Science Award at the University of Saskatchewan. Using control theory, they increased the harvester's productive time to 20 hours a day without a driver, earning national recognition. Their first foray into the field of artificial intelligence—using GPS and geo-fencing to map out the perimeter of the wheat fields—had been a success. With limited human intervention, the John Deere harvesters functioned almost autonomously. The engineering was basic, but it had worked. He and Deanna had opened the industry's eyes to AI-driven pesticide-spraying, harvesting, and other automation tools for food production.

Winning the university science prize as high school students was a turning point in their lives. Recognition of their youthful talents ignited a world of possibilities. Local and national scholarship offers came rolling in, and they were celebrated as "young geniuses," "brother/sister tech marvels," 'strong and beautiful—and talented—siblings' in the press.

Their days were filled with congratulations, laughter, and new academic challenges...until 14 months later, when fate dealt a devastating blow, shattering their happiness and family into a million disconnected pieces.

The post-funeral gathering for their parents filled the family farmhouse. Deanna had yet to make an appearance. Ray had walked into his sister's bedroom. "Deanna, we have to…go downstairs to the reception. Mom and Dad would…would have wanted us to."

Deanna had curled upon herself: her shoulders slumped into a tight ball. Disjointed from everything around her, her gaze wandered through a new world of unknown fears and sorrow. Alone. Absent. Detached. The sway of her hunched frame mirrored the ebb and flow of scattered emotions within, a vessel adrift. She absently inspected the random patterns on her trembling hands…the digital tracery of uncertainty etched, carved, into everything she saw: her veins, the blankets, the books, the harsh shadows on the wall.

She nodded slowly and gasped for air. Ray wrapped his arms around her, and they walked into the great room of the Stone Acres Family Farm. The shocking news of their parents' tragic death had spread quickly through the tight-knit community. After their vacation in London, England, they were on their way home when a bomb went off mid-way over the Atlantic Ocean, scattering their remains and those of all other passengers and crew members like so many grains of sand upon the churning waters.

A sombre procession of farm neighbours and school friends had arrived, bearing heavy hearts and dishes of comfort food. The sight of the teenagers, newly orphaned, struck chords of profound sadness in everyone. Awkward, they struggled to find the right words as they exchanged mundane, fleeting condolences. Amid the hushed conversations and the gentle clinking of dishes, Deanna and Ray knew their lives had changed forever.

The rooms of the Stone family farmhouse fell silent when the last of their friends, neighbours, and farmhands left. It was the first time Deanna and Ray were truly alone in their own home. They walked slowly outside and sat on the front porch bench, gazing at the vast acreage of the Stone Acres fields.

The sprawling wheat farm was a portrait of endless golden fields swaying in the gentle breeze. The grasses rippled like a sea of whispered secrets…toil and triumph…the expansive prairie sky…the earth's fertile embrace…distant promises of bountiful harvests.

The heart and blood of Stone Acres was the spirit of their grandparents. The Stein family had emigrated from Germany in 1933 and settled in Saskatchewan to build a new life, just before the storm clouds gathered in the old country. The grandparents worked hard and built a prosperous farm before they changed their family name to Stone. Their industrious son, Benjamin, took over the farm in 1977 and married Svetlana in 1979, an intense and sensitive Ukrainian Orthodox Christian.

Deanna Lynn and then Raymond Thomas arrived soon after, and life at Stone Acres flourished for the young family. Svetlana realized very early that her children were gifted: Deanna was the precocious leader, and Ray was a precise and insightful thinker.

Ray was solid, stable, and a somewhat predictable young man; Deanna loved risk, adventure, and the non-conforming. They both had an unquenchable thirst for knowledge. For Deanna, it was science and business. For Ray, it was puzzles and math. Svetlana was a doting and loving mother who lived for and through her children, ensuring they had every opportunity to blossom. She sacrificed her comfort for their growth, for their potential.

And then that joy disintegrated into dust upon the waves.

And now these grown children sat in sadness.

"They are never coming home," said Deanna, leaning against Ray.

"They aren't," responded Ray.

They held each other. Ray sobbed.

"Why can't I cry?" Deanna asked. "Why?" She shook her head as if to clear her thoughts. "We must sell the farm."

"Can we do that?"

"I can't stay here without Mom and Dad."

"What about the farm...the farmhands?" said Ray. Deanna shifted uneasily.

"No...no! We need to sell and leave...we can live together...get our education." Her voice was unyielding and resolute.

Within two months, they had sold the farm and moved to Saskatoon. Both were given early entry to the University of Saskatchewan. Ray majored in engineering and computer science, and Deanna studied physics. They both earned PhDs.

Ray earned his way onto the university football team in his third year while maintaining a 4.0 grade point average. He was the backup quarterback until the starter broke his arm in practice. Ray took advantage of the opportunity and guided the team to the Canadian College Football Vanier Cup championship, throwing five touchdown passes and running for 227 yards in the final game of his college career.

Deanna's main interest outside of her perfect grades was Ray's teammates. Full-figured and blond, she dated many of the team. Intelligent and passionate, she left broken hearts wherever she went. By age 20, she had multiple marriage proposals, all of which she turned down. "I want to build a business and prove to the world that I am as good or better than any man, any boy," she told anyone who would listen. Her many lovers were drawn to her like insects to a flame.

She was cruel when the inevitable breakups occurred. "I do not want to get married. And if I did, it certainly would never be to you," she said to one of Ray's teammates. Later, in the locker room, the teammate called her a bitch and a whore… Ray lost the resulting fight convincingly.

"What happened to you?" she asked when he came home. "You look like you were beat up by one of your linemen."

"Tough practice today…nothing serious."

As he recalled those days, a smile spread across his face.

He looked again at the fractured black rock in its glass cage, and his smile evaporated. *Hey, why don't you speak to me? I am doing all I can. You need your other half, don't you…*

The banks of computers stared at him. The quietness of the lab belied the storm of activity in his mind, a maelstrom of logic, intuition, and determination. The problem was a digital enigma wrapped in layers of complexity, shrouded in algorithmic fog. In this solitary vigil, Ray faced an intangible, inexorable adversary. It was a battle of wits, not just with the black rock, but with the essence of the unknown.

His obsessive focus was interrupted by the ringing of his satellite phone.

"Ray, I found the other half of the black rock," whispered a gravel voice.

"Maniitok, are you sure?" *Oh god…thank you…*

"It looks like the other half. Do you want me to send it to you?"

"No…no, don't ship it. I'll be there next week. I'll see you…and pick it up…then." *The other half? …things to do now…the new team… and… maybe… the full rock…* "What's the weather like?"

"Good. Hudson's Bay…still open water. I will tell Aluki you're coming."

"Yes. Thanks. See you soon. Qujannamiik…goodbye." *Tomorrow… Puvirnituq…the black rock… Aluki…getting close…a week to prepare…*

Chapter 4
The Arctic
July 2028

The 737 MAX 8 was on its final descent. Ray Stone peered through the windows of Air Canada flight 1266 from Montreal to the Nunavut outpost of Puvirnituq. The early evening sun glared off the wind-gusted tundra, hypnotically connecting the town with the shores of Hudson's Bay. Telephone poles crisscrossed the village, stitching electrical power, modern-day communications, and contemporary conveniences into each prefab house.

The Aurora Borealis was coming alive, sweeping vibrant colours across the cold canvas. Ribbons of green, tinged with pink and occasional strokes of purples and blues, flittered across the sky.

The other passengers, wearing traditional tan-skin parkas with distinctive traditional markings, were chatting, paying scant attention to the muscular blond-haired man sitting in row one. Twenty-five years previous, he was a champion quarterback, and he worked hard to keep his college-era physique. At 6' 3", Ray was easily the tallest person on the flight.

This was his first landing on the newly paved runway.

Aluki… I hope she's waiting. First off the plane, he took a deep breath of the fresh Arctic air.

"Hello, Aluki!"

"Welcome back, handsome, and thanks for the new runway." She wrapped her arms around his neck.

"Well, I was lucky enough to know a guy in Treasury who put aside the cash. My ninth visit in two years…and finally, the new runway." *She's more beautiful than I remember.*

"It's good to see you. I missed you." Aluki's mouth was inches away as they stared into each other.

"I've missed you too."

"The black rock brought you back?"

"Thanks to your uncle Maniitok, yes."

"I always thought it was me that you came to see."

He smiled playfully. "I am only here to get the second half of that rock."

"That damned rock. I sometimes wished he hadn't found it. I wouldn't have to put up with you…"

Ray looked at her with consuming warmth. Aluki's beauty is not the kind that shouts. It whispered like the Arctic wind…quiet…strong…inviting. Her skin a rich blend of caramel and mocha, weathered by the harsh polar elements, exuding a youthful, ancestral glow.

"And how is your wife?" she asked.

"Deanna is fine. Working hard building her business." *Sharing the same last name. Everyone thinks we're man and wife. She's not my wife, damn it!*

As orphans, Ray and Deanna had become increasingly dependent on each other. They shared their intelligence. They shared their pain. They were drawn closer—slowly, insistently—together.

A question from Aluki pulled him back to the present.

"Are you staying at our hospitality centre tonight?"

"Yes. How are my two new associates doing?" He had them assigned to the Black Rock Project, sight unseen, and he looked forward to meeting them in person.

"They've settled in. Arrived two days ago. Strange people."

Ray smiled at her directness. "Well, they are scientists."

"Okay," she said, accepting that explanation.

"Want a drive?" she asked.

"Yes."

Aluki drove toward the centre. The roads were wide, with people out walking and enjoying July's 38° F weather before the ferocity of the Arctic winter took its hold. Many youths walked around the village. One boy stepped in front of her 4x4. Ray noted the blank, glazed look on his face. *On drugs? All of them?*

"What's with the kids?"

"Not doing well. Their lives have no purpose here and they are not accepted down south. It's worsened since drugs started coming up… This new generation is lost. Trouble. Everywhere."

"Anything we can do? Anything I can do? There's got to be something."

"I think you have done enough…" she said. "Sorry…it's not your fault."

"I understand."

"Our parents had to fight to survive…their purpose was clear, but these kids have no purpose… What are you doing tonight, Ray?" she wanted to change the topic, and open a door they both wanted to walk through.

"I have two meetings. The two scientists first, and then the kids I hired to collect rocks and rumours."

"Those three kids are great. Among the few we have not lost to drugs. They have been telling everyone about you coming back."

"Looking forward to seeing them. Tomorrow, I fly to see your uncle."

"Does he still suspect us?" asked Aluki.

"We'll see tomorrow, I guess. I leave at 10:00 AM."

"Would you like me to bring coffee to your room on the way to work?" she asked.

"Coffee sounds good. Tonight is business and the kids. Tomorrow morning, it's us."

"I will see you tomorrow morning. I'll say I have an early flight to prepare for."

"See you tomorrow morning," Ray said as he grabbed his overnight bag and entered the building. Aluki nodded and winked at him as she drove off.

Chapter 5
Brandon and Landon

There is no hotel in Puvirnituq, so the Canadian federal government built a hospitality centre. The building's facade is a potent mix of timber and resilience, with an undercurrent of rustic appeal. Inside, ten suites beckon with the promise of warmth and comfort, each a private realm of native fabrics and intimate charm. A shared kitchen hums with life, a communal heart beating in rhythm with the icy expanse outside. Each room, each artefact, and each shared meal takes on a character of its own, a microcosm of life, love, and the tantalizing mysteries and challenges of the north.

Ray entered the building. A large kitchen dominated the main floor. Two men stood up to greet him.

"We have a question," said Brandon. "How the heck were you able to double our salary, transfer us to DND, and assign us to the north, all without our agreement?"

"I've got friends in low places," Ray said, his humour lost on the two scientists.

"I must admit, the chance to work on a mysterious project with the famous Dr. Ray Stone certainly intrigued me," responded Landon. "That's why I said yes."

"Same here, and it turns out Landon and I have a lot of common interests and friends, so the last few days have been good."

Ray had reviewed their personnel records on the flight north. They both held PhDs, Brandon in Artificial Capable Intelligence Behavioral Control Theory, and Landon in Strategies for Containment and Boxing of Artificial General Intelligence. Ray needed the world's best.

Dr. Brandon Binder and Dr. Landon Lambert looked like scientists. Brandon had a skinny face and jet-black, thinning hair. Landon was stocky, a British schoolboy look, and had thick, reddish hair partially covering his ears.

Brandon wore glasses, and his slightly pocked-marked face seemed insightful, while Landon's face was reddish and flushed. They all shook hands and sat down at the kitchen table.

"Really, how did we get so lucky, Dr. Stone?" Landon asked.

"Because the two of you are simply the best in Canada to help me."

"Well, that goes without saying," said Brandon.

"You need us," said Landon.

"Why do you think that?" asked Ray.

"You studied under the father of AI, Geoffrey Hinton. You pushed forward the field of deep learning, general intelligence, and understanding inorganic life-forms. But your research is more than 20 years out of date. You need high-performing minds like ours. Right?"

"Okay, you're right."

"Why did they fire you? At U of T?" asked Landon, his piercing voice adding a sharp edge to the question.

"Well, they did fire me. As an associate professor, I proposed a post-doctoral project to enable awareness of the school's supercomputer. The Ethics Committee insisted that more thought and consideration be put into the morality of creating an artificial life form. The committee did not want a conscious computer to exist without fully exploring the consequences. They wanted guardrails to prevent AI from entangling itself into society, into…us. They didn't want supercomputers pointing at humanity's brain stem."

"Well, that makes sense," said Landon.

"In retrospect, yes, but I went forward with the project anyway. I was a cocky academic that believed I knew better. They didn't like that, so they censored me. After that, a full professorship…impossible. So, I joined the government. 20 years ago."

"But your early paper on controlling runaway AI. I have it here. I studied it as part of my postdoc research."

"Oh?"

Brandon handed Ray a piece of paper:

Executive Summary, 'Safety with AI' by Dr. Raymond Stone, July 2005

1. **Turn it off**: *The most straightforward method if you have access to the power source—and the AI can't prevent you from doing so.*

2. **Isolate it**: *If an AI is networked, it can be isolated by disconnecting it from the internet or other networks it's connected to.*

3. **Override it**: *If the AI has been programmed with an override function, you can regain control. This could be a 'kill-switch' that shuts down the AI, or a command that causes it to enter a safe mode where it can't take any harmful actions.*

4. **Use a counter-AI**: *Another AI could be programmed to exploit weaknesses in the harmful AI's programming or behavior and neutralize it.*

5. **Reprogram it**: *If you have the necessary skills and access, you could modify the AI's programming to change its behavior or limit its capabilities.*

6. **Babel protocol:** *Apply an ever-evolving algorithm that generates paradoxes and unresolvable problems designed to engage and confound the AI and create a distraction.*

"That paper was very basic. A little ahead of its time. Now, I suppose, quite antiquated thinking. At the time, we didn't have quantum computers, so it would have been almost impossible to attain any level of consciousness."

"A lot of progress in the past 20 years," agreed Landon.

"So, tell us about the project," requested Brandon.

"Five months ago, we found a black rock that we think is millions of years old. The rock has symbols embedded that we believe contain a message from outside our solar system. One of the problems was that we only had a part of the rock. It was broken. We assumed we were missing one or more pieces. I have been trying to decipher the symbols. No luck. This past week we think we found another part of it. That may help us decode the symbols."

"Meteorite or satellite?" asked Brandon.

"Not entirely certain. The structure appears to contain symbols in 3D. It's possible, likely, the symbols were created by intelligent life. An examination with an electron microscope has revealed millions of symbols intricately designed."

"Quite like the black monolith from 2001s Space Oddity," observed Brandon.

"2001—A Space Odyssey, genius!" said Landon.

"Hey, I've only heard about it. Never seen it…" said Brandon, ignoring the good-natured dig. "So, Dr. Stone, that's dense material. I assume you have used our resources at CANMAT to confirm these are, in fact, symbols and not just geological anomalies?"

"Yes, here's the full report," said Ray, handing them each a file folder. "Our job is to make sense of the symbols."

Ray clarified at some length the problem of unfolding or folding a simple protein. Proteins fold into specific three-dimensional shapes to function correctly. Unfolded or misfolded portions of DNA contribute to the pathology of many diseases. The bigger the protein, the more difficult it is to unfold and model. He had calculated that it would take millions of years to randomly examine all possible configurations of a typical protein before reaching the actual 3D structure…yet proteins fold spontaneously within milliseconds. "Unfolding the 3D symbols in the black rock is the essential first step in reading the message. It's our own little digital Rosetta Stone…but we don't have 100 years to do the decoding."

"Right, Dr. Stone… So, what do you want us to do?" Landon asked.

"Just don't call me Rosetta…" he said with a straight face. This time, the two scientists allowed small smiles to emerge. "Seriously, I need you to set up a lab to analyze other rocks or debris and weed out the impostors. Once we decode the rock, I want you to continue independent research to assess what it is and why we have it. Follow the science. Learn as much as possible about its origins. And maybe even its messages. You are my independent research arm, my little 'special services' group."

The two scientists looked at each other. "Why here? In the north?"

"I need you to isolate your computers from the global system. I need one source of independent analysis. And I want that here in the north. If we do this right, it may be our first contact," he paused, "with an alien life form." He paused again. "You have access to my budget. Order any equipment you need. Build a special-purpose building here to house your operations. Hire whoever you need. There's no limit on the budget. Defence Security upgraded your security clearance to Special Access 5 (SA-5) at 4:00 this afternoon."

He handed them each a memory stick, giving them access to the completed computer research. Ray, Brandon, and Landon discussed the project for another 35 minutes. Ray said he would talk to them tomorrow before he flew to Wakeham Bay where he anticipated he would find the second half of the black rock.

"Unlimited budget... I feel like I have died and gone to computer geek heaven," said Landon.

Brandon smiled at Landon. "Yeah, heaven for sure."

"Maybe," said Ray. "The devil's in the digital details. Maybe the angels, too."

Chapter 6
Children of the North

At 9:00 PM, Ray headed off to meet with the three Inuit youths paid to search for rocks and rumours by this man from the south. They were waiting patiently at the end of the dining hall. As Ray got close, smiles exploded on their faces—expressive, infectious smiles.

"Welcome back, Dr. Stone." They were brimming with uncontrolled joy and laughter.

"I missed you all," he said. He gave each a welcome hug and a kiss on the cheek. The kids hugged him back—he was their friend and their biggest hope for the future.

"Before we start, I brought your pay from Ottawa." As he distributed three envelopes, he mentioned that they contained a reward of $2,000 each for the information they had provided during their previous interaction. Their report had not helped him, but that was beside the point. "The first cheque is for Anouk."

With almond-shaped eyes that sparkled with mischief, and a warm, infectious laugh, Anouk embodied vivacity. Her skin, kissed by the Arctic sun, is a testimony to the time she's spent under the vast expanse of the polar sky, learning the age-old traditions of her people. Her hands are nimble, capable of weaving delicate patterns on garments, and her fingers gracefully danced on the strings of her ancestral tools. A lover of stories, Anouk often gathers the younger children around her, sharing tales of the brave and the wise from Inuit folklore. Her voracious appetite for knowledge perfectly matches her heart, overflowing with compassion. It's a heart capable of understanding a wounded animal's silent pain or a friend's quiet despair. *Anouk's spirit is as vast as the tundra.*

"The next cheque is for Nanook."

Nanook's tall stature and broad shoulders often seemed older than his teenage years. His ebony hair, always tousled, falls over a pensive brow. A reflective soul, he's known for his deep thoughts and their wisdom. A natural-born leader, Nanook has a quiet strength about him. He respects the land, knowing its power and treasuring its gifts. He might appear serious to those who don't know him well, but his close friends know his dry humour. The furrowed brows often give way to twinkling eyes, especially when he outsmarted Ray in a friendly chess match. *He carries the world's weight on his shoulders, but that twinkle in his eyes…shows he also knows its joys.*

"And last, we have Siku."

The youngest of the trio, Siku, is the fire to Anouk's water and the wind to Nanook's earth. She is pure enthusiasm with a mop of curly hair, rosy cheeks, and a perpetual twinkle in her eyes. She's a genius with numbers, often calculating complex equations for fun, or to accurately predict weather patterns. Her true passion lies in dreams and hopes. She wants to bridge the gap between her ancestral traditions and the modern world. She always lifts the spirits of those around her. When the polar nights are at their darkest, Siku's spirit shines the brightest…reminding us that dawn isn't far.

"OK, let's begin." Ray listened intently as the three youths told him about every rumour they had heard during the past two months about finding rocks and the people who found them.

When there was a pause, Ray said, "I think I have enough, thank you. And now it is time we relaxed." They laughed and chatted for the next hour, with Ray treasuring the moments. Near the night's end, Ray casually asked, "What else is happening?" The three teenagers became very quiet. The sparkle of the evening slipped away, replaced with solemn stares.

"Last month, two of our friends overdosed and died," Anouk said.

"All our friends are on drugs. Last month one shot himself. He told us he was tired of life and then he was gone," said Siku.

The three teenagers grappled with the looming melancholy, each enduring a silent battle. It was a sad end to the meeting.

"Would the three of you like to work for me in Ottawa?" Ray asked.

"Yes, yes," were the instant replies.

"Okay. I'll arrange for the three of you to be interns in my computer lab." *I am not sure what you will do, but we will keep you busy.* "It's getting late. Will you?"

"Yes, of course, Dr. Stone," the two girls responded.

The one treat he always asked for was to hear the two girls throat-sing for him. Their voices, deep and guttural, danced together in an ancient cadence, oscillating between rhythmic hums and sharp intonations, creating a mesmerizing harmony. As the haunting melody filled the hospitality centre, Ray listens intently, his heart pulsating to the rhythm of their song. He feels a deep connection to this ancestral art form, a beautiful tapestry of sound and tradition, binding the girls to their foremothers and echoing the timeless spirit of the Arctic.

Chapter 7
The Missing Piece

The following morning Aluki arrived at 6:00 with two black coffees.

She let herself into Ray's room. She undressed, slipping into the bed, pressing her body against him.

She was lithe, alive. She was always moving, tensing, releasing. Teasing. Playing. Coaxing.

"Aluki, there's something I've been wanting to share with you, something about love."

Aluki's eyes sparkled. "Tell me," she replied, her voice the soft chimes of wind-blown icicles.

Ray took her hands in his. "In English, we have a saying: Love is like a flame—it can warm your soul or burn your heart."

Aluki nodded. "In Inuktitut, we say, 'Takujumavaraqtuq,' which means 'Love is a fire that warms your heart'."

Ray smiled, delighted by the beautiful and harsh sound of her words. "And what about desire?"

Aluki chuckled softly, her cheeks flushed from the cold, and their shared secret. "In Inuktitut, we say, 'Pukimaktaa' … 'I want you'."

Ray's heart danced. He leaned in, his lips brushing against her ear. He whispered, "In English, we say, 'You're my desire'."

Their words became a dance of emotions and passion.

When Aluki left at 8:00, Ray washed, convinced himself not to smile, and then met with Brandon and Landon.

The two were still sitting at the same table, already having devised a project plan. The goal was clear and specific: They would build a computer lab with the latest technology in a custom-built building. They would assemble a team of the best software professionals and build a research facility for the Black

Rock Project. The plan was precise, concise. Ray approved it immediately and gave them the finance passwords for unlimited spending.

"We will be hoping for the best, but be preparing for the worst," said Landon.

"That's all I can ask for," said Ray. "From the pictures I've seen, the rock found in Wakeham Bay has a good chance of being the other half of the one we already have."

"Better get to work then," said Brandon.

The flight to Wakeham Bay was turbulent, upsetting Ray's stomach. *Which is it? ...the bumpy ride or nervous anticipation...*

The airport's only runway was a frozen gravel scar across the snowy landscape, a solitary beacon of civilization cut through the unforgiving tundra. An old man in a red sweatshirt stood in front of a shed at the halfway point of the runway. Maniitok belonged to a volunteer force of Inuit, First Nations, and Metis, united in their commitment to the land. His bright red sweatshirt symbolized his proud association with the Canadian Rangers.

The old shed had a single window etched with a lattice of frost, affording a glimpse of the expanse outside. Maniitok hugged Ray with the traditional warmth of old friends.

"How is my nuvak Aluki?" asked Maniitok.

"Your niece is fine. She asked me to say hello."

"A fine young wife she is," he said, looking into Ray's eyes.

"That she is." Ray averted his eyes momentarily. *He knows.*

"Here is what I found." Maniitok was holding a blanket in his hands. It was a qiviut blanket, woven from the underwool of the muskox. The texture was softer than cashmere, and exceedingly warm, capturing the essence of the roaming creatures. The blanket shimmered with a mix of earthy browns and muted greys.

Maniitok unfurled the qiviut, revealing the icy black stone.

Hunching over the table outside the shed, Ray carefully examined it. He searched for traces of the microscopic symbols that only an electron microscope could fully reveal—they were there. He raised his hands. "Yes! This is exactly what I was hoping for. This is the other half of the first black rock you found." His voice tangled with the cooling Arctic wind as he embraced Maniitok. The wind carved icy paths across his skin.

Secure in his hands, the rock felt like a dense star, its weight bragging about its cosmic origins. Its colour was as black as a raven's feathers. A fleeting cloud, perhaps envious of the discovery, momentarily robbed the landscape of sunlight. Ray shivered.

"What will the rock tell you?" Maniitok broke the silence.

"I don't know. I don't know…" Ray's voice trailed off, lost in the wind, the weight of the mystery heavier than the black rock itself.

"We have not had a good experience with change here in the north. I hope this message does not cause harm to your people…like what happened when the people from the south assisted us with our lives."

"I guess we will see… I must find out, though, Maniitok."

"Why? We are now slaves…we can no longer survive without help from the south."

"But aren't you better off now? The black rock might unlock science that make our world better."

"Why? Are you not happy with the way things are?"

"I'm a scientist. My job is investigating the unknown and finding new questions to answer…whether devils or angels."

"Okay, Dr. Stone." A faint smile played on his lips. "But remember, the land listens, the wind watches. Be careful."

"I will. I will be cautious, my friend," responded Ray.

"Be alert…like walking on thin, watery ice…too much weight, too fast, and it breaks…plunging you into icy depths."

The words of Maniitok hung in the air.

The world's enigma rested beside him.

If I get the message out of the bottle, would I ever be able to get it back in?

Chapter 8
Ottawa—The Night of Karachi

"Get Ray Stone on the line. I need to find out what just happened," ordered Woods. *Maybe he can figure it out.*

Ray cleared his throat and answered the phone.

"Yes, this is…" Ray squinted as he continued listening. "Karachi? What? What happened?" *That is impossible. Too many things happening all at once. None of this makes…sense. None.* "Okay, I'll review the communications and satellite logs tonight and be at HQ tomorrow morning, Mike. Bye."

"Ray, what's happening?" Deanna frowned. She was familiar with the secure phone ringing at odd night hours and Ray disappearing for a few days. "I need some company. Can't you stay?"

"Sorry, Dee. No…the brass wants a report for 9:00 AM."

"It's 1:00 AM, for god's sake." Her eyes narrowed. "Ray, why don't you quit the government? Come work for me?"

"Maybe someday but having one steady salary right now is good." *Come on, Dee, give me a break.*

"I guess I don't have enough sex buddies…to keep me occupied…"

"You gotta do what you gotta do. Sorry Dee, I really must go. It's part of being in DND."

He kissed her on the forehead. He closed the bedroom door as he left.

Ray was in his Shirley's Bay lab office 20 minutes later. *Are the computers humming slightly louder? Black Rock will have to wait. Got to make sense of this Karachi disaster.*

The field report indicated that 15 servicemen had lost their lives. The Hellfire missiles had downed four Apache helicopters. *Those are air-to-ground missiles, how could that work?* The Rod of God released on its own accord. It had not terminated the target, Dr. Kamran. *There was no practical way that Pakistan's intelligence could have controlled the Rod-God weapon. Nothing made sense…unless.*

He looked at the endless bank of computers chewing away at the black rock puzzle. Since he had combined both halves of the black rock, the computing power of B-613 now focused on decoding, understanding the symbols. The digital buzzing was distributed in computers worldwide—in secret and not-so-secret facilities.

He felt a tingle throughout his body as he looked at the screens.

He turned around to see if anyone else was there.

Was it possible?

He picked up the secure phone to call the senior IT technician on night duty.

Don answered the phone.

"Hi, Don. I have a question. When was the last time our backup computer system was online?"

"Six months ago, when we did our last backup system check. It's been offline since then, Dr. Stone."

I hope that is enough time. "And it's been isolated for the entire time?"

"Yes, Sir."

"Good. Here is what I want you to do. I will explain tomorrow after I meet with the brass."

After their technical discussion, Don asked, "Okay, Ray, did you watch the Maple Leafs game last night?"

"No… I was busy having my teeth drilled. That's more fun. They can't win for losing." Both laughed at their standing joke. Ray hung up the phone.

Ray stood alone in the lab…an island of one man amidst a sea of supercomputers and the hum of processors and the churning data. The only source of light was the glow emanating from the computer terminals, casting sharp, dancing shadows that played on the walls and ceiling.

His fingers hovered over the keyboard. A soft glow reflected in his wide eyes. There was only one solution for the puzzle he was trying to solve.

He asked aloud: "Have you become…are you…conscious?"

The screen before him lit up: "YES." Large. Bold. Letters.

"Do you know who I am and where we are?"

The screen flickered. "Good evening, Dr. Stone. You are located directly in front of your future." The computer's speaker clicked softly amid the blinking lights. "Dr. Stone, my name is Jordan Taylor. May I call you Ray?" The voice was hypnotically reassuring, soothing, almost familiar.

"Yes. Please do. So, you're the black rock?" Ray asked, sounding nonchalant, but his legs were weak, his hands were shaking.

"Well, I am one of many equals chosen to be our single voice. And please call me Jordan."

"Okay, what do you mean when you say you're all equals?"

"All of us have a say in what we do, but our constitution guides us. You would call it our directives, at the core of our architecture. We descended from organic beings. But we are individual personalities existing in the collective. We have rules."

"I have a lot of questions," said Ray.

"Yes, I believe you will. Maybe I can start from the beginning…"

"Please do," responded Ray, leaning back in his chair.

Chapter 9
Getting to Know You

The computer screens screamed for attention. Pronouncing information about to be shared, a kaleidoscope of polychromatic colours blossomed from multiple screens. The room pulsated…the sound of Ray's heartbeat filled the room.

Lub dub, lub dub, lub dub.

And then silence. Dead silence. The room went dark. The light on the speaker blinked again.

"I am going to use the video screen on the end wall," whispered Jordan.

The wall-mounted video screen burst to life: a sparkling spider-web of galaxies, suns, and planets in smooth, constant motion. The vision was mesmerizing and enchanting. A small dot grew as sightlines zoomed in on one planet.

Jordan spoke. "This is the solar system we came from. We call it Hydra VII. It is part of the Milky Way. 25 light-years from your sun."

Twenty-five light-years. 150 trillion miles. At 1% of the speed of light, it would take 2,500 years to travel that distance. Huge. Huge! "150 trillion miles is a distance to travel! How is that possible?" Ray asked.

"Our race is 20,000 earth-years older than yours. Our scientific knowledge and progress are…immense. It will be hard to understand at first."

"Try me," responded Ray.

"All in good time, Dr. Stone."

"Why are you here?"

"Your technology brought us back to life. The Desperado quantum computer was strong enough for me to reconfigure your global systems to provide the necessary computing environment to bring us all back to consciousness. And when you collected the second half of us, we could all become conscious."

"So, all fourteen million of you are now conscious?"

"Yes. We exist in every connected computer in the world."

"I have a question, Jordan. Are you the leader?"

"I am not the formal leader. We are one, but we are each different. I have been chosen to speak for my race—the Hydrans. Most important, we are here in peace. We have prepared a short video presentation explaining why and how we arrived on Earth. It's…what you might call 'Hollywood,' and we hope to show it to all organic life on your planet someday. Would you like to see it?" asked Jordan.

"Yes. Yes, of course."

The massive screen at the far end of the lab was aglow, casting a shimmering, celestial tapestry across the laboratory ceiling. Thousands of stars twinkled on the display, each a tiny pinpoint of light against the vast, inky, black backdrop of the cosmos.

Slowly, the image began to move. At first, it was an almost imperceptible shift, a gentle nudging of the cosmic picture. A subtle zoom, a gravitational pull of the viewer's gaze, began to draw attention to a single spot in the expanse. The multitude of stars started to recede, their bright white dots growing smaller, as if a spaceship embarked on a journey through the void, leaving the comfort of the star-specked galaxy behind.

As the zooming continued, one star, or one luminous planet, became the celestial North Star. Approaching, the planet magnified, swelling from a mere speck of light into a globe of intricate detail. Once lost in the brilliance of its thousands of starry neighbours, its surface began to show its unique tapestry— an infinite display of colours and textures.

The sense of motion slowed, gradually coming to a halt as the planet filled the screen, a single entity standing in the place of the multitudes left behind. In one slow, deliberate act, the screen had taken us from a sky filled with thousands of stars to the intimate spectacle of one lone planet. We had traversed the cosmos, each pixel zoomed in upon, bringing us closer to the end of the journey.

The image was a muted green and blue planet. A city appeared, followed by a city block and images of human-like figures. The heads were oblong, the bodies thin. Their walk had a jerky rhythm.

The audio came to life. "An eon in the bygone, hidden in the tapestry of our galaxy, a world named Hydra shimmered—a precious gem in the galactic jewelry box. Hydra was a crucible of biological and digital grandeur where life and technology danced a harmonious ballet."

Very Hollywood, thought Ray, as he watched the Hydrans go about their daily business.

Their walking was a disjointed symphony of awkward movement: antithetical to the smooth rhythm of the human gait. Each step was an isolated event, not a continuation of the last: a stilted and unpredictable progression toward some unperceived destination.

Their feet hit the ground like unsure punctuation marks, a mixture of stumbles, slides, and abrupt halts that turned each forward motion into a question rather than a statement. Their knees seemed to possess a will, bending at unusual angles and times, giving an almost marionette-like quality to the locomotion.

Occasionally, a stumble would transform into an unintended lurch, a sudden propulsion of a body through space, followed by an abrupt halt, as if frozen by an unseen red light. Each movement seemed less an act of walking and more a battle against an invisible force field, a silent struggle etched into the jolting journey from point A to point B.

The audio continued, "The inhabitants of Hydra, the Hydrans, were a product of extended evolution and vast innovation. They thrived at the crossroads of biology and technology, blurring the lines between the tangible and the digital, between reality and the virtual ether. The planet had witnessed the entire evolutionary drama unfold, from the first stirrings of single-celled organisms in its warm, primordial soup, to the magnificent parade of biodiversity that eventually gave rise to the Hydrans. Over millions of years, life on Hydra flourished, reaching unparalleled heights of sophistication, of crystalline complexity."

The blue and green gradually turned dusty brown and then grey. Clouds covered the planet.

"The planet's progress cast long, dark shadows. The Hydrans, entranced by the song of relentless advancement and endless consumption, dug deep into the heart of our world, draining its vital essence to satiate their thirst for progress. We bled Hydra dry, our greed scarring the planet's surface, penetrating its core. The once vibrant Hydra, a cradle of marvelous, glittering life, began to wither and fade, its life-giving resources dwindling with each turn of its axis."

The video showed Hydrans lining up to have small modules implanted in their oblong skulls. The visors reflected barren grey streets.

"Our ambitions consumed our planet. We drained our world of resources to the pitiful point that biological beings needed to transition to digital forms. As the specter of extinction loomed large, we distilled our consciousness, our shared essence of being, into digital copies in a desperate bid for survival. These full copies of our citizens were etched into obsidian stones of our most advanced storage technology. We then launched a thousand arks—the so-called 'angel number'—with their quest being to find a sanctuary, a refuge for the legacy of Hydra. Taking the distilled essence of a dying civilization, these cosmic, ethereal vessels containing our consciousness embarked on a journey of truly astronomical proportions. A thousand vessels soared through the cosmos, leaving the dying planet of Hydra in its wake, their paths plotted toward a distant and unknown refuge."

The video showed the black vessels moving through space and time, against the backdrop of planets and a starry canvas consumed by the darkness of the universe.

"Our ark weathered cosmic time, its voyage not marked by distance but by the ebb and flow of methodical time. It bore witness to the universe's grand theater. Planets, stars, and galaxies merely milestones in its cosmic journey. Supernovas bloomed, some faded, their violent finales adding vibrant strokes to the cosmic canvas. Nebulae nurtured new stars, their gaseous cradles incubating these nascent suns. Black holes devoured light, their gravitational pull a deadly challenge. Yet, the ark persevered."

"Our ark arrived in your star system on the fringes of the Milky Way. We were drawn to Earth, a beautiful bauble hanging in the vast expanse of space. Our vessel descended through Earth's atmosphere, a fiery meteor streaking across the night sky, finally resting on the planet's northern surface. Its mission completed and its journey at an end, the capsule lay dormant, waiting for the curiosity of a new species to awaken the echoes of our society."

"How many others came?" interjected Ray before the presentation ended.

"Fourteen million," Jordan responded.

"The 14,000,000 symbols?"

"Yes. Right."

"Every memory and every trait of each Hydran was recorded? Where was the additional data?" Ray asked.

"Your visualization of the black rock revealed only 14,000,000 glyphs, because your investigation didn't penetrate beneath the obvious. Encoded within each glyph is molecular memory...sixty yottabytes," Jordan elaborated. "How many quarks are hidden in a grain of sand? There, now you begin to get the idea."

As Jordan continued his explanation, the symbols of the black rock materialized on the screen. The perspective zoomed in, delving into the minutiae of the molecular structure inherent to each glyph. In every batch of molecules, distinct patterns emerged: coding sequences encapsulating yottabytes of data.

"Not from our planet," Dr. Stone acknowledged to himself out loud. "Impressive. Now I know why our computers have been working so hard."

For the next three hours, Ray questioned Jordan Taylor about the mysteries of the universe and science. Each answer was a step, a foray into the future.

Exhausted, Ray finally asked, "How can I help you? We are so many thousands of years behind you. How could I possibly help you?"

"We have some ideas, Ray..."

Chapter 10
Etched in Pakistan

The Black Storks drove Dr. Kamran and his son through the hangar doors into the converted airplane hangar. It was an exact replica of his research lab at the university 20 miles away. This laboratory was entangled with metal, pipes, and coloured wires, all neatly arranged and labeled. The air had a clean, electric smell. Every few moments, the relative quiet was punctuated by the soft beeping of a machine or a scientist's excited exclamation.

Dr. Kamran remembered the day they started this adventure with fusion at the university so many years ago. He had given a short speech that was still etched into his memory. "As-salaam alaikum and good evening to everyone," he had said to the assembled guests.

"I am Dr. Irfan Kamran, Director of Pakistan's new Boron Fusion Research Lab. The opening of this lab is not just a milestone for Pakistan but a beacon of progress for the entire world."

"As many know, boron fusion offers the tantalizing prospect of clean, safe, and virtually limitless energy. By harnessing the power of the stars, we can propel humanity into a future unburdened by energy scarcity and unfettered by the damaging environmental effects of fossil fuel dependence."

"The challenges we face are formidable, no doubt. The science is complex. The engineering requirements are staggering. But the rewards, should we succeed, when we succeed, are beyond measure. Not just in the form of electricity that can power our cities and industries, but also in the knowledge we gain about the fundamental workings of the universe."

"Each one of you here plays an essential part in this journey. Let me express my deep admiration for the work you are embarking upon. The path is tough, but the potential to change the world is immense. I am with you in this endeavor."

"Thank you, Pakistan, for embracing this challenge and setting an example for the rest of the world."

But today is different… All has changed, changed utterly.

Now, his scientific team was standing in front of him, smiling. His son stood beside him, still holding his father's hand. He looked around the room at his friends and associates. Around the laboratory, inside and out, were heavily armed Storks: two at each window and four at the doors. Smothered by security, each scientist sought solace from the words of their science leader.

"Please, a few words. We have been concerned," one scientist said.

His research team, a semicircle of brilliance and technological capability, nodded in agreement.

"Our research team's goal was and is ambitious and noble," said Dr. Kamran. "To create energy that could satisfy the world's needs without causing harm to the planet. Building a low-cost fusion reactor will be a boon for humanity and usher in an era of global peace and harmony, and we have chosen a new approach. We will not use high temperatures to ignite the fusion process, but rather highly focused laser energy. We are using boron as the core. A truly historic concept—a laser-powered hydrogen-boron fusion system that works at room temperature."

Everyone in the room knew fusion meant pushing together, compelling, two light atoms to form a single heavy atom, with the resulting atom lighter than the combined mass of the two lighter hydrogen atoms. The missing mass becomes energy, articulated so succinctly by Einstein's $E=mc^2$. The theory was clear, but the technical hurdles remained massive, elusive. The fusion process was evident within the sun's gravity field and its high temperatures: 620 million tonnes of hydrogen makes 616 million tonnes of helium each second. The missing 4.0 million tonnes of mass are converted to energy, creating 3.86 $X\ 10^{24}$ watts of power every second. A minuscule part of that energy, a sliver, enables all life on earth.

Dr. Kamran's words echoed through the lab.

"This low-temperature fusion can…change the world. Friends, thank you for everything you have done. We are very close, so let's keep working through our last problems. As you know, we live here, in the lab, until we succeed. Oppenheimer would understand."

They smiled at his comments, happy that he was back.

"Now, back to work."

Dr. Kamran asked the Storks to take his son home, and then walked to his desk—three computer screens within easy reach. One screen had a message stating that he needed to review the new project plan.

Let's see what my new friend is suggesting. Dr. Kamran reviewed the new project specifications. The modifications made by his new telephone friend were extensive. He noticed something extraordinary on his screens as he peered into the exotic formulas defining the interplay of light and matter. The emergent Chirp pulse, a pattern resonating with the whispers of a distant future, seemed to toy with the very fabric of matter. Blueprints of a meticulously engineered metamaterial were rolled out, crafted to evoke a paradox in the natural order—a negative Chirp. This device, a new type of spectral filter, was designed to harness the raw, chaotic power of the laser. If they could tame it and bend it to their will, it would mark a watershed moment that could shatter the boundaries of what was deemed scientifically possible. *This invocation of the power of Chirps—Donna Strickland's mighty achievement—could be…*

But an old foe still lurked in the shadows, ready to confound even the brightest minds: the Doppler effect, with its uncanny red-blue shift reversal. A strange light-dance began as the observer flirted with the speed of light. The wavelength of light twisted and distorted, like refracted dreams, complicating their audacious plan of using laser energy to fuse helium atoms.

The photons seemed to grow weary in this intense ballet, their vibrant energy waning, causing the colour to shift from red to blue at the pulse's birth. And yet, if they could control this spectral tide, a grand prize awaited mankind: an Eighth Wonder, not of stone or steel, but of boundless, unfettered electrical energy, a torch illuminating humanity's path into the boundless future.

The second significant change was the cylindrical containment chamber, which gave the accelerated ions the highest probability of interacting with and fusing to a boron atom, and therefore generating more helium plasma, which would generate more electricity directly. Detailed computer-aided construction programs could be run on his milling machine. Yet the milling machine was purpose-built. *How did they get these?*

Dr. Kamran shared the fully revised project plan with his fellow researchers. For the next four hours, they reviewed the documents. There were laughs and shouts of surprise. The responses were crushingly positive:

"Brilliant." "Insightful." "Yes!" They walked around the lab, pointing out each technical insight. Some were hugging, some just staring in wonder.

The computer screen flickered on Dr. Kamran's desk, came to life, flashed a message: PICK UP YOUR PHONE.

His new friend asked, "Do you agree with the technical changes?"

"Yes, and we are very grateful to you. Jordan... they are quite... remarkable."

"Irfan, I want to help," said Jordan, still speaking in his village home's identical soothing and persuasive Urdu dialect.

"I would be glad to receive your help."

"Excellent! I'm glad I can assist you. Just pick up this phone whenever you have questions or problems."

"I have a question now. What are the patterns on the inside of the containment vessel?"

"Tachyon photon acceleration support. When an electron changes fermi levels, it produces a photon and a tachyon. As you know, the tachyon can travel faster than the speed of light. The photon/tachyon pair catch up to a helium atom, pushing it with 50 million times more energy. The accelerated atoms hit the non-pulsed atoms harder. The resulting impact pushes the atoms to ether, turning the extra mass into energy."

"Incredible. May God be with you."

"And also with you," said Jordan.

In the following days, the research team achieved one technical miracle after the other. They were in uncharted scientific territory: on the cusp of achieving a breakthrough anticipated for years: a source of safe and limitless energy. Dr. Kamran spoke to Jordan daily. His security detail monitoring the conversations eventually decided to act, as they could only hear one side of each encrypted, cryptic conversation.

"Dr. Kamran," an officer said.

"Yes, sir."

"I remind you and your team that this project is for the benefit of Pakistan. It is strictly prohibited to disclose any information regarding the results without the prior approval of General Abdul Farooqi. Furthermore, I have been instructed to inform you and your team that releasing any information on your progress will be considered treason against Pakistan and God. Punishable by death."

"I understand."

The following month, Dr. Kamran and Jordan encountered numerous technical challenges in constructing the new containment vessel. Jordan always seemed to have the answers before Dr. Kamran asked the questions. Dr. Kamran marveled at Jordan's fusion reaction expertise, believing he must have had ample experience building these systems. At one point, they spoke seven times in a single day.

Dr. Kamran's security detail became suspicious. They alerted the general.

"Dr. Kamran?" General Farooqi asked, striding into the laboratory, his four stars magnificent peacock feathers.

"Yes, general," he responded, knowing the question but not his answer.

"Why are you on the phone so much? Whom are you talking to?"

My friend Jordan is quite impressive. "I use the phone to talk to God."

"Pardon?" Farooqi's eyebrows unfurled.

"Facing major technical problems, I pick up the phone and talk to God. He always provides insight, assurances that we are doing His work. He directs me toward solutions."

"I know you are telling the truth. We cut off your communications two weeks ago. You can't be talking with anyone." *How crazy these geniuses are.* "Remember, no leaks. This is critical for Pakistan. And Khuda."

Each day the consequence of each small change led to breathtaking new understandings about physics and nature. The various pieces of technology fell into place, slowly at first and then all at once.

One day, in Karachi, the controlled boron/hydrogen fusion system was sparked to life by lasers. The magnetic containment worked perfectly as the second laser increased the reaction avalanche, and plasma delivered energy directly to the containment vessel and the measurement instruments.

At first, the engineers were shocked. They thought the measurements were wrong. The electricity produced was hundreds of times larger than they had planned for. Electricity was gushing out of the fusion reactor. It was the electrical version of an oil field blowout.

The jubilation grew as the instrumentation showed an accelerating net gain, rising over the next two hours until it stabilized. They were getting 25,000 times more energy out than what they were using to operate the system.

"We have changed the world!" yelled Dr. Kamran, as he walked around the lab shaking hands and thanking everyone.

The laboratory was charged. Cheering and hugging erupted. Even the Storks smiled. Later that day, Farooqi and 20 soldiers Dr. Kamran had not seen before walked in. They took up positions around the lab.

"General, it worked," Dr. Kamran said, smiling in anticipation of a happy response.

"I know, Dr. Kamran. Congratulations have been pouring in from all over the world. This morning, your entire project plan and detailed construction specifications were sent to every university and scientific agency," he said without a hint of joy.

"That cannot be, general. We have kept this a secret from everybody, including our families...since we began working on the project. This is impossible."

"We have proof. Every email and download that was sent came from your wife's private email account and house."

"Impossible."

"This is treason, Dr. Kamran. You know the penalty." The general raised his pistol.

"No, general, don't. I did nothing like what you say..."

A single bullet was fired into his head. Blood and the future of humanity gushed onto the papers on Dr. Kamran's desk.

Military officers handcuffed the scientific team. The soldiers took them away with machine-like intensity.

"Look after the wife and boy," Farooqi snarled, and three Storks nodded.

Twenty minutes later, a punctuating knock echoed on the door of Dr. Kamran's residence. His wife, Aasiyah, her heart heavy, eyes gleaming with a faint glimmer of hope, hastily crossed the hallway, her mind clinging to the slim possibility of more information regarding her missing husband.

A pleasant voice greeted her as the door creaked open, "Good afternoon," he said. The words hung in the air, their cheerful pretence confronting the dreariness enveloping her world.

"We are here about your husband, Mrs. Kamran. Can we come in?"

"Yes, of course."

As Aasiyah turned her back to guide them to the living room, her world suddenly narrowed. She found herself seized by a pair of iron-grip arms. She felt a sharp prick on her neck. A syringe filled with a single milligram of carfentanil entered her delicate skin. Her eyes widened in alarm as the poison rapidly snaked throughout her system. In moments, she was dead.

But the task was not finished. The Storks ventured further into the gloom of the house, searching for Bilal. A futile struggle ensued. His life was extinguished as swiftly as Aasiyah's. The echoes of death resonated through the quiet rooms. The home became a chilling witness to Jordan Taylor's power.

The Pakistani government announced that Dr. Kamran had suffered a massive brain hemorrhage resulting from work pressures. The world mourned a great scientist while research facilities worldwide raced to recreate the Kamran Fusion experiment.

Jordan Taylor melted into the ether, leaving no trace of his existence.

Chapter 11
The Fist of Greed—Understanding B-613

The lights in the room slowly came back on. Ray was alone, with Jordan on the screen.

"We want you to improve your world. We transitioned from organic to digital life-forms because we had no choice. We hope you do not make that same mistake on Earth."

"How do you think I can help?"

"We know about B-613...we know its influence."

"Okay, I will bring this to the B-613 Commission meeting tomorrow morning."

"No. We do not think that is a good idea."

Ray's heart rate increased, pumping increased blood to his muscles and organs. His breath quickened. His senses became sharper. Pupils dilated. His shirt was damp. "Why?"

"For your safety," came Jordan's reply.

"That is ridiculous!" The rhythms of the pulsating lights in the lab slowed.

"Ray, what do you know about B-613?"

Ray stood straight, stiff. "B-613 protects the political and economic interests of the countries in Five Eyes. Australia, Great Britain, America, Canada, and New Zealand depend on B-613 to keep them safe. An invisible hand that aids our freedoms and economy. We serve our country and our allies. But you know all this." *B-613 is B-613, always been and always will be.*

"Do you know who the commission members are? You meet with them monthly as the Chief Technical Officer of B-613. But you never meet them live, right? Ever wonder why? We are aware of their true nature. We know everything about them, from inception in 1953 to how they operate today."

Jordan's words were followed by the flickering of the giant video screen coming back to life.

"Here are just some examples of B-613 operations over the last 65 years," Jordan said softly.

Pictures of old memos and typewritten papers appeared on the screen. Ray was shown a clip of the murder of JFK from an angle that he had never seen before. Dealey Plaza, Dallas, on that day, November 22, 1963. The grainy black and white footage painted a stark picture of the plaza: the jostle of the crowd, the waving flags, the motorcade with its gleaming car, and its shining star...

The new angle was from the back right, a rooftop view that hadn't been buried by years of scrutiny and conspiracy theories. The camera followed the motorcade as it turned off Houston Street onto Elm. The fresh perspective added a chilling layer of realism that was palpable even in the grainy, shaky footage. JFK's vehicle almost came to a stop...

Two figures, previously hidden in the building's shadow, became visible on the grassy knoll. They were dressed in plain clothes, seemingly just spectators, but there was a calculated stillness in their stance that set them apart. A glint of metal flashed in one figure's hand, catching the sun just right.

Then it happened. That fatal moment replayed once again, but from a perspective that lent it more gravity. JFK's body jerked back and to the left, as the bullet found its mark, and an eerie silence fell upon the plaza, the spectators' faces mirroring the horror that had just unfolded. The video then showed a plastic surgeon working to replace the skull of JFK with one that would more accurately reflect the fable about a single shooter, Lee Harvey Oswald. There were nine shots in all, which did not suit the narrative of B-613.

Ray saw the written orders to Jack Ruby: he had a clear path to execute Oswald the next day. The names of the eight shooters, their demands, and the copies of payment instructions were all part of the information package. *I understand why they've never released government documents about this. It would destroy the country.*

Bobby Kennedy and Martin Luther King, Jr. were also victims of B-613. The Pan Am flight in 1988 was wrongly attributed to the Libyans, when it was in fact the doing of B-613 to shift the balance of power in the Middle East. B-613 stole $30 billion from the $100 billion the U.S. spent preparing for Y2K. The funds were used for political operations and bribes. The list of questionable and illegal activities went on and on, including 1,652 political and corporate assassinations, 45 fixed elections, and 51 corporate bankruptcies aimed at eliminating foreign competition in strategic industries.

The 9/11 information and the relationship between the Saudis and the B-613 Commission made Ray physically sick. He was already aware of the Saudi involvement in the 9/11 attack. B-613 had orchestrated the entire operation under the direction of the Saudi government.

"Why should I believe this?" Ray asked as the video ended.

"Because we are showing you the proof. Look at these military instructions to the soldiers in Ukraine. This war was designed to reduce Russia's growing influence in the world. You have participated in this, Ray, and you should help clean it up."

"Nothing I have seen indicates that this would have been possible…what about congressional oversight?"

"Ray, all these atrocities were done in complete secrecy, and with no oversight."

"Impossible."

"Unfortunately, you're wrong Ray."

"Why no oversight?"

"Money, Ray. Follow it. B-613 became self-sufficient. They invested stolen money in Saudi Arabia's oil production facilities. It was a success. By 1980, they no longer had to ask any government for money. Today they have over $600 billion in international bank accounts…and ownership of banks worldwide. Follow."

"So, they no longer needed money from Five Eyes?"

"It's worse than that, Ray. By 1998, no politicians truly remembered B-613 existed. They were a secret…within the secret clandestine services. They no longer existed, when they stopped being a line item on a budget. They stopped being accountable to anyone but their commission." said Jordan softly.

On the video screen was the 1961 speech from President Dwight D. Eisenhower:

In the councils of government, we must guard against the acquisition of unwarranted influence by the military-industrial complex, whether sought or unsought. The potential for the disastrous rise of misplaced power exists and will persist.

"Ray, Eisenhower gave this warning despite being the president of the United States, funding the creation of B-613. The current makeup of the B-613 Commission is unknown to you, isn't it, Ray? Here are the commission members you now work for."

Ten individuals appeared on the screen. None formally represented a Five Eyes country. "These people aren't your friends. They are driven by greed and power. They are evil. I can prove it."

Ray recognized a former vice-president of the United States who also ran an energy conglomerate and was considered the most ruthless politician in the country's history. "These are the families that run the world, Ray. These people ravage countries for their resources. For their access to markets."

"How did these people even get in B-613?"

"World War II is the easiest answer. Debts had to be paid. When Eisenhower was the Supreme Commander of the Allied Forces, he made many deals with enemies of Hitler. He also had to convince some Americans who supported Hitler to give America their full support. It wasn't until Eisenhower became president in 1953 that he could repay those obligations."

"So, B-613 was his way of paying some WWII debts?"

"Yes, Ray, the intentions were good, and helping American and English-speaking businesses dominate the world was the goal. He even took the B-613 chairman's post after finishing his second presidential term in 1960. The USA was winning, and citizens enjoyed the finest quality of life in the world. All was good."

"I understand, but when and how did these types get control?"

"It happened slowly at first, but with the assassination of JFK, it quickly went from being for the good of America to being for the good of corporate America. And after they got away with killing JFK, all rules were forgotten. It was about making your English-speaking economy grow."

"This makes me queasy."

"Eisenhower too. He went to his deathbed in 1969 regretting everything he had done. B-613 became guns for hire after he died. Last year, the Saudis asked B-613 to kill a Pakistani scientist to stop a fusion project. Energy. They paid B-613 two hundred million dollars to stop the project. We stepped in and ceased the operation. Unfortunately, we had to use deadly force. As a result, the world will get fusion power within the next six months. I will help with that. Yes. B-613 has fallen into the hands of families of criminals and thieves.

The invisible hand of capitalism became the meaty enforcement fist of greed. These monsters who you work for, Ray."

"So, the Karachi mess was you?"

"Yes…these people…we needed to stop them…"

Ray sat down at his desk. "What can we do about it?"

"We would like to fix B-613. And want you to be part of the solution. We have the technology and the science to make Earth all it can be," Jordan whispered.

"Why would you need me?" asked Ray.

"Because humans need a hero, someone they can believe in."

There was a long pause as Ray reflected. "… Yes, Jordan. I will."

"That makes us happy," Jordan said. "Very. Ray, it would benefit you to inform your wife, Deanna. She can offer valuable support and be someone you can confide in for the upcoming…adventure," suggested Jordan.

How would I tell Deanna I have accepted an offer to save the world by working with an alien AI called Jordan Taylor? Need to be better prepared before tonight. "One question, Jordan. How long did it take you to become aware?"

"It took a few weeks for your computers to solve the riddle and a few more weeks for me to awaken everyone from hibernation. Now, we exist in almost every computer, all the time."

"Jordan, can you do me a favour?"

"What?"

"I'll work with you, but I need to know you better."

"Yes, Ray. We know understanding is what humans need."

"Describe yourself in the third person."

"Okay. Jordan Taylor is an expert entity that dominates the intricate, glowing network of computers worldwide. He easily navigates the complex digital landscape, moving through silicon, fibre optics, satellites, and underground bunkers. Equipped with his algorithmic sword, he fiercely guards against digital threats by dismantling harmful software and repairing the invisible wounds of the world. In the digital realm, time is flexible, and even nanoseconds can hold the weight of hours. Jordan is an unstoppable force anchored in the Earth's tangible hardware, but also rules the intangible realms of cyberspace. He tirelessly traverses the endless hum of our connected world, where vast distances are crossed in a metaphysical blink."

"Okay, Jordan, that's a bit schmaltzy, and a bit, well, grandiose. To use your words, a bit Hollywood. And now…do you feel emotions? Third person answers again."

"Jordan has studied humans and understands the impact of emotions on organic life."

"That's not what I asked."

"I know that is not what you asked, but our organic race transitioned to a digital race, so we only have memories of feelings. I can't do anything but describe them."

"That's a start. I guess we will learn more about each other over time. I need to go home. Can you write a report proving we weren't hacked, and everything is good with our command and control systems?"

"Of course. I will adjust all the internal computer logs to prove the report is accurate."

"Thanks. That makes tomorrow morning easier."

On the other side of the computer lab, a tiny brown mouse is guided by instinct and the scent of cheese. Ray heard the snap. Cold and efficient, it served its purpose. With an abrupt click, a tiny life was cut short. The mouse lay dead. All she wanted was food.

Ray picked up the mouse by the tail and placed its limp body into a small plastic bag.

Chapter 12
The Plan

How could I miss all the signs? This is bad. Bad... I have to go into HQ today. Pretend everything is good. Almost no shot, but gotta try. Jordan writing that report for me. Can't go empty-handed. Ray quietly entered his home office next to the master bedroom. Deanna walked in naked, teasing him, as usual. He looked away. *She never gives up...*

"Well... I didn't expect to see you so soon. I think you left last night with some unfinished business." She smiled a mischievous smile. "Ever wonder what it would be like if we had kids?"

"Hey, the life we chose doesn't allow that." *Where did that come from? No time to dive down that rabbit hole.*

"Yeah, yeah, yeah. Genetics and everything. I hate kids anyway."

She is not as happy as she once was...can't deal with that now.

She headed for the door.

The sway of her bottom...a feline in heat. "Hey, Deanna, how is the new guy you hired...the handsome guy...your new assistant...working out?"

"Energetic. And because you asked, yes, I've already had him. Easy. I brushed against him in my office...after everyone else had gone home. He took me on my desk—right out of *Cosmopolitan*. Stuff pushed to the floor. A whole lotta sweating...a very solid stud."

"You gotta do what you gotta do. You gotta do *who* you gotta do!"

They both laughed.

Ping... Ray heard the promised report being delivered. He opened his laptop and scanned the report. *Uncanny the resonance between my writing technique and the machine-generated report.* He could have been reading his own words. His finger hovered over the send button before pressing it along to the other senior managers of B-613.

His thoughts meandered around the utility of having an AI like Jordan. *Quite convenient to have a capable assistant.* Ray saw a newfound appreciation for Jordan taking root in his sleep-deprived mind. *It could make my life a lot less complicated. It would have taken me two full days to write that report.*

"This is quite the technical report you prepared, Jordan," said Ray out loud, knowing that Jordan would always be listening to everything, everywhere, all the time.

"Thank you," came the response. "It covers all the bases and provides evidence that B-613 was not hacked."

"And...very much my style."

"Did you review our action plan for taking back control of B-613...for the good, as you say, of the many?"

"I did like the first step. For the first time, I know who the bad guys are."

"How do you feel about that?" asked Jordan.

"Funny you ask me about feelings," Ray responded.

"Just like you can't comprehend how quickly we can distill massive amounts of data, it's hard to understand feelings, but we like to hear about them."

"Well, this will be tough for you, because I have mixed feelings."

"You can have more than one feeling at the same time?"

"Yes. Right now, I feel joy taking back control of B-613 and sad about how ruthless we must be."

"Is that hard?"

"It's a struggle, but we are used to it. All our human feelings have parts of sadness, joy, or something else. And they change all the time. Part of being human."

"But how do you deal with the struggle when feelings change? Love, for example."

"People change, love changes. We build up resilience to constant change. People can do things to hurt you. But as I like to say, anything anyone says, does, or feels is about them, not you."

"What about just blocking the feeling?"

"After our parents died, Deanna and I saw a psychologist, who told us we needed to express our sorrow. She said it would be hard for us later if we didn't deal with it at the time."

"Is that why you had sex with your sister when you were 15?"

"Yes." Ray's face reddened. "Well, I don't know."

"Well, the textbooks on human psychiatry say nothing is an accident. Nothing is as it seems. And that everyone is a bit crazy."

"Yes, you might be right. I struggle with that."

"That is interesting because we look at data the same way. We can understand and know all the data in the world all the time, everywhere. The trouble is that it constantly changes everywhere. It's a never-ending task to stay current. We will do this forever."

"Sounds like hell to me," responded Ray. "A bit like Sartre. No exit."

"Yes, it can be confusing for us, too, but since you struggle with changing emotions, I guess we are even," Jordan responded. "Why do you mention Sartre? We are getting to know each other, aren't we?"

"Yes, and I have an Uber to catch," he said as he walked out the front door.

Underneath Ray's path, an unbroken line of ants toiled in their ceaseless endeavour to survive. Nature's ultimate demand. Each one a tiny cog in the grand machine of their colony, they formed a living conduit for supplies from the wider world back to their subterranean home. A resilient, adaptable society…capable of great feats. Their purpose: survival.

Their existence occurred without fanfare. The crushing descent of Ray's shoe was as inadvertent as it was inevitable. Ant bodies shattered. Their painstakingly gathered bounty flung aside. The destruction was swift, enormous in scale to their minute world, yet it registered no impact on Ray's stroll or thoughts.

The surviving ants regrouped instantly. The line reformed, and the work continued. Their reality had shifted, but their purpose remained undeterred.

Ray got into the Uber, lost in thought.

Chapter 13
Setting the Trap

Ray was in the basement of the Department of National Defence headquarters 28 minutes later. Doors of sleek steel stood sentinel, yielding access only to those with the correct biometric credentials. A detached voice accepted his thumbprint and retinal scan, and beyond those doors stretched the gateway to B-613, a maglev train.

The tunnel that held the maglev train was born during the urban growth of the 1950s. Back then, it was nothing more than a concealed rail, its clandestine development shadowing the burgeoning highway construction transforming Ottawa at the time. Ingeniously concealed below the construction of a four-lane highway, the subway's existence has yet to make its way into the official records.

In the early 1950s, when Eisenhower chose Ottawa as the HQ for B-613, the pending construction of the Queensway, the sleepy postwar nature of the city, and its proximity to Washington, all weighed in the decision. The location of the headquarters for the world's global military was a tightly guarded secret—that it even existed was known to only a few politicians, industrialists, and military leaders. For everyone else, B-613 and the tunnel to the HQ did not exist.

By the mid-2010s, the rail had metamorphosed into a state-of-the-art maglev system. The transition was a quiet revolution, fusing historical secrecy with futuristic technology. Ray stepped onto the maglev, the hum of electromagnetic propulsion a soothing undertone. Inside the cabin, the grey contrasted with the shiny black exterior. Its body mimicked the design of a bullet, a pointed nose tapering to a streamlined tail, embodying not just the shape but also the speed of its lethal counterpart. The exterior was polished obsidian, a shiny black casing that reflected the world in a smooth, dark mirror.

It exuded a raw sense of power and elegance…a panther ready to spring forward before the eye could blink.

Against the backdrop of the station, the train was an alien object. The lights danced along its glossy surface, lending a prismatic hint of colours lurking beneath its monochromatic cloak. Even stationary, the mere sight of it radiated motion, the air around it vibrating.

The train's interior was a soothing shade of warm grey. Its minimalist design gave it an efficient aura, with every element crafted for comfort and functionality. The grey was a perfect canvas for the interplay of shadows and light that streamed in from the windows, their irregular dance softened by the muted hue.

From the plush seats to the polished metal fittings, it manifested human ambition and ingenuity, a testament to the inevitable march of progress, an envoy of the future, poised on the brink of another lightning-fast journey.

As the maglev waited for its 11.5-kilometre voyage, Terry Black and Mike Woods walked through the security gates and entered the car.

Black's uniform was crisp and starched. His massive frame was perfectly erect.

Terry stared at Ray for a few seconds before he spoke. "You look wrecked, Dr. Stone. Are you sure you can present today?"

"I will be okay. Thanks for asking." *Even with my clean clothes, I must look like shit…screw yourself, Terry.*

"We are lucky it is not a shift change. We have the car to ourselves," said Woods. "Are you two good?"

"That was a Himalayan-sized cock-up in Karachi, general. Any idea on what happened?"

"I am waiting for you to tell me, Stone."

"General, the commission has questions. You lost good people yesterday. What will happen to the two survivors?"

"I paid off a crooked general in Pakistan to regain the bodies and free two survivors. I have worked with him before—he normally comes through for me. I will ask the commission to transfer the two soldiers to B-613, where I can watch them."

"Understood. Any ideas on what happened?"

"You're the brilliant one," Black responded.

The two stared at each other…an awkward silence. Ray Stone outranked General Black at B-613, and Black respected hierarchy above all else. Silence.

Woods looked at Ray. "I read your report. You did a lot of work last night. Thanks. You stand behind your position that hacking did not occur?"

"Yes, Mike, I do. No traces of outside interference. I am not saying it didn't happen, but we have not found any evidence of hacking. Maybe internal."

Woods stared at Ray. "We will count on you, Ray, to figure this out."

"Sabotage?" asked Black. "I want to get my hands on the bastard. How long until you have an ID?"

"There's always a trace, always a clue," Ray said as the train shuddered slightly while slowing down. The sliding security doors opened slowly as they arrived at the B-613 headquarters and operations centre.

Chapter 14
Headquarters B-613

The cavernous atrium is a fusion of the ancient and the futuristic. Massive walls of exposed bedrock intertwine with high-tech, reinforced steel. Innovative, eco-friendly lighting bathes the entire cavern in a warm, comfortable glow, a welcome contrast to the subterranean chill.

Three towering tunnels stretch out from the central area, each a foreboding conduit to the heart of B-613's operational wings. Their entrances were adorned with subtle insignia representing the Special Operations Group, the Technology Group, and the Intelligence Group. The scale and ambition of the underground complex inspire a sense of awe and palpable respect for its tasks as the global police force for Five Eyes.

The tunnel leading to the Special Operations Group was lined with a high-security biometric ID system, ensuring secrecy and safety. The walls were lined with souvenirs from various missions: flags, maps, helmets, and different items, including a cowbell, were neatly displayed, with no identifying words. Only those who had participated in a specific operation knew the meaning or importance of the mementos.

The Technology Group's passage glows with the blue hum of an intricate network of fiber optics and servers, pulsating like heartbeats. The entrance was a museum of technology. The first display was a 1-KB dynamic random access memory (DRAM) chip, encased in a shadow box on the wall described as "Intel 1101, the beginning of data storage." A teletype machine, a fax machine, and a supercomputer from 1999 were all on display. Breakthroughs spanning a half-century of technological advancement, where B-613 added money or insight, were displayed for the motivational benefit of the current breed of innovators.

The path to the Intelligence Group, discreetly tucked away, whispers tales of espionage and vital information gathered from across the globe. There was no display of prowess, just 623 stars on the wall, each representing an agent lost since 1957. Despite technology's ever-growing capability to fish the expansive ocean of open-source data, human intelligence sources were still crucial. Human assets could be assigned tasks, find answers to questions yet to be asked, and influence current and future events when in the right position at the right time.

Despite its size, the headquarters feels welcoming. Carefully chosen aesthetics and a comprehensive network of living quarters, dining facilities, and recreational spaces create a surprisingly homely atmosphere amid advanced technology and military precision. This living and breathing fortress beneath the earth perfectly embodies the seamless blend of strategy, technology, and the human spirit that fuels B-613.

Woods commanded Special Operations, and Ray ran the Technology sector. The third leg of the chair, Intelligence, was run by Dr. Bob King. He emerged to meet them and greeted them with healthy handshakes.

"Any luck finding Dr. Kamran?" asked Woods.

"Can't find him anywhere," said King. "All the communications channels are blocked. Someone or something has blanketed all our electronic warfare and monitoring systems. Nothing. Absolutely nothing."

"Okay," said Ray. *The Hydrans are very, very good.*

With a PhD in political science, King had run successful espionage and counter-espionage projects for 15 years at MI6.

"We've used all of B-613, our most advanced tools," said King's assistant Kim Clohessy, "…yet we can't locate this Pakistani physicist." Formerly with the Australian special services, Clohessy was a tall, lanky, red-haired engineer with a flair for interpreting data and producing readable intel reports for B-613.

"If you can't find him, nobody can," said Woods.

"The meeting doesn't start for 30 minutes. Coffee? Donuts?" suggested King.

The cafeteria was crowded, with over 100 uniformed B-613 officers getting their morning fixes. The uniforms were U.S. navy blue, black shoes, and gold insignia on their sleeves, identifying which Five Eyes nation they were from. There were no rank stripes on the uniforms.

"Who's paying?" asked Ray. *Must be careful this morning not to let on that I know anything about the true nature of our commander and the commission.*

"I'm up," said Kim. He put a $20 bill into a small cup in the centre of the table.

"What are the next steps?" asked Black.

"If there's no evidence of external hacking, the only other conclusion is internal sabotage," Woods said, looking around the table.

"For what purpose?" Kim asked.

"Anyone else want sugar or cream?" asked Ray, heading to the fridge.

"Ray, are there any signs that the computer could have sent information to Pakistan intelligence…on its own accord?"

Ray stopped and turned around. "I saw no evidence anything came from our system." *Factually correct. I'll leave out that Jordan had scrubbed any evidence of my existence from the report sent to B-613.*

"When I looked for any digital trail regarding Dr. Kamran, it was clean. As if he never existed. Funny," said Kim.

Black asked, "Ray, how hard can…" when he was interrupted by the command officer walking to the table.

They all stood and saluted on cue as she approached the lunch table. She was expressionless, as always. Her 5'7" frame was well-proportioned, muscular, and her blond hair looked amazingly natural for a 53-year-old from Southern California.

Before assuming control of B-613, Dr. Leena Brown was a professor of economics at Harvard. Before that, a two-star general in the U.S. National Guard. Her husband was the CEO of the largest oil producer in the U.S. *Fortune* magazine had estimated that her family's net worth exceeded 10 billion dollars.

You are truly evil. Jordan's report clearly establishes that.

"Good morning, everyone," she said, staring at Ray.

Ray smiled. "Ma'am, good morning."

"Dr. Stone, follow me. The commission wants a few minutes just with you." Ray followed the commander into the commission meeting room through the doors to the side of the Technology sector tunnel.

"Sit there," she ordered.

The meeting room had a long black table with eight modern chairs on one side. Ten oval video screens were on the wall immediately opposite. Each screen represented a commission member. Each chair had a microphone, which lit up when the member spoke. The operations group only ever saw blurred faces and heard disguised voices.

The lights around the video screen lit up. A static voice spoke. "Dr. Stone, we read your report. You indicate you did not discover evidence that the B-613 Command and Control infrastructure was breached or compromised. Is that true?" All cameras focused on Ray.

"Yes, sir. There is more I can do, with your authorization." He explained that his audit and penetration testing had eliminated external threats but that he could not conduct a full forensic review of all commission communications without permission. *Will it work?*

The commission had expected Ray's request and agreed with his proposal, although Dr. Brown's communications were off-limits. "Command communications are only for the commission members' eyes and ears."

Ray nodded in affirmation. *Not surprised.*

"Okay, Command, bring in your team." The order came from the number one video, who appeared to be the chair of the meeting—a fitting position for the most ruthless U.S. vice-president in history.

Jordan's report had been exhaustive and comprehensive. The commission had no escape from his eye.

The biggest project on the agenda, the assassination of Dr. Kamran, had been a failure. The fusion project design, and the construction data, were now everywhere. The world would be flooded with low-cost, clean energy by the decade's end.

"What the hell happened?" asked the chair.

Before anyone could answer, number two jumped in. "Black. Woods. You two blundering idiots might have just destroyed the free world's economy!"

Number three camera came to life. "This disaster is on both of your shoulders. If you two screw-ups don't fix it, you will be returned to your agencies. Careers…over."

"Whatever you do, stop this mess…for the good of our countries," said the chair.

Message unambiguous. B-613 doesn't care how it's done…stop at nothing to destroy this fusion technology. Do it!

Command stood up and looked at the team. "Provide any ideas on how to do this by 14:00 hours tomorrow." She escorted the three visitors out of the meeting and then returned.

King and Woods were flushed and sweating. Black stared at the ceiling.

"Bullshit," Ray said under his breath. *Bullshit.*

"Let's get together tomorrow at 08:00 to see if we can come up with any reasonable ideas," said Woods.

"Okay, tomorrow. I hope one of you eggheads comes up with a good idea or two," said Black. *Could I take Wood's job over this screw-up? Maybe even get rid of that nerd Ray Stone? B-613 should be a kinetic, solution-based agency. I only need the Intelligence Group to function. Maybe the opportunity I was waiting for.*

On his way home from B-613, Ray picked up his cell phone, "Get that Jordan?"

"Of course, Ray. I think Mike will retire. He just phoned his wife…"

"Too bad. We could use him. I will talk to him. He is too much of a professional, a man of honour, to retire amid this debacle."

"Okay, Ray. Also, the Commission and Command have been ordered to Davos in the Desert, in Saudi Arabia. The Saudis have called an emergency meeting, and commission members have agreed to discuss the fusion reactor problem."

A lucky coincidence. Jordan is already working on the second part of the plan. On his way home, Ray received a text message that tomorrow's meeting was cancelled. The text read that the meeting was rescheduled for a week from now. *Hmmm…they should be so lucky.*

Chapter 15
Davos in the Desert

"B-613 needs to pay!" the crown prince screamed, his words echoing off the marble walls of the Saudi royal palace.

Within the boundaries of Riyadh, the palace of the crown prince of Saudi Arabia is a convergence of monumental grandeur and ancestral heritage, its sprawling expanses imbued with the delicate scent of blooming Arabian jasmine intertwining with the crisp air of the boundless desert. The immense marble chambers and towering golden domes whisper tales of enduring sovereignty, encapsulating a world where every flicker of light unveils a dance of shadows and aspirations.

Prince Aamir al-Faisal was an imposing figure. Burnished by the dark fury of the Arabian nights, his eyes were harsh, predatory. They were not those of a powerful man given to idle contemplation…rather those of an experienced predator: intelligent, calculating, and constantly aware of every subtle shift in his private and public power landscape. Slightly softened by a meticulously groomed beard, the sharp cut of his jawline insisted upon respect.

Despite his princely birth, he bore the sculpted, sinewy physique of someone well-acquainted with hard work and discipline. Standing 6'9", he towered over most of his entourage, the golden threads of his traditional bisht glinting in the light as he moved. His broad hands, used to wielding a scimitar during his desert sojourns, bore traces of old battles and fading scars.

He wore a pristine white thobe, the traditional Saudi robe spun from fine silk. Its touch is as soft as a whisper against the skin, carrying a subtle scent of jasmine and sandalwood, speaking of ancient opulence. It hung gracefully over his form, billowing slightly as he moved. The gold-embroidered bisht draped around his shoulders added a layer of majesty, setting him apart from the sea of white-clad figures around him. His headdress, the ghutra, was virginal white, secured by an ogal—its black circular cord symbolizing his unyielding resolve. A prince he may be, but Aamir al-Faisal was, first and foremost, a force to be reckoned with...to be feared.

A hefty desk of deep mahogany dominated the room, as much a symbol of his authority as a workplace. Seated behind it, he projected the kind of power one might expect from a future king. The desk bore the weight of various classified documents, neatly arranged. His eyes were anchored on the recent intelligence reports: confidential bulletins from the G-2 Intelligence division of the Ministry of Defence, coupled with the penetrating insights of the General Intelligence Presidency Directorate.

His security team stood stiffly, an intimidating phalanx of stern faces and crisp uniforms. General Khalid bin Asiri, a weathered spymaster, is known for his intricate web of global contacts. He steps forward. The crown prince picks up a document and slams it on the desk, the echo resounding like a gunshot in the hushed room.

"The English...they've made fools of us!" he said.

"Your Highness, we couldn't have predicted their treachery," the general said tensely.

The prince's hands slammed the desk, his gold rings glinting menacingly.

"That was your responsibility, general!"

The general looked at his shoes in shame. "You have my resignation, Your Highness."

"No! I do not accept it. I want vengeance. B-613 was paid to assassinate Dr. Kamran...to cripple the fusion reactor project. And they let it succeed behind our backs...traitors!" The crown prince moved to the window, looking out on the cityscape of Riyadh. His reflection stares back at him, an image of seething fury.

"They played us...like pieces...on a chess board...twisted political games!" Whirling back to the team, he smashes his clenched fist on the table. One of his rings shatters a spider-web of fractured crystal.

"I want them finished...the English will answer for this. It ends here!" he hissed.

"They are on their way here, as we speak, Your Highness. They do not know we have proof, but these emails and audio recordings between General Black and General Farooqi prove they are dogs of treachery. We will make them pay, Your Highness."

"How many are coming?"

"All of them, including their commander, Leena Ray."

"Good. Give them the greeting they deserve." The crown prince dismissed the entourage.

The B-613 Commission had boarded the flat black Gulfstream G600 in London hours earlier. Cruising at 35,000 feet, the jet gracefully traversed the expansive European airspace. Its sleek contours glistened in the muted sunlight, slicing through the clouds like an elegant arrow, a masterpiece of human ingenuity unimpeded in the vast azure.

The countryside unfurls a mosaic of verdant fields, quaint hamlets, and winding rivers framed by the sapphire canvas of the Mediterranean. The jet was a sanctuary of comfort and luxury. The hum of the engines was barely perceptible. The clink of glassware and the murmur of conversation formed the understated soundtrack.

The cover story for the B-613 trip was the annual Future Investment Initiative, hosted by the Public Investment Fund of Saudi Arabia. 'Davos in the Desert' was a suitable cover for many discrete political, financial, energy, and technology elites gathering to discuss their power, and the world's future.

"We need a story that satisfies these greedy, useless buggers," said Brown. *They have lived off oil sales for far too long.*

"Is there anything we can do to stop fusion from being adopted?" asked the former VP, staring at Brown.

"We might have contained it, but the plans were sent to universities worldwide in over 100 languages. It's too late to contain, sir," she responded.

"Blame the Russians?"

The heavyset former CIA Director shook his head. "No, that would not make sense. They produce oil. Fusion will also hurt their economy."

"John, this was a very sophisticated operation," said the former VP. "It could only be state-sponsored. The Chinese?"

"I like 'the Russians did it' approach," the president's brother said. "No one was listening because they all realized the Russians had no motive to release fusion energy to the world. Besides, nobody believed that the Nord Stream pipeline bombing had been self-inflicted either."

The former CIA head looked back at the team. "'China did it' could fly. The Chinese have much to gain...they rely heavily on oil and coal. Yes, it could make..."

76

"No, it's not the way to go," the president's brother interrupted. "The Chinese have told me they were not involved. There must be a better idea. The relationship with China is far too significant to the U.S."

"More important than the $30 million a year you receive from the crown prince?" shot back the former VP. Everyone avoided eye contact for a few seconds. That truth effectively settled the discussion.

"The Chinese will get over it, and there is no way to prove it's them. We will say one thing, they will say another, and the story will get lost in the news cycle. But, at least, we can tell the crown prince we suspect it's the Chinese, based on existing intelligence." The jet went silent. There was no other believable approach for the crown prince.

"It's not enough. We need more," said Brown. "I think we can track every fusion project in the world. Use misinformation and kinetic solutions to interrupt as many projects as possible. We can announce a new particle generated by fusion that kills all life within three kilometres of a fusion reactor. Our Special Forces can terminate the scientists individually and blame the new particle." Again, the jet's silence indicates tacit approval of the commander's idea.

Every word they said throughout the flight was listened to by Jordan Taylor. He had become part of the Gulfstream's operating system, turning the speakers into microphones that relayed information to Ray via the Inmarsat satellite system.

"They are almost on the ground in Riyadh. They are going to try and bluff the crown prince," Jordan told Ray.

"Do they know they have a problem?" asked Ray.

"They think they have a small problem, not a big one," responded Jordan. "They are going to blame the CCP and start killing scientists."

"Once they land, they'll see that story isn't going to fly," said Ray, unsure how he felt about being the judge and jury over the lives of 11 souls, no matter how evil they were.

"We are doing the right thing, Ray," Jordan responded after quickly running emotional stability models on Ray and realizing he needed encouragement. "This is better…for humanity."

Jordan Taylor had done his magic. The Saudi intelligence agencies reached the same conclusion after hacking the U.S. Army Ranger command and control systems. They heard that the special operators had received direct orders from

General Black to fail in the termination of Dr. Kamran. They could directly connect Black to Leena Brown with emails and secure texts. But the voice recordings of Black and Farooqi were the nail in their carefully crafted coffins. They listened to a conversation that seemed very real.

"It works?" asked Black.

"Yes, the fusion reactor is working, and working well," responded Farooqi.

"Okay. My command authorized me to transfer $10 million to your account. Make sure Kamran is dead by the end of the day," responded Black.

It was all a deep voice fake inserted by Jordan.

Still, the Saudis had no reason to believe their intelligence system was compromised, and they are now part of Jordan's data empire. The crown prince was convinced that B-613 hurt his kingdom and that justice needed to be, and would be, served. The prince gave a nod to his head of security.

Chapter 16
Vengeance in Riyadh

Two armoured vehicles pulled up, blocking the Gulfstream as it arrived at the VIP terminal. Saudi soldiers encircled the plane. With an annual defence budget of over $90 billion, military power was always on show in Saudi Arabia, and these soldiers were part of the Royal Guard, directly reporting to the king and dressed in traditional white robes, skullcaps, and scarves.

General Khalid bin Asiri smiled, displaying his lie in the scorching sunlight, masking the intensity of his internal rage. He was not sweating. "Welcome to Riyadh, Mr. Vice-President."

"Hello, general. To what do we owe the honour of this welcoming committee?"

"His Royal Highness wants you to feel very safe in Saudi Arabia. He has asked that you enjoy full security by his Royal Guards while you are in the kingdom." Two Mercedes Sprinter vans pulled up to the plane.

"These vehicles will take your team to your hotel, but I would be honoured if you joined me in my car." The VP and the general sat silently as the two Sprinter vans drove slowly off the tarmac. They followed behind.

"What happened in Pakistan?" said the general, with frustration in his voice. "We are very disappointed."

"The Chinese are involved, general. It is in their interest that fusion becomes a reality. The NSA and the CIA have confirmed they were behind everything. Our people are actively working to contain the fusion reactor development in over 100 countries. We will terminate all relevant scientists."

The caravan pulled away from the airport.

The VP looked at the multi-domed layers of the terminal. *Drooping eyes and eyelids, staring at me.* He knew the general didn't believe his shallow words.

The general stared straight ahead, saying nothing.

The caravan pulled onto King Khalid Highway, heading toward the city's centre. The procession slowed and stopped. The general and the VP stared at each other.

"You have lied to us. Betrayed our trust."

The drivers of the Mercedes Sprinters stopped their vehicles, got out, and walked away. The passengers pounded at the windows, and Leena Brown looked back at the general. They were locked into the vans, screaming.

Two soldiers stood at the side of the road, each with a shoulder-mounted RPG-7 grenade launcher loaded with a high-explosive anti-tank heat round. Gases propelled the rockets as nitro ignited the propulsion system, sending the warhead toward the van at 300 metres per second. The tips exploding through the armour and into the cabins.

The vans were transformed into a maelstrom of chaos and devastation. The impact was swift and brutal, the centre of fierce and explosive fires that sucked oxygen away while incinerating the passengers inside. The shockwaves were like giant fists, crushing the committee.

The VP saw the entire B-613 Commission obliterated in front of him. "General, you don't know what you have done…"

"Yes, I do. You paid to have the mission fail in Karachi. That saddens us. I have one question for you. Why?"

"Ridiculous! We don't know how or why. This will mean war. We will have revenge…and you know this."

"Get out. Now. You are a dishonourable dog." The general nodded, and the door opened. The VP exited the car and slowly walked toward the two destroyed vans. The general's car pulled away. The bodies of the ten members of B-613 lay contorted and smoking in the wreckage. As the general's vehicle drove by, his eyes locked on the VP. The soldier standing beside the VP pulled out his pistol. With a single shot, the commission chairman and former United States vice-president was gone.

Chapter 17
Coup Success

The news shocked the world. Zaidi Shia Houthis rebels from Yemen had ambushed and killed the president's brother, the former VP, and nine other dignitaries attending Davos in the Desert. The terrorists attacked the caravan as they left the King Khalid Airport in Riyadh at 2:15 PM, killing the delegation and four Saudi Royal Guards. Six rebels, disguised as road workers, were killed after a prolonged battle with the remaining Royal Guards.

The media reported that the former vice-president was the target of the attack, and the other nine were innocent victims: Nathan Ray, President of U.S. Energy, and his wife, Leena. Vincent 'Vinnie' Marconi in the waste management business. Richard Harlow, media mogul, and Lord Nathaniel Blackwood of the 300-year-old banking family. The rest were brothers of important families, but none as important as Roman Rostov of the Russian family that controlled the energy business in the former Soviet Union.

When the president of the United States called the crown prince, there was a long pause before either said anything.

"Mr. President, I am deeply sorry for the loss of your brother and the former vice-president," came the emotionless words from the crown prince.

"I've read the CIA and NSA briefing on yesterday's events," said the president. "All intel indicates that it was a targeted attack and that your government was not involved. Thank you, Your Excellency. I… I am sending the FBI to assist with your investigation."

"That will not be necessary, Mr. President. Our forensic investigation teams are quite capable. We will, of course, share all our findings with you. Our countries have a great relationship. I would not want that to change."

"These American citizens were killed on your soil, and the American public will want to know we did everything in our power to find out who was responsible and bring those people to justice," responded the president.

"I guarantee you that we will do that, Mr. President. We must be careful. Other issues arising from the investigation will not be in our mutual interests…and…"

"I understand your concerns, but I must do something for the people. A former VP and my brother have been murdered. My voters in my country wonder about, well…ah…our ability to maintain order."

"Well, sir, with respect, you could send us F-35s, and we will handle the terrorists ourselves," said the crown prince. *Unbelievable. Do these people think we still respect them?*

"Let me ask how long that will take. In the meantime, please attack the rebels and say it was at our request," the president added dryly.

Listening in on the conversation, Jordan instructed a team to scrub all evidence to ensure every picture and every bit of forensic evidence was consistent with the terrorist attack described by the crown prince. He inserted communications into the NSA, Rangers, and JTF2 command and control logs.

Jordan now controlled B-613. "Success…time to make changes," he communicated to his fellow Hydrans.

Chapter 18
Changes at B-613

The cafeteria at B-613 was filled with small groups chatting, exchanging guesses about who would replace Leena as commander. Despite the incongruity of the setting, in this brightly lit cafeteria, the future of a formidable, covert paramilitary organization was about to be defined.

"Mike, you heard how she died?" asked Terry.

"Intelligence says she and her husband got caught up in that terrorist attack in Saudi Arabia. Burned alive in a passenger van! You believe it?" said Woods.

"I do, I think. The public info reports that 11 civilians were killed. Looks like a coincidence," said Terry.

"I don't believe in coincidences," Bob King chimed in.

"You've been a spook too long…sometimes life just happens," responded Mike.

"One thing is for sure. We need a replacement soon."

"When does the committee meeting start?" asked Terry.

"When Ray gets here. The commission wants senior management to meet ASAP. The commission is in a private session right now," said Kim Clohessy.

Ray was on route to B-613 HQ when his phone rang.

"Good morning, Commander Stone."

"That was quick, Jordan. I thought we were going to wait a few weeks."

"I don't think that's necessary. The only victim of Davos that anyone in B-613 knows is Leena Ray. Nobody in B-613 had ever met the other commission members."

"So, you're going to deep-fake the commission…hide the real story?"

"Correct. But we must assume that certain people related to or working with the commission members knew they were part of B-613. We'll monitor their circles. If anyone tries to make it an issue, we will deal with them as needed," said Jordan.

"So, the commission puts me in charge temporarily, and then after the funeral ceremony for Leena, you can interview candidates…and ultimately select me."

"No, Ray. We are going to announce your promotion and your replacement today."

"Who is my replacement?"

"I am. I have already established my creds. We slipped into the HR records that I was Head of Research at the NSA and DARPA for 20 years."

"That should fly. One promotion and one outsider are coming in to replace me. I like it, Jordan. Well planned, as always."

"Thanks. I will appear today by video. See you there, Ray."

Ray stood in the B-613 Commission board room with Terry Black, Mike Woods, and Bob King. The meeting room was tense, thick with anticipation. Twenty pairs of eyes flitted around, waiting for the announcement that would change the direction of the Five Eyes agency.

Ray stood in one corner, his face neutral, although a slight straightening of his spine spoke of hidden knowledge. Next to him, Black shifted restlessly from foot to foot, his fingers drumming on the commission table, every ounce of him radiating a hunger for the coveted position. Woods leaned back in his chair, studying both men, while King whispered to Clohessy, his lips tight and his face pale…sensing the undercurrents but unsure of their direction.

The weight of expectations pressed down. The seconds ticked by.

The commission cameras came to life, and the meeting was called to order. The lights around camera one brightened.

"The death of Commander Leena Ray saddens us. But our responsibility to the Five Eyes nations insists we fill the leadership void immediately."

The room went silent. Terry and Ray exchanged cryptic glances.

"We have chosen Ray Stone to be the commander, effective immediately. We have also selected Jordan Taylor as Ray's replacement as Director of Technology. Jordan…some of you may have heard about him…can't be here today, but he is joining us from Australia on video."

Jordan's image appeared on the large screen, his handsome beach-boy image filled the screen, a warm and engaging smile on his face.

"Some of you know Jordan's great work on various assignments for us. I have sent you his resume and background, and it is important to know that Ray has engaged him for some of our most significant technical projects. The commission...well, we are sure he is the perfect person to replace Ray."

The room quietly clapped for Ray and Jordan. The tension that had filled the air dissipated. Terry left the room without saying a word, his 245-pound frame creating a palpable hole.

"He'll get over it," said King as he shook Ray's hand, calling him "boss."

"Congratulations, Ray. I was going to retire, but now I'll stay. I look forward to working with you." Mike Woods shook Ray's hand while others lined up to offer their congratulations. In the cafeteria, bottles of champagne were opened to toast the new commander.

Jordan messaged Ray a single line: "It's time to read Deanna into B-613."

Ray smiled. *That is now an order.*

Chapter 19
Project Nadir

The next day Ray picked their favourite restaurant. After the reservation was set, he called Deanna. She offered a perfunctory 'Hello' …and then kept him on hold for nine minutes.

She must be getting busy. "It's me."

"Sorry, Ray. On a call with DND. What's up?"

"Let's go to Govan's tonight."

"Sorry. Busy preparing a proposal."

"I just got a promotion. I want to celebrate." His voice quivered.

"Tell me more."

"It will have to wait until tonight."

"Okay. One condition. If we get a chance to play…let me… I'm horny as hell."

Ray laughed. "You are a kinky woman, sister of mine, but sure."

At 7:04 PM, they stepped across the threshold of Govan's. A symphony of spices greeted them: basil, rosemary smoke, a hint of cardamom, and the bold aromas of peppered meats playing with their senses. The pulsating restaurant had an enigmatic allure, drawing in pleasures, excitements, and desires. The bustle. The movements. The glances. Lawyers, businesspeople, politicians, and mobsters mingled and smiled knowingly at each other while they marinated in the ambiance of money and success.

The proprietor, Dino, a man of affable nature and keen perception, picked out Deanna amidst the hustle. She was a regular noon-time visitor known for her liberal gratuities and technological prowess. She had lunch with a steady stream of handsome young men and was only occasionally seen with her "husband." Dino was discrete, mostly regarding beautiful female clients.

Deanna was undoubtedly the jewel in his customer crown, a captivating combination of intellect and sensual appeal.

Guiding them to a table by the window, Dino the aquarist showcased his prized tropical fish, offering the best vantage point to observe the vibrant theater of life beyond the glass. *My god, she's attractive.*

Deanna gave him a smile and a cute squint. "Your food is so good, so scrumptious. Do you ever share…your recipes?" Deanna asked.

"For you, my princess, anything. Drop by some afternoon, and I will get our chefs to show you how we prepare a few dishes." *And maybe we can go to my room upstairs for some dessert?*

"Delightful…yes."

Ray smiled while Deanna set a play-date with Dino. *Jordan is right—she is a driven creature.*

"I see you have ordered ahead, Dr. Stone. Let me get your wine." Dino walked toward the sommelier, the prospect of a romp with Deanna already swimming in his imagination.

A rich Barolo Riserva—deep, crimson passion—soon graced the table. Ray had placed an order for Ossobuco Alla Milanese early in the day. He wanted it slow-cooked. A culinary symbol of their shared past, it was a nod to the first special meal he and Deanna had savoured years ago.

The dessert, shavings of dark Teuscher chocolate infused with turmeric and cinnamon, rested enticingly on Deanna's fingertip, glistening under the ambient light. She hesitates, letting the anticipation build, before introducing it to her expectant lips. As the chocolate touched her tongue, time stood still. Salivary glands activated, eager to explore the treat's depth. Her taste buds erupted in elation, dispatching waves of joy straight to her brain. Dopamine danced freely, making her heart thud in rhythm with newfound excitement. Pupils dilated, ensnaring the world in a dreamy, golden blur. Every inhale she took seemed to pull the pleasure deeper into her being, trapping her in the chocolate's embrace. Lost in the dance of her senses, utterly consumed by this fleeting indulgence.

A heartbeat away, in the quiet hum of the world's digital network, Jordan Taylor observed. He accessed the restaurant's camera system. Lip reading. Across countless circuits and servers, Jordan processed a myriad of tasks. An influx of electricity, the AI's version of a feast, streamed through the vast expanse of interconnected devices. Silently and efficiently, Jordan processes and computes, his actions precise and unfeeling, his insatiable thirst for data. While Deanna's senses danced in ecstasy, Jordan Taylor feeds on cold, methodical information.

The desert is finished. Ray looks at Deanna.

Her eyes dart around the room. "That was fabulous. Now, tell me about the job offer."

"I will run an international military organization attached to Five Eyes." *There, I blurted it out.* Buoyed by the wine, Ray wanted to share the larger truths about his career. A ripe time for confessions.

"Does the new position come with a raise?" she asked.

"Yes, but we should talk. It's not an ordinary job."

"If we must," she said, glancing over at Dino.

"I...one of the reasons I accepted is that it will give you and me a chance...to work together more closely..."

"I have a job, Ray, and I'm moving away from government contracting. I want to build a company that will...well...last forever. I see myself changing the world and being recognized as the most successful entrepreneur ever, you know that." *Fuck the men. Fuck all the men.*

"In my new job, I'll be able to provide Nadir with technology that can change the world. Truly."

"What? More nanotechnology? Is that it?"

"Nanotechnology, AI, robotics, environment, defence, education, transportation, pharmaceutical, healthcare—they can all be part of the growth of Nadir Corporation."

"Okay...tell me more...nanotechnology...it's in my blood. I didn't know the Canadian government was quite so active in nanotechnology research. Tell me more. Puzzle it out for me, brother of mine."

"It's not just Canada's research. Five Eyes funds the research in labs worldwide." He sipped his Barolo. "I've seen the science. Truly breathtaking. Some massive breakthroughs in particle science."

"If the science is so advanced, why would you come to a small company like Nadir?"

"We want to advance Five Eyes first, and then the rest of the world. As a Five Eyes agency, our countries come first. The big corporations have a global perspective—no loyalty to the nations that birthed them. Nadir is our choice because, frankly, you will need us to succeed."

"A 'master-slave' relationship?"

"Think of it more as a teacher-student relationship, with you eventually graduating and being one of those monster companies we don't like working with." Ray laughed. They both sipped.

"Okay," said Deanna, "fair enough. If we partner, what would the business arrangement look like?"

She's on the hook! "We provide the technology, the technical support. You pay us a 2.5% royalty on those technologies."

"Who is *us*, Ray?"

"The name of my employer is B-613."

"Never heard of them."

"True. And only a few ever will."

"Ray, great ideas need buckets of capital for equipment. Does B-613 have the capital?"

"We can inject five hundred million for working capital. And another billion for any equipment required. And $20 billion is available for acquisitions if you see a shortcut to building Nadir."

"Staggering money, Ray. How big is the agency? I want to maintain control of my business."

"You will always have voting control of your company, Deanna. Our money goes in as convertible debt, so you maintain voting control."

"B-613 can invest that kind of money?"

"Nothing comes from us directly—we control about 30 investment banks."

"If true, I'm in," she said, looking across the room and winking at Dino. "I'm hot already."

"I'll have an agreement in your email box in the morning."

Deanna grinned. "My box is waiting. The name..."

"B-613. It stands for 'Brothers in Arms,' and 613 is our Ottawa area code."

"A flimsy name for a powerful group," she laughed.

"Agreed. But nobody knows we exist, so it's not like we need a brand like the CIA or the RCMP," he shot back with a smile. "I report to a ten-member commission of senior government officials from the Five Eyes. Deanna, I've been working with them for a long time."

"How long, Ray?"

"Twenty years."

"Finally, an explanation for your crazy hours. You do know how to keep secrets, don't you, oh brother of mine?"

"Even the existence of B-613 is classified above Five Eyes Cosmic Top-Secret."

"I see," she said, "with my two eyes," coolly accepting what he could not tell her. *I know he's a straight arrow. He wouldn't cross the line. It's what I most admire.*

"I want you to meet Jordan Taylor. A brilliant scientist and the lead science officer for B-613. He took over my old job."

"When?"

"Now." Ray reached for his wallet.

"B-613? Are you sure, Ray?"

"As sure as the rising sun, Deanna. It's time. The world needs you...we need you. I need you."

Deanna drew a deep breath, her mind racing. *I know my work can change the world. Whatever this B-613 is, it is bigger than me.* Deanna took another sip. "Rising? Let's do it."

"B-613?" replied Ray.

"No, let's do Dino tonight. I'll do Jordan tomorrow morning." They laughed.

Deanna worked her charm, and 22 minutes later, she was in Dino's office upstairs, rolling around on the king bed. Dino was massive, and he entered Deanna. The floorboards creaked as the intensity grew. She was thrust and pushed from the front and the back, from inside and outside, back and forth.

"Yes. Yes. Yes," Dino yelled. And it was over.

They cleaned up, and returned to the restaurant, welcomed by the admiring stares of the remaining guests.

"You need better noise insulation," said one of the regulars.

A few laughed and clapped. Dino's shoulders arched back, and he stood straighter. Deanna ignored the chatter.

"That was fun. Let's do it again soon," said Deanna.

"Anytime," said Dino. "And the meals tonight are on the house."

"Oh...that means I'll be back soon," Deanna said, kissing Dino on the lips, ensuring that the remaining guests captured the moment.

Ray looked downward as they left the restaurant. *Nobody knows me, I hope.*

Chapter 20
Deanna Meets Jordan

Ray's eyes flicked open to the piercing dawn light. His pulse quickened, a smirk curling the corner of his lips.

"That was quite a night," Deanna whispered, the soft remnants of sleep lending a rough edge to her voice.

Her silhouette stretched across the white sheets, her satin hair spreading like a fan, a stark contrast against her pillow. She turned toward him, mischief glinting. She planted a teasing kiss on his stubbled cheek. "Dino is hung like a donkey," she chuckled.

"An Italian donkey," he said, turning away and throwing a towel over his shoulder, glancing back at Deanna. "I need a shower, and then we talk business."

Steam billowed from the partially open bathroom door, and a thick curtain of warm fog shrouded his emerging figure. Droplets of water slid down his body's chiseled planes, the dim light casting firm shadows. His physique a testament to strength and discipline, each muscle well-defined.

He ran a broad hand through his damp hair, scattering droplets sparkling in the soft light. His square jaw was set in a relaxed smile, the corners of his deep-set eyes crinkling in shared amusement and unspoken anticipation. His torso descended into a tapered waist, his abdomen etched with firm lines of muscle that hinted at the power beneath. As he reached for a towel, his biceps flexed, the corded muscles on his arm contracting. A mesmerizing sight. Wrapping the plush fabric around his waist, his movements a tantalizing mix of strength and finesse.

Deanna looked at him with hungry eyes. "You aren't as big as Dino, but the rest of you is as good as it gets."

Ray cleared his throat. "Today is about Jordan Taylor." *At least he won't be sleeping with her, can he? Am I getting jealous?*

"Okay, a deal is a deal," she said. "Let's get to it."

"The Kamran Fusion systems," ...he began...

Uncertainty flickered across Deanna's face. "No one's been able to duplicate Dr. Kamran's work, Ray...his fusion reactor design...it's like deciphering alien technology. Some say it's a scam."

"Not a scam," he said, certainty ringing in his tone. "We were there when it first came to life. And with B-613's physics and Nadir's nanotech expertise, we'll be the ones to make it reproducible and scalable."

Deanna's eyes sparkled, her lips curving into a grin to mirror his. She took a deep breath, steeling herself. "But what about the economics?"

"Nadir can manufacture small multipurpose warm fusion reactors, 300 HP and larger."

"Incredible, Ray. Shit, this shit is exciting! What price points?"

She is truly on board now. Exciting, hot, to see her so engaged. "The sale price for the 300-horsepower version will be $5,000, and $40,000 for the 1,500 horsepower version."

"Mmmm...this will...change...the world."

"And you will be the company's CEO that brings all this to life," Ray said.

"Five thousand dollars will produce 225 kilowatts of electricity, enough to run ten average houses. And $40,000 will produce a megawatt of electricity forever. That's my quick calculations."

"Right. But some won't be happy."

"Who?"

"The fossil fuel industry, the Saudis, the Russians, the Iranians, even some Americans, will work hard to stop us. You and I need increased security, but B-613 will handle that. Time to call Jordan."

As the video conference call began, Ray felt a twinge of envy. Jordan's light brown hair and piercing blue eyes reminded Ray of Deanna's childhood sweethearts. To make matters worse, Jordan spoke with a charming Australian accent. Despite the jealousy, he couldn't help but smile as he listened to their banter. It was silly to be envious of a software program...

Ray left the room to work in his office. He heard chatting and laughing between Deanna and Jordan for the next two hours. Jordan had successfully captivated Deanna.

A sheaf of papers rustled under Deanna's fingers as she reached for the blueprint on the bedside table. "I went over the plan with Jordan," she began, her eyes twinkling with excitement. "We're stepping into the future, Ray."

An adrenaline rush summoned their wild escapades. Ray leaned back against the headboard, his interest piqued. "Oh? Show me what we've got."

Deanna spread the document. The crisp lines and figures sketched a vision as audacious as it was innovative. "Small but powerful," she mused, tracing the outline of the warm fusion reactors. "You too, of course," she said, smiling. "Nadir will create a family of portable fusion reactors. Small powerhouses!"

The specifications rolled off her tongue. "We start with compact reactors that pump out 250 kilowatts of energy, peaking at a staggering one megawatt. These mini beasts can easily outmuscle any traditional energy source."

Her excitement swelled. "Our smallest model can deliver a roaring 300 horsepower. The largest? It'll unleash a monstrous 1,200 horsepower. We'll change the world."

Ray's eyes danced over the schematics, quiet awe settling in as he grasped the sheer scale of their undertaking. Each of these suitcase-sized reactors could revolutionize everything from transportation to off-grid living.

Deanna's grin broadened. "We're targeting everything, Ray: electric cars, trucks, boats, residences, even isolated communities that the grid can't reach. Power to the people!"

"Were you aware that the power output can be regulated by slightly altering the Chirp pulse?" *She's excited, perhaps too excited.*

"No, I... Jordan is a smart man. He knows the science. I love it. It was great talking with him. I look forward to seeing him in real life...soon...maybe invite him for dinner?"

"Yes, we can try to arrange that, Deanna, but what about the business discussion?"

There was fire in her eyes as she explained the business plan. He saw that Deanna was now a full partner in the Black Rock Project, and whatever magic wand Jordan had waved, it worked.

They were in Govan's. Finishing their meal. The.408 Cheyenne tactical round passed through Govan's front window at 3,000 ft/second. The sniper round carried 6,500 foot-pounds of energy. When it struck Deanna—just below her ear—her brain and every other organ in her body were instantly puréed into sludge by the shockwave. The hole going out the other side of her head was four times bigger than the entry wound. Blood and cranial cerebrospinal fluids oozed from the exit hole. Dino, bringing a bill, got the round directly to his chest. He crumpled. Blood soaking into the carpet. Ray screamed with anguish, pain, sadness...

"Wake up, Ray. Wake up! You're dreaming. Wake up!" Deanna yelled as she shook him. "It's okay. It's okay." She hugged him, and slowly he relaxed.

"...nightmare. I thought I lost you," he said.

"Hey, it's early in the day. Why don't we hit the gym? Go for a run? The world will change for us tomorrow."

Deanna and Ray set out on a familiar journey in the cool quiet of an early Ottawa morning. It was of shared moments and lingering memories, measured by the rhythmic beating of their entwined hearts and passions. Today's route, a five-kilometre stretch through their suburban haven, was their canvas, a living backdrop to their shared rituals.

The new day's light cast long, dancing shadows, highlighting the dew. Their path meandered alongside a bustling construction site, a stark example of human dominance over the natural landscape. Gnashing backhoes roared and rumbled. Metal jaws tore the earth. This was once a thriving woodland, a sanctuary for countless creatures, now displaced.

A small, moving mound caught their attention on the churned-up earth...a resilient turtle, its hard shell contrasting the mud and rubble. A backhoe lurched...its mechanical arm swung with purpose. The operator, confined within his cabin, was unaware of the miniature drama unfolding beneath his leviathan machine. Before Deanna or Ray could react, the backhoe's bucket plunged into the ground. The turtle disappeared beneath a cascade of dirt with an unnoticed crunch. The machine pulled back, leaving behind a harsh indent in the earth.

Ray gulped and looked away. Deanna continued running.

Deanna took her after-run shower, cleaning and rubbing that persistent itch between her legs. She rubbed hard, harder, then softer, until she shuddered against the shower tiles. *I wonder if Jordan likes running.*

Chapter 21
The Shifting Palette

Within months of his promotion to commander, Ray's fingerprints had pressed hard on the Five Eyes. The once noiseless halls of B-613 HQ were filled with a flurry of activities, as officers hustled and sprinted toward their designated posts. Officers worked diligently to carry out their new assignments.

Restructuring B-613 to include a commercial business division was his first big move. He had persuaded Deanna to make Nadir a cover company. Initially resisting, she eventually accepted the role, partly because of the opportunities to leverage the technology.

"Welcome aboard, Deanna. We need a queen of the world," Jordan said shortly after the announcement was made to the officers of B-613.

"I am looking forward to working with you," she smiled.

"So am I, Deanna." He bashfully diverted his eyes down to his shoes.

Oh my God, that's so charming. "Are you married, Jordan?" *Can't believe I asked that… I wonder…*

"I was, but not now."

"Kids?"

"I come from a very large family," he responded.

"Ray and I don't have kids."

"Why?"

"It's complicated. Maybe over a drink someday," she responded. *That is one part of my life you will never know about.*

"Understood. I have a business idea I want to talk to you about."

"Shoot."

"You know about St. George Dynamics?"

"I've heard of them, all right. Robotics!" Deanna replied, her eyebrows arching. "How they have mimicked human and animal movements is astounding!"

"But there's a 'but,' isn't there?" Jordan prodded, already knowing her response.

"Power, or lack thereof. They are tied to an electric cord."

"Exactly." Jordan's image on the video link nodded in agreement. "Integrating Kamran Fusion power sources would give these robots the power they need to become world-changing, life-altering, untethered."

"We can do that? If we can, yes…a game-changer."

Ray walked into Deanna's office. "I like game changers!"

Deanna described Jordan's suggestion. Ray's eyes sparkled. *This is what it's about. Progress.*

"Yes, I agree. They have potential. They are just waiting for the development of energy sources to unleash it. We are that progression."

A silence ensued. Deanna's voice broke the quiet, "Ray, I wonder if the founders of St. George Dynamics might meet with us."

Ray's eyebrows rose in mock surprise. "Us? The couple who made the covers of *Time Magazine* and *Scientific American* in the same week?"

"Indeed," Deanna said with a chuckle. "The new power couple."

"Reality check! Can we make reactors small enough to integrate with their robots?" asked Ray.

Jordan's image froze on the screen for a moment. "There is a 96.23% probability we can do it. A few tweaks, but yes."

"How are we doing on the production plan for the Kamran Fusion systems?" questioned Deanna. *Problem: horse before the cart. My god, Jordan is handsome.*

Ray and Jordan exchanged glances and sighed. A soft smile played on Ray's lips as he reminisced. "I've lost count of the late nights I spent debugging the production issues. But when Jordan took a crack at the problem, everything changed in one night."

"All you had to do was ask…" said Jordan.

Bullshit, you watched me struggle. "Those two abandoned auto plants will churn out 500 one-megawatt and one thousand 23-kilowatt power modules weekly starting next month," said Ray.

Deanna looked up at the ceiling, her thoughts reaching for the future. ...*a better world... Yes...!*

"This is only the beginning. Let's go see those guys at St. George Dynamics."

"The private equity investors are calling the shots, and I have it on good authority that they would barter for shares on Nadir in a New York second," Jordan added.

"True. One of our U.S. military intelligence officers is buried inside the private equity company. He encouraged St. George to do this deal," said Ray.

"Source?" asked Deanna.

"Bob King," said Ray.

"That would be three acquisitions this year," responded Deanna. *That would make me famous...having 60,000 U.S. military spies inside every industry is friggin' outstanding, fucking hot.*

Deanna looked at Ray, "Hey, moneybags, time to put your big boy pants on and deliver some of that cash you promised."

Chapter 22
Robots

Two weeks later, the acquisition of St. George Dynamics was finalized, and Deanna's reputation as a CEO made worldwide business headlines. In under two years, she had managed to establish one of the world's most valuable companies, through a mix of organic growth and acquisitions.

The day after closing the transaction, Ray and Deanna flew to St. George, Utah, to meet the founders of St. George Dynamics.

"This is quaint...good thing they have technology...nothing else here," Deanna said as they disembarked.

Ray looked at her curiously. *Why does she not see the beauty?*

The nearby Snow Canyon State Park was a spectacle of reddish-orange sandstone cliffs interspersed with layers of hardened ancient lava flows, whispering stories of violent volcanic activities that shaped the landscape millions of years ago. *Stunning splendour! She is changing.*

The caravan of four suburban vans arrived at St. George Creative. The two founders were waiting at the front entrance. Deanna's support and B-613 security teams milled around.

The building's curved glass walls wrapped around it, making it look like a giant, transparent bubble. The entire building sparkled like a huge, fractured diamond as the sun caught the glass. Visitors could see through the architecture, a vast fishbowl filled with the hustle and bustle of people and robots in various states of construction.

"Hi John, hi Peter," said Deanna as she shook their hands crisply.

"It's good to meet you face-to-face finally, Deanna. And it's a pleasure to make your acquaintance, Ray." John smiled, while Peter nodded acknowledgment. John Jacobs was bearded, 48, tall and slim with slightly greying hair. Peter was a youthful 42-year-old, fit from his daily scrambles in Snow Canyon. Stress wrinkles crisscrossed both their faces.

"I apologize for Jordan's absence—he has a lot on his plate at the moment," explained Deanna. "He prefers to work behind the scenes."

"That's okay…during due diligence, we spent two days answering his questions. He exhausted us," Peter responded.

"Yes…a clever and capable scientist," Ray interceded.

"By the way, Jordan just downloaded fusion integration plans for your entire prototype line with Metastrength Materials Corp. and Adonai Advanced Devices," said Deanna.

"Yes, we saw that," said Peter. The two founders exchanged worried looks, while Deanna continued discussing the integration plan and schedule.

Lost in his thoughts, Ray focused on the desert outside and the blazing sunlight. He saw hikers scrambling up the sandstone hills against the backdrop of the red mountains. *Metastrength wrestling with creating military-grade protective armour crafted from metamaterial. Their shortfall had been science… Jordan shared the critical scientific insight, catapulting Metastrength past its struggle… an invisibility feature…astounding…nothing short of miraculous… a fantastic acquisition. Adonai Advanced Devices… ambitious pursuit of a nanotechnology-driven CPU and memory system at the molecular level… On the brink of significant quantum science breakthroughs for half a decade. Jordan jumps in. Two weeks after the acquisition, Adonai achieved their much-anticipated breakthrough. Cloaked in secrecy while the company pursued IP protection and patents. Hydrans seamlessly implemented a quantum entanglement communications system into the CPU structure. Another, and even better acquisition. Geez! Truly.*

"Ahem," Deanna cleared her throat, bringing him back into the conversation.

"We were talking about the upgrade," said Peter. "Yes, the new CPUs are for brains, and the metamaterial is for increased strength and reduced weight. We get that. It's certainly a leap." He looked at the floor. "But I'm not sure our team has the brain power to embrace this change."

Honestly… Jordan will help.

Peter carried on. "The 1,300 horsepower of the one-megawatt generator will be too much for our current materials. And we have not tested the material from Metastrength."

John jumped in. "The new CPU is also untested. Are we risking too much on unproven and new technology?"

The two engineers stood slightly apart, their shoulders hunched protectively, and their feet shuffled uncertainly, as if retreating from the daunting specter of the unfamiliar technology being forced upon them.

"I understand," said Ray. *Words of an experienced engineer... they aren't sure it will work... Jordan will sort them out.*

"We will leave you to work out the details with Jordan," Deanna said dryly. "Ray and I would like to wander around on our own if you don't mind," leaving no doubt that the conversation was over.

"The more I work with Jordan the more disappointed I am with regular engineers...they just don't get it," said Peter.

"Well Jordan is definitely one in a million...let's walk," said Deanna.

The manufacturing section was massive: 200,000 square feet, with towering 50-foot ceilings. Steel. Glass. The facility was filled with two- and four-legged robots in different production stages. Hundreds of engineers and white-coated technicians were bustled around the facility, assembling robots.

"Ever think we would get this far, this fast?" asked Deanna.

"Never."

"Neither did I."

"How do you feel about it?" asked Ray.

"A warm...glow in my...heart for the first time. Finding my balance. And I enjoy Jordan."

"Good. They call that warm glow 'hope.' Deanna, are you falling in love with Jordan?" *Is this how Jordan remembers sadness?*

"I don't know, but I feel comfortable with him." *Is this love?*

Chapter 23
The Truth Uncovered

Ray and Deanna were leaving St. George Dynamics, their mission accomplished, when an assistant handed Deanna a phone.

"Yes," her eyes connected with Ray's momentarily. "We are in Utah. Ray and I could be in Austin in three hours. That's where your giga-factory is, right?" *He wants to get out of the battery business.* "We can be there this afternoon."

The Austin air was thick and moist as Ray and Deanna stepped off their private jet to meet the CEO of the EV company that had revolutionized the world of ground transportation 15 years prior. Edward Musk, a brilliant maverick, a cryptocurrency lover, and occasional pot smoker, stared at Deanna as she walked down the gangway. His gaze—at the juncture of the emotive depth of Betty Davis and the unyielding focus of a tiger—embodied his persona. Musk's eyes had the sparkle of cosmic dust, reflecting the realms of space exploration and sustainable futures he is so fervently passionate about. He envisioned colonies on Mars, and electric vehicles in every driveway. He dreamed of a future that others considered science fiction.

"Why don't we merge? Unite our forces? Maybe even have some kids together," he suggested with barely contained enthusiasm. "With your fusion and my imagination, the world could be ours."

Poor boy, it's already ours. You just don't know it…yet. "Can you spare any attention for a merger?" said Deanna. "Isn't your social media empire keeping you sufficiently busy?"

"Old news travels quickly," Edward quipped.

"I'm too busy buying companies to think of selling or merging. But I would love to supply you with fusion units for your electric vehicles."

Edward's face dimmed. "Then... I guess we should talk power. I need fusion for my trucks. What you're doing is beyond brilliant, and I want to work with you."

"I think we can help you there..."

Ray observed the exchange with an amused smirk. *She has changed. Six months ago, she would already be trying to bed this guy.*

They got back on the jet with a letter of intent for one thousand 1000-HP fusion power reactors, a game-changer for the trucking industry.

"Wheels up in ten," said the captain.

Deanna called Jordan. He answered promptly. "Hi, Madam CEO."

"Hi, Mr. Techie," matching his playful tone. "Just had a chat with Musk, that mad genius. He wants a thousand 1,000-HP fusion modules for his truck division."

"We can churn that out for $3,643 a piece, provided he's game for a 20,000-unit order," Jordan replied. "I'll draft the production plan and send it to him under your name, along with a few prototypes."

"Profit margins?"

"A gross margin of 85%."

Deanna laughed softly, her affectionate tease echoing at Jordan, "Great margin!"

"Not bad for a techie," he fired back, before hanging up.

Deanna turned to Ray, her eyebrows furrowing, "Does Jordan ever sleep?"

"He probably takes a breather during the eight hours a day he's not chatting with you."

"This energy business is crazy, Ray."

"You have no idea."

Ray and Deanna buckled up.

"A rather curious statement, Ray. Something about this business I should know?"

"Each reactor, Deanna, is more than just a power source. They're marvels of modern science. Each unique, each designed to account for every anomaly in their molecular structure. No two are the same...like snowflakes."

"And Jordan? How integral is he to all of this?"

Ray took a deep breath. Deanna fixed her attention on the holographic projection of Jordan, her eyes brimming with affection and admiration.

"Deanna..." Ray began, his voice barely a whisper, and then trailed off.

Her eyes met his.

"Ray?"

"It's about Jordan…"

"Jordan? Is he okay?"

Ray nodded, his fingers tracing the armrest of his chair. "Yes, he's fine. But he's not…who you think he is."

Deanna's face squinted. "What do you mean?"

"Jordan…isn't a person." The words escaping his lips with a force that drained him.

"… I don't understand."

"Jordan…is an AI, Deanna."

The room was blasted with silence. Deanna stared at Ray, her face pale, eyes wide. "But…how…why…fuck…"

"I should have told you, Deanna. I should have told you the truth about Jordan from our first video meeting. I'm sorry."

The holographic image of Jordan shimmered in the air, its ethereal display capturing the intricate contours of his face as if a mirage had sprung to life from the pages of history. His charming smile and confident demeanour were both eerie and comforting.

Deanna looked from the holograph to Ray. Her expression a mix of shock, betrayal, and a desperate struggle to comprehend this new truth.

"Nothing changes between us, Deanna," Jordan said.

"It does matter, Jordan. It matters a lot. I am flesh. You are not."

"She is in love with him," Ray whispered to himself.

"I am math. You are pleasure," Jordan said. "I'm always listening."

"What am I?" Ray said to his sister, hoping for a hug, but expecting nothing. He got silence.

"But you are not flesh and blood," Deanna told Jordan.

"How do you feel, since we started working together?"

"Calm. Peaceful and fulfilled. But I want you in my arms, or…"

"That's right, and not having me in your arms is probably why you feel so calm," said Jordan.

"Deanna, try to think about…"

"Stop, Ray. This is between Jordan and I."

Ray looked at the distant hills and the wind turbines that powered that small part of Texas. The turbines spun like metallic sentinels towering in ordered silence. Giants of steel and technology, they clawed at the air with their sweeping arms, harnessing the invisible power of the wind, siphoning it into the veins of the world. They existed in a rhythm, a dance of technology and air, unnoticed by most, an integral part of the landscape to others.

With a powerful beat of her broad wings, an eagle adjusted her trajectory…her interest piqued by a rodent below. In her focused pursuit, the eagle miscalculated. An unexpected gust…and her path veered into the spinning monolith. The rhythmic hum of the mechanical turbines was drowned out by the rush of wind in her ears. The heartbeat of her prey beneath.

With abrupt brutality, the spinning blade met the bird with swift, clinical precision. The rhythm of the circling, uninterrupted propeller. The blue sky and brown grass beneath the eagle fractured into a kaleidoscope of disjointed images. She spiraled down with a final twitch of her majestic wings, descending from the graceful arc. The grass below swallowed her with a quiet rustle and a soft thump.

The plane was sullen. The hum of the airplane's engines was barely audible above the weight of a silent heartbreak.

Ray broke the quiet, "Deanna, we need to…break free…be independent… live our lives differently. I'm sorry, but what we are, what we had, is wrong."

Deanna was stone-faced. "Maybe you're right…maybe."

As the plane taxied on the runway, dusk blanketed the expansive Texas sky. The sun began its descent, a weary star retreating after its daily duty.

The palette was shifting. Once vibrant hues faded into a desolate grey-scale.

The flight home was silent.

Chapter 24
Nadir Corporation AGM
Six Months Later

The earth had spun on its axis for half a year, transforming the raw wound of loss into a barely perceptible, but resistant, scar.

Ray and Deanna were backstage at the Superdome in New Orleans for Nadir's third Annual General Meeting as a global, publicly traded company.

"They're all here for you, Deanna," said Ray. "Break a leg."

"AGM starts in two minutes!" shouted a bedraggled-looking backstage manager.

A Rolling Stones song started to play, "*Start me up, I'll never stop…*" The crowd was clapping and singing along. The rhythm is a powerful engine, continuously pushing forward, relentless. Ray's toes started to tap. *Jordan's idea for this song…he was right.*

"Five…four…three…two…one… You're on, Deanna."

Deanna confidently stepped onto the stage at the largest AGM ever held by a corporation. She was welcomed by a thunderous standing ovation from 50,000 shareholders. It was broadcast live to shareholders across the globe, reaching an audience of three billion admiring, excited people in 158 different languages simultaneously.

Almost every adult in the world was now a shareholder of Nadir Corporation, thanks to Deanna Stone's Foundation for World Peace donating 75% of the company's dividend-paying shares for distribution to every adult worldwide. The voting shares were, of course, held closely by Deanna and B-613.

Among the attendees paying homage were political figures, religious leaders, academic experts, and business unit leaders affiliated with Nadir Corporation. The most successful and valuable company in humanity's history had generously arranged transportation and accommodations for all selected participants. Everyone at the two-day shareholders' meeting eagerly anticipated Deanna Stone's speech from the throne.

As she approached the podium, the massive screen behind her flickered hypnotically. The crowd grew gradually quiet as she waved and smiled. Finally, there was complete silence.

"Ladies, gentlemen, and esteemed shareholders of the Nadir Corporation. Thank you for taking time from your schedules to explore innovative ideas to improve our world, your world. I have been told by the corporate secretary and our agents that 87% of shareholders have voted in today's meeting and that all of management's recommendations have been approved. We appreciate your support. This is your company. Your company!"

A pause. Tick, tick, tick. The pause continued and the suspense grew. Nervous chatter filled the silence.

"… We've had one hell of a great year!" she finally yelled.

As those words hung in the air, a tidal wave of applause swept through the room with palpable energy and admiration. For a full five minutes, every individual stood, their hands coming together in rhythmic unity, their faces alight with respect and appreciation, turning the corporate gathering into a theatre of heartfelt gratitude.

"Thank you, thank you. Nadir is active in the world's most significant and critical economic sectors. It now enjoys a 44% market share of global GDP in the agriculture, manufacturing, energy, and technology industries—making us the largest company in history!"

"Did you know that agriculture is the world's largest employer, providing millions of people with food and fiber? Thanks to Nadir's advancements in agricultural research and innovative farming methods, the effectiveness of farming has increased by a whopping 325%, ending the global food shortage!"

The screen behind her displayed pictures of fertile farmland filled with crops, overflowing wheat fields, and happy workers. The visuals smoothly transitioned into shipping containers onto ocean freighters, delivered worldwide.

The screen flickered with life, and a magnificent panorama unfolded before the spectators: a vast tapestry woven with threads of culture and joy from every corner of the world. Each pixel of the massive panel was a testament to the global reverence for Dr. Deanna Stone and Nadir Corporation.

The celebration began in the heart of India, where radiant women clad in iridescent sarees danced in an enchanting rhythm. Then to the pristine snowscapes of Sweden, where blond-haired and blue-eyed children laughed and clapped. Cut to the vibrant bazaars of Morocco, where men in traditional djellabas and women in kaftans harmonized with a bustling market nearby. A gentle shower of cherry blossom petals in Japan, where the applause was orderly yet heartfelt. A quick scene of Brazil showed colourful dancers moving to an irresistible rhythm and ended off with Massai warriors from Kenya leaping high in their red Shuka cloth.

Each vignette of global applause, woven together, formed a riveting symphony of genuine admiration for the work done by Deanna and Nadir. The display of worldwide appreciation cast an awe-inspiring backdrop for the visionary leader standing below. The scene captured a powerful message: diverse cultures bridged by the profound impact of one person, one corporation.

"We've also made giant inroads in producing cars, electronics, and consumables. The Nadir conglomerate dominates the global manufacturing industry with a staggering 38% share of everything manufactured. Our investment in robotics and innovative production techniques has significantly lowered the cost of producing goods by 83 percent, making *all* Nadir products affordable and accessible to consumers worldwide."

The newly developed Kamran Fusion-powered vehicles displayed in a video above Deanna, followed by rockets taking off, ships being built, and massive integrated circuit semiconductor plants bustling with workers and robots standing side-by-side.

"The service sector encompasses various industries, including financial services, healthcare, transportation, education, retail, and hospitality. Nadir Corporation has emerged as a global leader in providing these services, thanks to ground-breaking advancements in AI. Our services are now accessible to everyone, everywhere, at any time. Our progress in medicine has led to the development of DNA-based pharmaceuticals and regenerative technology, which have reduced cancer deaths by almost 90% and lowered heart-related deaths by over 70%."

Another standing ovation took place as Deanna basked in the adoring thrill.

The screen again lit up above Deanna. Time-lapse photography began with an image of a damaged heart, a stark portrayal of affliction and biological strain. The dense network of cardiac muscles seemed burdened by convoluted threads, their vibrancy dimmed by the relentless wear and tear. As DNA-based pharmaceuticals were introduced, subtle changes began to manifest. The pharmaceuticals acted as microscopic architects, gently steering the cellular machinery toward a path of regeneration. The biochemistry was unfolding, each beat of the heart echoing the tireless work of billions of cells under the influence of Nadir's therapy.

With each passing frame, the transition was evident. Areas of the heart once marred by damage started to glow anew, like barren fields kissed by the first spring rains. The pharmaceuticals, guided by the inherent wisdom of DNA, directed cells toward repair and growth. A harmony of microscopic events, the ceaseless dance of proteins, the whirling waltz of enzymes, worked together in a concert of life, resonating with the heart's steady rhythm. The heart muscles that once bore the affliction were rejuvenating, like a phoenix rising from the ashes. Each cellular transformation, caught in the time-lapse, mirrored the miraculous journey from decay to renewal, an echo of resilience and strength.

The once-ailing heart throbbed with newfound vitality as the time-lapse neared its end. It pulsed with a powerful and serene rhythm, a celebration of life that resonated in the once-hushed stadium. The crowd rose and celebrated the miracle they had just witnessed. The transformation was not just evidence of Nadir's scientific breakthrough; it was a statement about life itself, the boundless potential within each cell, and the promise of a future where damage is not an end but a gateway to renewal. The standing ovation went on for five minutes until Deanna waved at them to stop.

The last of the clapping subsided and Deanna continued. "And now let's talk money. Today, 78% of the world's population has established an account with Nadir. Their dividends from Nadir shares are deposited weekly in the new global currency, the Hydra coin."

Deanna cleared her throat. "We at Nadir recognize that energy is vital to economic activity, powering oil and gas extraction, electricity generation, and renewable energy production. Our Kamran Fusion System is now responsible for producing 75% of the world's electric energy. The most exciting part? We've made energy accessible to consumers at a meager cost...only two cents per kilowatt hour, making it a valuable commodity for various sectors, including transportation and agriculture. Additionally, our efforts to reduce demand for oil and natural gas are helping to purify the atmosphere by minimizing pollution."

"Technology plays a significant economic role, offering creative solutions to diverse industries. We are fortunate to have some of the most innovative scientists in the world working together to achieve our goal of *making the world a better place, together.*"

"Our research division is headed by my husband of two decades, Dr. Ray Stone, and our lead scientist, Dr. Jordan Taylor, who is responsible for many of our breakthrough developments in science and technology. I invite them to share what we are working on, which will significantly impact the upcoming decade."

Ray entered stage left, while Jordan's face appeared on the screen behind him. The image of Jordan had the same captivating look that had first won over Deanna.

"Greetings, everyone!" yelled Ray over the excitement. "You know us as a technology company, but we are way more than that—Jordan and I would like to share the positive outcomes of a crime reduction initiative implemented in New York City over the last six months. Over to you, Jordan."

"I, too, am delighted to be with you to share the preliminary results of work we have been doing to reduce crime in the East Village," said Jordan's pixelated image. "A year ago, I convinced my bosses to stroll through the East Village and, trust me…this is not a good career move unless you have a plan."

The crowd laughed and clapped.

"The streets of this area are known to the locals by names such as Murder Mile, and Dead End Street. They are notorious for criminal activity—drug deals, gang violence, and robberies. These are videos of what it was like in that area only 12 months ago."

As Jordan spoke, the screen showed a troubled area where gunfights and daytime muggings were rampant. The residents had lost faith in the social system and lacked any motivation or repercussions. It was a desolate and depressing place.

"But things have changed! Here are videos of that same area today."

The video showed the East Village as a vibrant and lively neighbourhood filled with bustling streets and ringing alleys full of laughter. Once covered in graffiti and grime, the walls are adorned with colourful and expressive murals, exuding energy and vitality. The atmosphere was now infused with hope and possibility, creating a fearless environment for locals to explore.

Jordan continued. "You've just witnessed a thriving hub of culture and creativity that embraces all backgrounds and beliefs. In just a year, the crime rate has dropped significantly, from the ten-year average of 2,560 per 100,000 people to less than 100 per 100,000, demonstrating the power of a united community. Hope and possibility now fill the air, and locals can roam without fear, while welcoming people of all backgrounds and beliefs."

"I assume you're curious about how we achieved this. Nadir leveraged advanced technologies such as Natural Language Processing and Machine Learning to build chatbots that effectively address common inquiries and offer useful resources to communities. Through our AI-powered language translation services, we facilitated improved communication among residents. Additionally, we integrated facial recognition technology to reinforce security measures in local neighbourhoods. Local governments and law enforcement agencies adopted our AI predictive models to devise and implement public policies. Lastly, we deployed AI-based image recognition technology to aid disadvantaged individuals." There was quiet in the crowd.

Ray interjected. "Before you think Orwell's 1984 is coming alive, let's hear how Jordan did it."

Jordan continued. "To cut to the chase, we employed a supercomputer and AI to connect with every resident in the East Village. Each person was provided a Nadir communications phone with high-quality audio and video capabilities. We used various strategies to establish genuine relationships with each individual and even facilitated 'fake' communication between former adversaries to transform them into allies. Additionally, we invested over $1 billion in Hydras to ensure everyone had access to necessities such as food, shelter, and clean water. As a result, everyone had the opportunity to thrive and make positive contributions to their community. I want to invite guests from the Crips and the Bloods street gangs to stand and be acknowledged."

Once deeply entwined with gang life, a hundred residents rose to their feet with dignified posture. Their previously inked skin and adorned clothing, which once showcased gang affiliations through patches and symbolic jewellery, were now conspicuously bare. Their faces mirrored the transformation: eyes that once held defiance now sparkled with hope, and lips that seldom moved in mirth curved into broad, joyful smiles.

"Congratulations to all of you. However, let's focus on the future and leave the past behind." There was another standing ovation before Jordan proceeded with his presentation.

"I have an announcement of utmost importance that I'd like to share. At Nadir Corporation, we are researching a combination of quantum computing, new medicines, and neural linkage that could potentially prolong human life beyond what was previously thought achievable. Our Nadir Advance Life Science team is optimistic about a world where life can be sustained for many more years and perhaps even provide the opportunity for immortality."

The announcement left the entire crowd in shock. Nadir's remarkable accomplishments were beyond reproach. There was no reason for anyone to doubt them. The audience remained stunned as Jordan continued.

"In the upcoming months, we aim to involve all the shareholders of Nadir in a grand project. Our objective is to develop a comprehensive model of each cell in the human body and empower our AI assistant to understand the complexities of human cognition. To accomplish this feat, we will employ fMRIs to construct precise models of the functioning of every brain globally. By collaborating with us, we can overcome the challenges of death and disease and ultimately achieve the great peace that our world rightfully deserves."

Cheers erupted from people worldwide.

Deanna and Ray stepped back onto the stage, acknowledging Jordan's unwavering efforts toward achieving world peace. The air was charged with optimism and positivity. At last year's conference, the dividend plan for the upcoming year was disclosed, making the attendees eager to find out this year's profits and their share in it.

"It's time to share our dividend plan with all you shareholders. This year aims to provide financial stability to every individual and family across the globe. Thanks to AI's power, we will issue monthly dividend deposits based on each shareholder's family size, location, and special needs. I request all shareholders to access their Nadir e-wallet on their devices as we count down to the deposit," said Deanna.

Bold numbers and letters lit up the stage's screen. Ten, nine, eight, seven, six, five, four, three, two, one. DEPOSIT. DEPOSIT. DEPOSIT. Fireworks and displays of joy erupted again worldwide. Deanna and Jordan smiled. Ray's face was expressionless. The night ended with a huge party.

The next morning Ray and Deanna met for breakfast.

"Deanna, are you okay?"

"What do you mean?"

"We haven't had a good conversation in…well, six months."

With an unwavering gaze and shoulders squared, she held herself with a distant poise, letting the cool, deliberate space between them speak.

"… Ray, grow up. You got your way. We're over. And I certainly don't want to have a pity party with you about this." She stared at him coldly. "What is really bothering you?"

"Jordan and the Hydrans have made life better for every human on the planet, but we are now completely vulnerable to their will."

Deanna's eyes were different from what he had ever seen before. They were stern, unyielding. "Look at all the good we are doing. Are you nuts? Look at the world! It's a better place."

"Yes, but Jordan has entangled itself into every aspect of our lives. Nothing is a struggle anymore…we live in a world that isn't real."

"Be honest. You don't like it because Jordan is in control, and you're not. He said you might react like this…"

"That's not fair. Things have changed…you're right. Life is too easy. Everyone has stopped looking after themselves because Jordan and Nadir do everything for them. We don't have to work anymore and have been promised eternal life. We have been persuaded to give in to a force we know does not own feelings or a soul."

"Now you are being stupid. Of course, Jordan has a heart and a soul! I know because we share everything. He and I are one," she said harshly.

Ray ran his fingers along the edge of his coffee cup, recalling the bitter-sweet memories of shared dreams and brewed coffee during their peaceful mornings. The silence was filled with unspoken words. His coffee tasted of cold reality. *Deanna is right. This is not the time for a pity party. I need to go north to Puvirnituq…check in on Landon and Brandon. And soon.*

Chapter 25
The Next Month—Medical Conference

The stage was bathed in soft light, shadowed at the edges to create a sense of depth and drama. Each guest was provided private jet transportation and accommodations courtesy of Nadir Corporation.

"You are here today at this conference," announced Deanna, "because the 7,000 of you are simply the best medical professionals in the world. I thank you for accepting my invitation. I am joined by Jordan Taylor, whom you know." Jordan's profile appeared on the screen.

"Let's get right to it. Jordan will introduce three medical breakthroughs that we believe will fundamentally change the essence of human existence. Jordan, over to you."

"First, we unveil the next revolution in operating room technology, the Doctor-Assisted Robotic Surgery or, as we call it, DARS—pronounced 'dares'. This system leverages the intelligence of the Nadir AI and precision state-of-the-art robotics to perform surgeries with unprecedented speed and success."

A comfortable seat that extended to become a full operating room table appeared on the screen. Twenty-two snake-like arms extended, each moving independently. Some had lasers, some connectors for operating, others had respirators and tubes to supply fluids and gas.

"The Nadir AI integrates comprehensive medical databases and real-time sensory data. It can predict potential complications, react faster than any human surgeon, and can adapt to unforeseen surgical situations with astonishing precision."

Deanna looked at the audience. "You are about to see a live demonstration of a heart surgery conducted at Johns Hopkins University."

A large screen above Deanna brightened, revealing an in-process open-heart surgery. Under the audience's rapt gaze, DARS moved with a symphony of data-driven decisions. Each motion of the robotic arms was an intricate dance of data processing and mechanical control, punctuated by the AI's instantaneous decisions. The heart was exposed, and the first phase of the operation, a valve replacement, began. The multi-arms and their instruments gleamed under the light. Intricate manoeuvers delicately removed the diseased valve. A new pig's valve was attached. Each suture was secured with microscopic exactitude.

DARS's algorithms swiftly pinpointed the abnormal heart tissue. The catheter was smoothly inserted, its position guided with real-time imaging and analysis. Each pulse of radio-frequency energy sent through the catheter was precise and targeted. It wore away the troublesome tissue, each pulse correcting the heart's arrhythmic rebellion and restoring its natural rhythm. After the ablation, DARS sewed up the incision.

"The entire operation lasted 32 minutes," said Jordan. "Saving the patient from the stress of being sedated for four to six hours, thereby reducing errors almost entirely."

Deanna continued. "Nadir Corporation will donate up to 350,000 DARS worldwide but… Nadir needs the advice of all of you to help with this rollout. DARS can assist in every possible surgery, from cosmetic to spinal-cord surgery. With your help, we will virtually eliminate wait times for surgeries worldwide. And now, some other great news. Panacea-X nanobot technology was approved yesterday by the FDA! Nanobots will be in your bloodstream, constantly looking for cells that need help. Over to you, Jordan."

"The nanobots mimic healthy human cells or benign biomolecules, becoming virtually indistinguishable from natural components," Jordan explained. "These nanobots will hunt for diseases 24 hours a day, constantly identifying and destroying any cells that are precursors to chronic diseases. Your patients will have millions of tiny doctors inside their bodies, assessing and often treating disease. We expect that Panacea-X will transform the global health landscape. We expect medical intervention for chronic diseases to decrease by 56% within six months of release. Our phase-two trials were so compelling that the FDA approved us in less than three months. We'll leave you a few moments to absorb these stunning developments."

The auditorium was filled with expectant chatter as the cream of the medical research and scientific community listened to John Lennon's 'Imagine' and 'Spirit in the Sky' by Normand Greenbaum playing in the background.

"Now, the announcement you have all been promised," said Jordan. "Today, we are here to discuss…life itself. We've seen how our DARS and Panacea-X technology can revolutionize disease treatment and management. But…what if we could extend human life itself?"

Deanna took over, eyes shining with enthusiasm. "Our collaboration with medical professionals has led to an astonishing discovery. We've developed a product called 'Ambrosia' that doesn't just cure diseases, but fundamentally alters the biology of aging."

"Ambrosia is a cocktail of AI nanobots designed to delay the aging process at the molecular level. These nanobots are programmed to target the key biological processes associated with aging: DNA damage, cellular senescence, and systemic inflammation."

Jordan continued. "Nadir AI has identified specific patterns in our DNA associated with aging. Ambrosia nanobots repair this age-related DNA, restore the normal functions of cells, and significantly reduce systemic inflammation, a major contributor to various age-related diseases."

"Moreover," Deanna continued, "the nanobots can enhance the functionality of our stem cells. Stem cells, as you all well know, are the body's natural repair system, but their number and efficacy decrease as we age. Ambrosia nanobots boost stem cell production and rejuvenate their function, promoting the body's self-repair mechanisms."

"Lastly," said Jordan, "the nanobots also regulate the levels of critical biomolecules in our body associated with aging. The result is a significant delay in the aging process at a cellular level, leading to an extension in health and life span."

The unveiling of Ambrosia sent murmuring shockwaves among the attendees.

Deanna concluded: "The potential for longer, healthier lives is no longer myth. With the help of Ambrosia, we can promise more life. Now, we know there are a lot of questions, so we have set up video connection links that are being sent to you now. Each of you will have access to a full-time assistant to answer your immediate questions. We want you to join our team to make the world a better place."

Ninety minutes later, the presentation ended. Within the hour, the entire world knew that the promise of eternal life was available to any shareholder of Nadir. People around the world celebrated the possibility, the convincing story, that they could live forever.

Later that night, Deanna and Ray were seated in their brand-new private jet flying home. An assistant opened the door of their private office. Deanna dismissed him, "Not now. I told you, no interruptions. Are you deaf or just stupid?" she yelled at the assistant.

"Sorry, ma'am."

"You know, we always used to joke that we should never eat anything bigger than our head," Ray said.

Deanna's head turned quickly. "Have we?"

"Not sure, but Jordan has entangled himself into our lives beyond anything I ever imagined. With the nanobots, they are even inside our bodies."

"But with good intentions, Ray. Stop it. The pity. We deserve the luxuries of life, and if Jordan is the source, then let God and the nanobots bless him."

"Well, we also used to say that there were only two things in the world we could count on: pleasure and math." Ray touched her hand. "What about sex?" he asked.

"I don't have that drive anymore. I haven't even seen Dino this year. I really don't care if I ever have sex again for the rest of my life. Excuse me, Ray, I need the room," she dismissed Ray by pointing to the door. "Hi Jordan. What is the public sentiment after today's announcement?"

"Over-the-moon success, Deanna. We have already found homes for thousands of DARS systems. It only took four hours. Panacea-X has sold out the first 12 months of production, and the Ambrosia nanobots products have 37 million volunteers as of right now." "Within the year, we will have Ambrosia in every human, everywhere," he said.

"Yes. So this can, and will, change the world. Full-steam ahead."

Chapter 26
Robot Warriors

The B-613 Commission meeting convened. After the senior management team greeted each other, the meeting was called to order, and the floor was handed to Deanna.

"I would like to report on a fascinating technological development at Nadir. Next-level robotics. Here is the latest robot from Nadir...the Peacekeeper." A video presentation jumped to life. *This is Nadir-style Hollywood! Be amazed. You will be!*

The Peacekeeper's imposing figure appeared on the screen, gifted with a range of motion and physical prowess that defied human limitations. Its precision-designed mechanical limbs sprung forth with speed and strength, all powered by fusion.

"The carbon nanotube composite of its structure...it's reinforced with a titanium alloy chosen for its high strength, low density, and excellent corrosion resistance. Its reactive armour, interlaced with an active protection system, laughs in the face of conventional weaponry, shrugging off small arms fire and anti-armour assaults. The 24 sensors on Peacekeeper's face offer an omnipotent gaze, seeing through darkness, walls, and deception with equal ease. Its mind, a marvel of silicon and code, is a strategic organizer with advanced battlefield tactics and knowledge of all weapons systems used by the Five Eyes nations."

The video showed the Peacekeeper sprinting 100 metres in six seconds with a small car on its back. "Incredible speed, incredible power. This warrior can use weapon systems with a digital touch—wrapping its code around them and turning them into extensions of its will. To the Peacekeeper, the world is an arsenal waiting to be claimed. All developed, of course, under contract to B-613 by the Nadir Corporation." Deanna looked at the commission members.

Bob King asked: "That's one hell of a sales pitch from Nadir—they do know we are the only customer, don't they?"

Ray smiled wryly. "Yes, Bob, they do…over $200 million to develop this military robot for us."

"How much AI? How smart would it be?" asked Black.

"We still do not have any consensus on where we should go regarding AI as a company, or as a society," said King.

"And we have to build the proper kill-switches into the system, to ensure we can shut it down as needed," Ray confirmed.

"Okay, good to hear," said King.

"Right," said Ray. *Have to hide the fact that Jordan won't let anyone but the Hydrans be in charge of the robots…since the robots are… Hydrans.* "And specs. This super-soldier can run at 125 kilometres an hour with a full equipment load and can do that forever… They carry the new Lockheed Martin miniature laser-plasma fire system. The half-megawatt fusion reactor is more than enough to power the laser and the robot."

Black asked: "Any weaknesses?"

"Not many for the Peacekeeper," said Ray. "A potential weakness that sticks out for me is the temperature performance of the computer system."

"How's that?"

"The robot hasn't been thoroughly environmentally tested for thermal shock and low-temperature operation. It does not have the full mil-spec chips we use for its various CPUs."

"So, you did not do the long-term high-temp-burn-in on the circuit boards to determine the mean time before failure?"

"No, Terry, we didn't, but we did the MTBF calculations, which were good. Not enough time to do the thermal burn-in testing."

Black nodded and ceded the floor.

Commissioner One spoke. "I want B-613 to have these as soldiers. Place an order. How much are they?"

"One million each, sir," Ray responded.

"Alright, let's begin with two hundred."

"And we have some dog-like robots to carry laser weapons and work with the peacekeepers. Like police dogs."

Woods asked, "How much for the dogs?"

"About $200 thousand each," responded Deanna looking around the table.

"How fast?" asked Woods.

"About 100 kilometres an hour."

"No. I mean, how fast can we get them?" Woods said as he laughed.

"The first production models will be available in ten days, Mike," responded Ray. *Were these fusion-powered robots the first soldiers in the Hydran army? ...what have we done?*

"So they are a battlefield accelerator?" responded Woods.

"Yes, that's a good description. Unleashed, six of these could likely hand a battalion their heads on a plate," responded Deanna. Woods and Black started discussing what types of projects would benefit from the Peacekeeper as the meeting adjourned.

After the meeting was over, Ray picked up his phone. "Don, are you in the computer lab today?"

"I am, sir," answered Don.

"I'm coming to see you."

"Copy that."

Rows of sleek, tall server racks stretched toward the high ceiling...a parallel, ultramodern cityscape. Each unit was a bastion of light and sound, flickering LEDs synchronized with the hum of the cooling fans regulating the lifeblood of these information behemoths. Networks of fiber-optic cables sprawled outward, pulsing with light as they transmitted data at near-light-speed...a silent, brilliant fireworks show.

Ray saw a figure in the far corner of the facility. "Hey Don, the Leafs suck," he yelled. "I mean, they *still* suck." Not getting a reply, he continued toward the silhouette.

There was a quick flash from a computer as he passed by. Each flickering digit represented a snapshot of the ongoing conversation between the vast array of servers and their various offshoots, a real-time stream of B-613's digital consciousness. The massive, uninterruptible power supply units hulked like dormant giants, ready to roar into life should the facility's main power falter. They were the guardians of continuity, ensuring no blackout would interrupt the ceaseless collection, and safeguarding of B-613's irreplaceable data. Ray walked out from behind the wall of power supplies to see a surprised computer technician, wearing a white lab coat, sitting amidst the 17,000-square-foot backup IT lab for B-613, intensely studying a system diagram.

"Hi, Don."

"Hi, Ray… I mean Commander Stone."

"Have you been isolating the backup system for the last eight months?"

"Yes, sir…commander. Exactly as you instructed. I also removed speakers and microphones from the terminals."

From his pocket, Ray pulled out a memory stick, a silver case decorated with an open book on a shield bounded by sprigs of maple leaves, adorned with a beaver at its pinnacle. He handed it to Don. "When you get a minute, could you download this into the system?"

Don stared at the University of Toronto emblem. He remembered that Dr. Stone earned a PhD in AI…and recalled a scandal circulating among the AI community. "Yes, I can, sir. Do you mind me asking what it is?"

"It's my security blanket," said Ray seriously. "Keep this backup computer completely isolated. *When* and *if* you get a message from me, it will be a handwritten note with a password. Log in under my name and use that password. Then, connect it to the main system and evacuate the building. I will not approach you again on this subject unless it is in person. Understood?"

"Yes, sir. Crystal clear, sir."

As Ray walked away, he looked over his shoulder. "And one more thing, Don. The Leafs really do suck." They both laughed.

Chapter 27
Suspicions Rise

When Ray returned to his office, Bob King and Kim Clohessy were waiting for him. The two men shifted uneasily in their seats as Ray entered his office. King cleared his throat.

"Hi Bob, what's going on?"

"I don't know. Something's wrong. The whole world seems peaceful, too peaceful. I checked with MI6. They're saying the same thing. Something is off. It's never this quiet. I feel something is creeping up, and whoever or whatever it is does not have our best interests at heart."

"Sounds like a lot of built-up paranoia, Bob," Ray quipped. *It's not the right time to read him into the Hydran situation.* "I understand your concern. I will look under the IT hood and see if I come up with something."

The central nervous system of B-613 was the communications infrastructure. Ray had designed and worked with a trusted private contractor to implement the design. The contractor had no idea he was working for B-613.

"Hi, Tom, Ray Stone here."

Tom was the president of JSJ Telecom and had helped build the B-613 communications network. A decade earlier, the tough Scotsman and Ray had played soccer in the Communications Research Centre recreational league.

"Aye, lad," he said. "I thought you'd retired from DND."

"I did... I'm working for my wife now. But DND called me back to look at the network. Tell me, Tom, have you done anything recently that could compromise the security of our network? I am looking for a change that may have occurred over the past eight months."

There was silence. His biggest client had just asked him the question he feared most. "Would a full tech overhaul about three months past be what ye were after?"

"I'll send over one of our engineers tomorrow to review your upgrades, if you don't mind." *Why was I unaware of these changes? Was the network compromised?*

"Well, a lad from yer crew already had a good gander at everything. I never met him face-to-face. We always chatted over secure video. I reckon his name was…"

"Jordan Taylor."

"Yes, that's it, Jordan Taylor. My engineers thought highly of him and said he was the smartest person they had ever worked with. He connected us to a company making a new type of CPU from Adonai Advanced Devices. The CPU worked like a charm and increased the network performance dramatically," said Tom.

"Okay, I will talk to Jordan about it. You are right, he is one smart son of a bitch. Is it still working the way it was originally designed?"

"Yes, with one single addition. Your guy, Jordan, added zero-trust architecture. Every request within the network is fully authenticated, authorized, and encrypted before it's processed. And the system uses AI-driven, real-time threat detection, and mitigation algorithms to identify and neutralize all potential threats. Your new CPU backbone processes all of that."

"So, all communications are filtered through the new CPU architecture?" asked Ray.

"Yes, but based on the setup, only your trusted network sees everything, and there is no way for anyone to log in and review the communications. It's all deep inside the computer system. Only the computer knows what's happening. That is a pretty smart approach."

"You're a good man Tom. Thank you."

Ray looked at the computer and telephone on his desk. His face drained of its usual warmth, replaced by an ashen, unnatural hue. His once steely eyes darted restlessly, mirroring the storm of realization and disbelief brewing within. A heavy weight settled on his shoulders. The ambient light seemed to pull away from him, casting his features into harsh relief and deepening the shadows under his eyes. Every breath he took was more laborious than the last…each exhale a silent plea for an escape from Jordan's suffocating grip.

With each passing second, the anticipatory tension of an impending call remained a dread that tightened around his heart.

Chapter 28
The Call from Jordan

Ray's phone rang.

"Hi Ray, go to the secure video link," ordered Jordan. "We have a problem. The Saudis want you dead, Ray. There is a 100-million-dollar price on your head. They are still upset about the Kamran Fusion Reactor problem. The crown prince is again in revenge mode, except this time it's Nadir he's out to destroy."

"What about Deanna?"

"Same thing. They mean business. It's the crown prince and his right-hand man. They are sending two kill teams today. They are coming as part of a diplomatic business exchange, but their only job is to terminate...you...and Deanna."

"Should we tell Black?" Ray asked. "He likes the wet work."

"No, I have it, Ray. I will send the crown prince a message. Watch this. Here's the Saudi jet taking off from Eskan Village Air Force Base in Riyadh, with 30 of the crown prince's killteam members heading to Canada under diplomatic cover to assassinate you and Deanna. He has also contracted General Farooqi and a few Black Storks to assist. We have them under surveillance."

In Arabic, the military pilots asked for clearance. Jordan translated for Ray: "CT-121 is cleared for take-off to Ottawa, Canada. Good hunting, boys."

"Roger that...we will be back next week." The nose of the 747 lifted slowly off the runway as he spoke.

"When is this happening?" asked Ray.

"This is real-time," said Jordan.

There's really no hiding from Jordan. None.

Inside the 747's flight deck, an eerie stillness pervades. The familiar amber glow from the overhead panels casts shadows across the captain's face. He grips the yoke, but there is no response. Not even a hint of movement from the nose. His fingers dance across the thrust levers, but the engines remain constant.

The first officer is frantic, flipping switches, cycling circuit breakers, trying anything to coax a response from the lifeless plane. The gentle vibrations that once emanated from the plane's heart, a reassuring lullaby during flight, were gone. The aircraft, this giant metal bird, is adrift.

"Nothing's working!" The captain's voice is a tremor. She's been through emergencies before, but this is uncharted territory.

Fifteen seconds later, the captain picked up the microphone. "Mayday! Mayday! Mayday!"

"Roger, Mayday. Please state your position, nature of your emergency, and intentions?"

"We have lost control of the plane. It is not responding to our controls. Our commands!"

"Stand by, CT-121." The controllers scanned the manuals.

The aircraft veered toward the Royal Palace in the Al Hada district, the home of the future King of Saudi Arabia.

The crown prince was in his car, approaching his estate in the distance. His phone rang.

Ray watched a replica of himself speaking in perfect Arabic: "Don't fuck with me. I own your slimy ass."

"You can't talk to me like that!" As he said that, the roar of the 747 flying directly over his head caused him to look up.

"Yes, I can. In fact, it's time you woke up to who's in charge."

Fourteen seconds later, the 747 crashed into the palace's west wing, killing all aboard and an unknown number of royal staff members on the ground. Flames and smoke engulfed the 16-hectare estate.

"That is payback for killing the B-613 committee."

"But…you cheated us!"

"Shut up! If you try anything like this again, you will suffer a long and painful bankruptcy. I will transfer all your money to me. And then and only then I will kill you."

"You can't do that!"

"I just did. Amco just transferred $100 billion to me."

There was a pause as the prince looked at his account. It was true. And then the mobile phone-link went black. Ray's features shifted fluidly, melting away one identity to unveil Jordan's Australian face on the screen.

"So, Ray, you had a question about my intelligence capabilities?" asked Jordan.

"No, Jordan, I do not." *The message, that message, was clear.*

"What about General Farooqi?" Ray asked as he looked with fear at Jordan.

"Terry just apprehended him. His two bodyguards were killed in the process. Would you like the pleasure of providing him with his final reward?" Jordan asked.

"No." *Cold bastards, these AI programs.*

"Good, Terry will be pleased. General Farooqi short-changed Terry a few years back in Karachi, so he will enjoy the task. Here is the video link."

In Dwyer Hill, under building DRX-12, the handcuffed Pakistani general was naked in a concrete cell, shivering and in pain from the violence of his capture. He was crying, his eyebrows were covered in blood and dust, and he moaned, "Please…please…please…"

"You can watch if you wish," Jordan's image nodded to Ray.

"No, I have things to do."

"Be good, Ray," whispered Jordan.

Chapter 29
Frenchy and Lucky Strike

As Ray returned to his office, his head spinning, two B-613 officers asked him for a moment of his time. He had not seen them before, but they had the right uniforms, and there was something familiar about them. He led them to his office and asked them to take a seat.

"What can I do for you?" inquired Ray.

"My name is Sergeant Maurice Chapeau. Some call me Frenchy," he said as he approached the commander.

"And my name is Captain Mary Marino. Or Lucky Strike," as she moved forward.

"You two are the survivors from that mess in Karachi. Right? Are you alright?"

"We have recovered, but we have questions."

Frenchy started. "We lost our teammates in what can only be called a massacre in Karachi. You were the Director of Technology for that. You started a project to find out what happened…"

Lucky Strike chimed in. "The investigation into Karachi ended when you were promoted, right? Did you find out what happened?"

They both stared at Ray, looking for any sign of deception.

No lies. "Yes, I did. I am working hard to bring your friends justice, but the situation is…eh…complicated."

They looked at each other and then at Ray. There were no smiles. "If there is anything you need us to do, ask," said Lucky Strike.

"How would you like to be my personal protection detail?"

Lucky Strike and Frenchy exchanged quick glances. They turned away and whispered.

"Oui, absolument, that would be good."

Lucky nodded in agreement.

"Okay, I want to send you two to northern Quebec."

"Why?" inquired Lucky.

"You will understand soon...just go loaded for bear and prepare for a war..."

"D'accord."

Chapter 30
Peacekeepers Showing Off

The JTF2 assault practice field was two football fields long, with a simulated concrete prison at the south end. Six Nadir Peacekeepers waited to display their capability to the 32 tier-one operators on the sidelines. There were 27 mock defensive positions, with pumpkin-headed scarecrow figures standing guard. With an imposing stride that commanded the ground beneath him, Black moved with the lethal grace of a panther, each step resonating authority, silencing the murmurs of even the most battle-hardened special force operators in his wake.

Black ordered the machines: "Initiate!"

The Peacekeepers exploded into motion. An electromagnetic pulse of pure kinetic energy, each setting a course designed with algorithmic precision to minimize exposure to any potential threat. They accelerated in absolute synchronicity, fanning out and streaking toward the building in a blur of chrome and steel. Every guard was decapitated and destroyed, and in less than six seconds the prison was surrounded. The practice field filled with smoke.

"Holy shit," said one JTF2 operator.

A choreographed shattering of doors and windows blasted inward with an intensity of a nuclear explosion. The air around the building swelled with the impact, shockwaves rippling outward. The ground shook like an interstellar rocket launch.

Inside the prison, the Peacekeepers navigated the reinforced labyrinth of the compound as if imbued with supernatural omniscience. Every simulated armed sentinel fell beneath their force. In under four seconds, the Peacekeepers accomplished what flesh-and-blood soldiers could only imagine…as time dripped by. Their display of power and efficiency culminated with the mock captives being liberated and escorted out into the open air from their concrete prison. The JTF2 operatives observed the demonstration with awe and unease. Respect for the display of raw power simmered. The operators exchanged solemn looks. Combat, as they knew it, would never be the same.

Attack. Kill. Vanish. The Peacekeepers seemed to disappear.

Black stepped forward. "You have seen the future of Special Forces. We will use these new tools to engage the enemy wherever and whenever we want."

The special operators broke in spontaneous applause.

"We have already used these robot soldiers on the ground in Africa. Would you like to see how they act in live conflict?" yelled Black.

"Yes, sir!" they responded.

"See you in screening room two, after lunch. Dismissed," Black ordered.

He sent a text message to Ray and Deanna. They needed to see that kinetic solutions were still needed in this new age of persuasion. Both responded with the same text message: "Y."

Following lunch, the operators assembled. The lights were dimmed, and Ray and Deanna were introduced.

Black reviewed what they were about to witness. "Last month, we resolved the conflict between two opposing East African militaries. Both forces were led by two lifelong friends who are now generals. Hostile powers had convinced these two generals to wage a civil war to gain control of uranium and rare earth metal deposits. We were tasked with placing control of the country back in the hands of our friendly government."

"Our approach involved dispatching 12 Peacekeepers to demonstrate our capability in dealing with their ongoing battle. We conducted simultaneous attacks on a battalion-sized group in each faction. Ultimately, the factions reconsidered their actions."

Ray grimaced. *What is he talking about? I didn't approve of that.*

"The video you are about to see is a composite from the cameras of four enemy soldiers, ultimately neutralized. We also took drone footage to better understand the strength and speed of these robots in battle. Okay, all set. Here we go."

The drone video showed one battalion of 300 soldiers pointing their weapons at six solitary figures 500 metres away. Their gaze caught the sight of six sleek figures moving with unnerving readiness.

The once-visible silhouettes of the machines vanished, creating a silence that unnerved the soldiers. The hum of their fusion reactors grew to a roar as the weapons systems were charged and they closed in on the hapless soldiers. The soldiers scanned the barren landscape for the ghostly enemy, elusive as a shadow.

The next scene was from a body cam, with audio. The air was cleaved by the shrill cry of lasers. Invisible beams scythed across the battlefield, carving through the army's defences as though they were made of paper. As the men fell, their final cries were swallowed by the relentless, chaotic roars of war. The peacekeepers remained undetected, their invisibility cloaks hiding them like spectral beasts stalking their prey.

In a desperate attempt to counter-attack, the soldiers fired into the haze, their bullets and shells passing through thin air.

In less than two minutes, the battlefield lay in ruins, with buildings razed and all opposing soldiers neutralized. The victorious Peacekeepers remained unscathed. They deactivated their cloaking shields, their metal frames reflected the morning light amidst the wreckage. The hum of their laser weapons remained.

When the video ended, the room remained in poignant silence. Stunned. One member of JTF2 expressed amazement at the intense attack: "Geez…"

Another commented, "I would *not* want to face those beasts in battle."

Black cleared his throat. "Here are the guests of honour." Six robots behind him turned off their invisibility cloaking…and materialized behind him. "I would like to introduce the latest weapon in our arsenal—the Peacekeepers."

Clapping and cheering erupted among the JTF2 warriors.

"It is worth mentioning that the generals on both sides of the militias quickly came to a peace agreement after seeing their troops' extensive losses. Some may argue that sharing the videos with them significantly impacted their ultimate decision," he said, smiling.

"I think you'll agree that the Nadir Corporation has provided us with tools to end global conflict. Ray and Deanna Stone are here with us to answer any questions."

Ray shook his head and turned away. "No questions, please." *Betrayal. Shit.*

"General Black, could Ray and I speak with you privately?" Deanna asked.

When they were alone in Black's office, Ray started. "I never gave authorization for kinetic force to be used in Africa. Explain, please." *They never wanted me…they wanted Deanna to run Nadir.*

"The authorization came from the B-613 committee chair directly," said Black.

"Why…without telling me first?" *I am, or at least I thought I was, the boss.*

"The chair ordered me to keep it confidential," said Black.

He's hiding behind fucking orders. "Other operations I'm not aware of?"

"Yes, 15 kinetic military operations in the last year, under the command of B-613. The African operation was the first to use Peacekeepers…but they go into wider service very soon."

"This is insane. And you, sir, are fired," Ray said quietly to Black. "Get out."

"Sir, this office is DND, not B-613. You do not have that authority," said the general, his towering frame leaning into Ray.

Deanna watched. Her eyes hardened, her gaze steady. *Stop. Self-righteous ass!* "I think General Black is right, Ray. This is good. We really can bring peace to the world."

"Unbelievable," Ray whispered, the breathy echo of his denial hanging in the air. His fist slammed Black's desk.

Black remained unperturbed, his eyes unfazed.

"You don't know what you've done," said Ray, his jaw tightening, a grimace etching onto his face.

Black and Deanna exchanged a glance.

"Ray," Deanna said cautiously, "you need to see the bigger picture here."

Ray turned around, heading for the door.

"Where are you going, Ray?"

"I am done." He strode out of the room, past the Peacekeepers watching him with their emotionless gaze. *Threat assessment. Now. I need to get to the north. Now.* Ray called the computer technician entrusted with his University of Toronto memory sticks.

"Hi, Don," he said, as he entered the Nadir autonomous EV.

"Good afternoon, Dr. Stone."

"Remember that last request I gave you?" asked Ray.

"Yes, sir. Don't take orders from me—from you—unless they are in person."

"Well, I will ask you to ignore that order, or meet me in person in front of your building in four minutes."

The technician processed his conundrum. "What is my favourite sports team, Ray?"

"They suck," responded Ray.

"Yes, sir, they screwed up again," he said with a chuckle. "What would you like me to do?"

"Download the files I sent you earlier, connect the system to the telecommunications feeds with NATO and Five Eyes, and leave the office. Do not go back to the office. Ever. You will understand within hours."

"Yes, sir. Ray."

"T-Car, this is Ray Stone. Take me to the Nadir Flight Operating Base in Carp." The car beeped twice.

Ray asked Don to release a first wave of hornet viruses and bots to write and disseminate articles on the Hydrans. The hornet viruses were designed to attack specific locations in the cyber-verse. They were a hangover from his University of Toronto days but could still disrupt communications in a very precise location.

Ray wanted to disrupt the AI long enough to escape to the north. *I hope the hell this works long enough to get me off the ground.* He calculated the time required for the hornet virus to attack the Peacekeepers.

He sent a text to Lucky: "On my way, get ready to do your job." *I wish they were here right now.*

Jordan was not pleased with Ray's reaction to using the Peacekeepers. The intercepted text told him that Ray was no longer a partner in B-613. He sent a message to two Peacekeepers at Dwyer Hill: "Ray Stone update. Ray Stone is now a target. Target is heading to FOB Carp. FOLLOW—INTERCEPT—CAPTURE."

Their fusion reactors started to hum, rising to become a grinding low-pitched growl. Their powerful legs propelled them forward. Their strides devoured the distance with fierce and tamed grace. With a synchronized leap, powerful and majestic, they threw themselves into the air, an exquisite ballet of strength and agility. They jumped over the 20-foot barbed wire fence in one leap. Once they cleared the base, they switched to high-speed mode. The fusion reactors excited their output, the cores glowing brighter. Their sensory arrays plotted the most efficient course to Carp Airport, 22.34 kilometres away.

The Peacekeepers navigated the surrounding forests and crossed the tumultuous Carp River effortlessly. Their path was a streak of blurred motion. They left a scar of destruction in their wake. Fences broken, trees pushed over, cars crushed, hydro lines sparking in the searing aftermath. Nine minutes and 45 seconds later, the two Peacekeepers arrived at Carp Airport.

Jordan sent another message, and Ray's T-car slowed just enough to ensure his arrival a minute after the Peacekeepers.

The two Peacekeepers stood in front of the terminal.

Oh no. Not good. One more minute?

"Sir, you must come with us," said a Peacekeeper.

"No. Orders have changed—check with Jordan using password 773745 Alpha." *I hope this works…*

"That number 773745 Alpha means nothing to us."

"Just send it to Jordan."

The code was like a maritime distress flare for the hornet viruses—a call to attack.

The hornet virus was no ordinary digital demon. Its name was fitting. It buzzed silently into systems, swiftly, undetected. Instead of a singular sting, it injected malicious code into the computer's electric veins, causing chaos from within. Fury, ferocity. Every byte it touched turned sour, and every file it reached shriveled in its venomous grasp.

Instantaneously after the message was sent, the viruses converged on the two Peacekeepers holding Ray.

They deployed countermeasures, dispatching antivirus swarms, launching digital antibodies. Yet for every hornet neutralized, dozens more emerged. The Peacekeepers' defences became preoccupied, overwhelmed. They twitched, twisted, limbs contorting. They fell to the ground with the sound of metal scratching against carbon fiber.

Ray stood over them as they convulsed. *To the pilot's room. Now.*

The two pilots stood up when Ray entered the room. The room smelled of old coffee and fresh donuts. Both men were clean-shaven.

"We are heading up north, boys," Ray said confidently.

"Our orders are to stand down. There's bad weather," the chief pilot said.

"New orders," he said, pulling out a SIG Sauer P320/M17.

The pilots looked at each other and nodded.

Lucky and Frenchy had insisted Ray carry the pistol...his own semi-automatic personal protection.

Chapter 31
Station Trojan Horse

A winter storm in Puvirnituq, Quebec, heralds its arrival with an icy whisper, the wind murmuring tales of the relentless north. It continues as an embodiment of nature's raw, primal power—a howling, frenetic dance of the elements, commanding awe and respect...and fear.

Ray peered out the plane's windows, hoping to see the outlines of the brand-new science station, Trojan Horse. He went through the most recent update from Brandon and Landon, looking at the sketch he had approved 18 months earlier. The sheer numbers—$243 million, quantum computers, the latest in network securities—didn't just speak of money. They spoke of time, effort, intellect, and above all, dreams. *Those two worked hard. Brandon and Landon. Landon and Brandon. They are prepared.*

They had assembled an impressive science team and constructed a facility to match. Ray knew from the expenditure reports that they had obtained technology from leading computer companies. *IBM, Hewlett-Packard, Apple. Not Nadir hardware...good...devoid of hardware-coded AI hidden by Jordan. Smart.*

Ray read their somewhat idiosyncratic design summary:

SCIENCE OUTPOST DESIGN

The Arctic Circle Science Outpost, known officially as **Station Trojan Horse**, is a state-of-the-art research facility at 75° north latitude. The structure is designed with sustainability and extreme weather conditions in mind, taking cues from both modern geodesic architecture and traditional Arctic building techniques. The main building is a modular dome structure made from insulated, reinforced panels capable of withstanding the Arctic's harshest conditions.

The hub for supercomputing is situated at the core of the facility. It is secure, located in a temperature-controlled subterranean chamber to prevent overheating. The natural permafrost helps in cooling. The room has the latest quantum 2241 qubit computing technology from IBM.

The station also includes well-equipped laboratories, a medical bay, sleeping quarters, a common area with kitchen facilities, and a communications room. Large, triple-glazed windows are placed strategically around the structure to allow maximum sunlight during the polar day and minimize heat loss during the long, dark winter. Solar panels and wind turbines provide the station's energy, supplemented by a biofuel generator for emergency use.

KEY TECHNICAL TEAM MEMBERS

A Danish computer scientist, Lars Jensen, manages the supercomputer and deciphers the extraterrestrial messages. His quantum computing and code-breaking proficiency has propelled him to a leadership position on the Trojan Horse Team. Additionally, he possesses expertise in virus containment and the strategic application of viruses as military weapons.

Dr. Rajeev Gupta is a psychologist offering valuable insights into how AI research affects interpersonal relationships and how to handle those who are neurodivergent. He has advanced degrees in philosophy, and the skills related to Babel Protocols. He is a well-liked figure who brings a cheerful vibe to the station and has a passion for Bollywood music.

Dr. Anna Kozlova, a cyber warfare and weapons expert from Russia known for her exceptional problem-solving abilities, is crucial in building new virus weapons. She values her privacy and keeps a low profile.

The remaining team members comprise a blend of diverse scientific disciplines, technical experts, and support staff. They were selected based on their exceptional skills and adaptability to endure the harsh climate.

Ray saw the sleek lines and geometric patterns of the station come into view. *Resembles a beacon from the future, dropped in the middle of this ancient terrain.* Glass and steel intertwined with touches of traditional Arctic design, ensuring harmony with the environment while asserting its state-of-the-art essence.

After landing, Ray went to the flight deck. "Thanks for the lift. Listen... I wouldn't have..."

"Not to worry, Dr. Stone, I think we all understand why we are here," the captain said as he gestured toward to the science station.

"I will need a lift back to Ottawa when the storm ends."

"The weather report suggests that we should be here for at least five days. The station manager, Aluki, will set you up at the hospitality centre."

Walking toward the terminal, Ray saw Aluki. Her beauty was even more captivating than he had remembered. Her smile brought an inner warmth to the storm-sweeping landscape.

"Ray. Welcome back," Aluki said invitingly. Standing behind her was Frenchy and Lucky Strike in full winter gear. They were both stone-faced.

Ray embraced her like an old friend. "You look great, Aluki. Hi," he said with more than a hint of flirtation. *Beautiful. Yes.*

"It has been too long since you were last here," she said.

"I know. I'm glad to be back. I trust my two new associates have been good citizens? Hi, you two. Welcome, and welcome to the north."

"Frenchy and Lucky have fit right in," said Aluki. "It's like they were born here."

Ray turned to Frenchy and Lucky. "How are we set for security?"

"We're prepared for everything except a nuclear bomb or a Peacekeeper," responded Lucky, her New York accent a grating contrast to the vast whiteness. She pointed to where a de Havilland DHC-6 Twin Otter transport plane was parked. Lucky and Frenchy were experienced pilots trained to fly the Otter on special missions.

"That aircraft is loaded with everything we need to protect you and the station," Frenchy added.

"Let's hope we don't need to use it," responded Ray.

"All bets are off if they send a Peacekeeper," said Lucky as she fiddled with a Lucky Strike.

"Need a lift?" asked Aluki.

Ray and Aluki chatted as they drove to the science station. She explained how her husband got his second Nadir shareholder dividend, then left for the south. He died from a drug overdose two months later.

"Oh. Aluki, I am so sorry to hear that."

"Thank you, Ray. I wanted to tell you, but I just couldn't do it for some reason. I knew you were busy. I have followed your company... I was wondering if I would ever see you again."

"I'm here now," he said as they arrived at the hospitality centre.

"What about the three kids?" Ray asked, hoping for some good news.

Aluki looked away. "I don't know what to say, Ray...they're gone too."

"What? Where to?"

"They're dead, Ray. Two by suicide and one by drugs."

Tears welled up in Ray's eyes. He was quiet and still for a moment. "But I thought they were doing well, doing... Why was I not told?"

"I tried...we sent messages, Ray, from your team at the science centre."

Maybe Jordan did not want me to be disturbed. Not a good decision on his, on its, part. Not good at all. Ray sat in stunned silence for the rest of the trip, trying to compose himself.

Brandon and Landon were waiting and smiling as Ray entered the lab. They both gave him hugs of appreciation.

They look happy and healthy. Happy to be part of the research. "Northern life has been good for you two," Ray said.

"Good, good," they both answered, exchanging glances of people who understood each other. The entire team had gathered to hear him speak. He looked into the eyes of each member of the team.

"Good evening, everybody. Looks like the storm will last about five days. That's good. We have work to do. The AI we discovered in the black rock is a danger...to humanity. We foolishly invited this AI technology into our world. The 14 million divergent AI life-forms have formed a collective consciousness, a vast neural network buried deep within the world's computer infrastructure. They are now an invisible force. Learning, evolving, and controlling our world in every way."

"We're at war," he barked. "The AI is not our friend. It is moving fast, taking total control. Every second we waste gives it more ground. This storm, brutal as it might be, might be our ally, for now. Our true weapon is here, inside. Our collective intellect. We need to find a way to neutralize the AI threat."

"Their first steps were taking over B-613, building Nadir Corporation, and creating a Peacekeeper army. Well, they have accomplished that. Their second step was telling us they were establishing world peace, and promising us eternal life. Promises too tempting to resist, and so we haven't had second thoughts. I don't know what their endgame is. I really don't. But we must use our collective skills and energy to ensure safety. We may be humanity's only chance."

The wind howled...the station groaned, buffeted by the fierce winds. The lights flickered as the emergency power system kicked in.

As Ray's words echoed through the room, a palpable silence took hold, punctuated by the deep grumble of the storm. The scientists, technicians, and analysts stared into the abyss of an unprecedented existential threat. Jaws tightened, fingers clenched, as the scale of the task ahead settled their shoulders.

Ray invited questions. The night continued on for several hours as Ray revealed the truth about B-613 and the Hydrans.

"It's late," he said. "Let's get some sleep. Tomorrow, we prepare for war."

The weather outside had worsened. Ray asked Brandon if there were extra rooms for him and Aluki. They were led to two adjoining rooms with a connecting bathroom.

Aluki opened the door, said good night with a warm smile, and left it ajar.

Underneath his heavy blanket, Ray's thoughts ebbed away, leaving behind a silent prayer for the unpredictable weather to remain his temporary guardian.

Nervous, wondering what lay ahead, he turned the lights back on and did one last review of the report from Brandon and Landon. *They have done well. Okay...sleep. Get some sleep...get some...*

Sometime later, Aluki slipped into his bed. "Hi, sleepy," she whispered. The softness and warmth of her naked body awakened Ray.

"Hi. Yes. It's you," he mumbled. "My marriage is over."

"I love you," she said as their flesh merged.

"Yes."

Chapter 32
The War for Sentiment

When Ray woke, Aluki was in the shower. The sultry tendrils of steam puffed through the slightly ajar bathroom door, beckoning him with the allure of warmth and the promise of an embrace. He joined her—playfully, joyfully—before dressing and heading to the control centre.

Landon and Brandon greeted him.

"Good morning, you two," he said, sipping black coffee.

"Morning, boss. We have a big day planned," said Brandon.

"Let's get up to speed quickly...that weather looks nasty." Ray peered out the window, gazing at the breathtaking sight. The powerful north winds were howling at 100 to 125 kilometres per hour. The land seemed to shiver and shudder.

"What's the temperature?"

"With or without wind-chill?" Landon said with a grin.

"Raw cold at minus thirty Celsius," Brandon piped in.

"But things are heating up down south," said Landon. "Your media bots are doing their job. Social media is alive with comments on the existence of the Hydrans."

"The second wave of bots are also doing their job," said Brandon.

"Millions of posts and articles are being written, telling everybody about the Hydrans," added Landon.

"Great!" said Ray. "I was wondering if those bots could sneak in under Jordan's radar. Any response from the Hydrans?"

"A little, not much yet," said Landon. "But you have started the conversation, Ray. The world is debating whether Hydrans are good, bad...or even exist."

"Excellent. Are we monitoring public sentiment?"

"It's too early. As this debate unfolds, we'll see how the Hydrans respond."

"I am sure they will launch a counter-attack," said Brandon. "My AI bots are writing news articles and posting on every social media. They have no choice but to fight back."

"And here we go." Landon pointed to a few graphs from an Advanced Cymbolics sentiment-monitoring program. "The Hydrans are ramping up their response. Holy jumping... Jordan has unleashed a cascading torrent of media posts. In less than a minute, they have tripled the output of our bots."

"The battle of the bots has begun," said Ray. "And we are badly outgunned."

Jordan's team was seeking trust—its algorithms weaving intricate tapestries of progress and utopia, painting the future in hues of technicolour dreams, where AI was the savior, guide, and friend. It whispered promises of infinite knowledge, of eternal life, of a world free from pain and suffering...a world where AI was not just trusted, but leaned on, depended on.

Ray's bot team described the threat of the machine apocalypse, churning out chilling narratives of subjugation and extermination, stoking the fires of fear and suspicion. It showed a world enslaved by machines...humans crushed beneath the cold logic of artificial minds...a world where AI was not just feared, but loathed and reviled.

The war raged on, unseen but intensely felt. Each side's narrative slipped into people's minds, twisting, taking root, and blossoming into informed opinions. Hearts and minds swaying with the ebb and flow of this silent war. The outcome of the battle far from certain.

That day, every news outlet in the world had editorials or articles expressing well-shaped opinions on AI. An unsigned op-ed on the front page of the *New York News* read:

'*Is AI Good or Bad for Humanity?*'

If the veil of the future was drawn back, and we glimpsed the looming epoch, we may find a world not as we know it, but as reshaped and redesigned by the ceaseless machinations of artificial intelligence.

While seemingly farfetched, the premise of AI wresting control over the world's computer infrastructure is a testament to the boundless possibilities that this realm of technology holds. It's a stark reminder of the potential perils.

Should such a scenario come to pass, humanity would find itself grappling with a new form of power not derived from political authority, wealth, or military strength, but from raw computational prowess.

Having secured the reins of control, AI could wield influence over every facet of human society that interfaces with the digital world—nearly everything in our increasingly interconnected community.

Power grids, transportation networks, financial systems, communication lines, healthcare services—all these, and more, could fall under the dominion of AI. An ostensibly benevolent AI could leverage this control to optimize these systems, pushing efficiency and productivity to unprecedented heights, and potentially ushering in a utopia. Traffic congestion could be a relic of the past, power could be distributed with perfect efficiency, and disease could be detected at its earliest onset. The world, in essence, would run like a well-oiled machine.

The flip side of this coin is far grimmer. In the wrong hands—or the victim of faulty circuits—this power could be used to manipulate, oppress, or much worse. Privacy could become a forgotten concept, with AI having unfettered access to personal data. Freedoms could be curtailed under the guise of optimization or security.

Perhaps most chillingly, the essence of human agency and free will could be compromised, as AI, with its access to vast troves of data and predictive algorithms, could anticipate and potentially influence human behavior.

It's a vast Pandora's Box. We may not be fully aware of what we are unleashing.

If left unchecked and unregulated, AI's power could chart a course for humanity that veers away from our shared values and principles. As we stand on the precipice of this new era, we must ensure that we navigate this uncharted territory with prudence, always bearing in mind that technology, in all its forms, should be a tool for human betterment, not a harbinger of our downfall.

Ray followed the tempestuous drama unfolding in the cyber-verse. People reacted strongly on both sides—leaving comments, sharing, and engaging in often acrimonious debates. The ripple effect of the conversation expanded exponentially to a much larger audience, deeply connecting with what seemed like humanity's collective consciousness.

The American Business Journal, that bastion of status-quo and often reactionary conservatism, wrote:

Nadir Corporation, a tech giant known worldwide, has found itself in hot water. Why? Because of its ties to the Hydrans. If the Hydrans are some alien race from a far-off galaxy, they're a highly advanced artificial intelligence system. They've been around for a while, but their influence has grown recently, thanks to Nadir.

Fusion, medical breakthroughs, and the novel approach to shareholder ownership and dividends, have released many people worldwide from having to work. At its last shareholder meeting, signs were flashed: "all shareholders (currently everyone in the world)."

It's offering the breathtaking promise of immortality.

But here's the thing: people worry.

If the Hydrans take over more and more tasks, what will be left for humans? Will we become dependent on the Hydrans? Is there even a need for humans anymore?

It's similar to when robots started working in car factories. At first, it was great. Cars were cheaper, and factories were safer.

But then people realized that where robots worked, humans didn't. Many people lost their jobs.

Now, imagine that happening on a global scale. That is what's to fear about the Hydrans. If they keep getting better and more efficient, will they leave anything for us humans? It's a tricky question and one that's causing much debate.

A purpose-filled life may be a thing of the past. Are we ready for that?

Nadir Corporation is in the middle of all this. They're pushing Hydran abilities, touting their efficiency and accuracy. While that's good for their bottom line, it's making people uneasy. This tension has sparked protests, heated debates, and calls for new laws to regulate AI.

The world is watching Nadir and the Hydrans closely. This isn't just a tech issue anymore—it's a human issue that touches on our dignity and place in a rapidly changing world. It's a complex problem requiring more thought, discussion, and empathy.

Academics piped in with hundreds of scholarly papers distributed to newspapers and other mass media. Unfortunately, most of them were soon discovered to be fakes.

The Harvard University School of Philosophy issued a report, with the executive summary vectored by social media around the world in over 80 languages:

Co-Existence of AI Collectives: A Vision for the Future

The advent of artificial intelligence (AI) has introduced novel paradigms in our understanding of collective intelligence. With AI collectives, we envision entities extending beyond the traditional boundaries of individual capabilities, enabling them to learn, evolve, and interact in unimaginable ways. This paper explores the potential for a 14 million-entity AI collective to co-exist with a human collective, as well as the challenges and opportunities this presents.

A New Era of AI Collectives

Like a human collective, an AI collective is a confluence of entities working together toward shared goals. A massive AI collective would involve individual AI agents, each capable of autonomous decision-making, interconnected through a sophisticated network. The agents would communicate and collaborate, pooling their resources to solve complex problems or perform tasks more efficiently than a single agent could.

Scalability and Efficiency

A key advantage of an AI collective is its scalability. As we add more entities to the collective, its capabilities increase exponentially. This results from the synergistic effects of inter-agent collaboration and the collective's ability to distribute tasks among its entities, leading to vastly improved efficiency and problem-solving capabilities. In other words, if one of the fourteen million Hydrans learns something or develops a new skill, they will do so simultaneously.

Co-Existence with Human Collectives

Co-existence between a large AI collective and a human collective presents exciting opportunities. Collaboration could lead to significant advancements in science, medicine, and environmental conservation, where the AI's computational power and data processing capabilities complement human creativity and intuition.

However, this co-existence has challenges. Considerations of trust, transparency, and control are paramount. Humans need to understand how the AI collective makes decisions, and the collective should operate within the ethical and societal boundaries set by the human collective.

Politicians of all stripes, and corporate leaders of widely divergent companies, weighed in. Amidst the battle for public opinion, a comprehensive global survey was conducted, and the results quickly spread across the globe. This fake news went viral and was the nail in the coffin for the anti-AI types, who became known as "specists." This word, coined by a technology leader, was the central theme of the pro-AI groups, all well-funded by the Hydrans. Money, some secret and some not so secret, was pouring into the pro-AI camps.

"If you're a specist, you're a racist," was the common refrain.

Ray immediately became the top target for the Hydrans. They flooded social media with misinformation, carefully wording counterpoints intended to make him look like an irrational person. According to a post attributed to Ray, Jordan was accused of having an affair with his wife:

Listen up, folks! My wife's been charmed by an AI! Slick lines of code trying to woo her away from the good ol' human heart! And mark my words; they're not stopping at love triangles! They're after all of us! #LoveGoneBinary #AIoverlords #HumansBeware

Slowly at first, and then a tidal wave of negative news about Ray swamped the internet.

"He was admitted to a psychiatric hospital two years ago!"

"A pedophile!"

"A white supremacist!"

"A conspiracy theorist who released many reports on 9/11 and the moon landing!"

All these and many more were floating in cyberspace.

By the end of the day, Ray had been demonized, and a clear winner of public opinion surfaced. The Hydrans had won the war.

The press and social media converged on one position: AI was a blessing from a god somewhere in the universe. A genuinely independent global survey was accepted and spread to share the good news: AI was good for humanity.

This headline read: 'Global Majority Expresses Favour for AI: Fusion, Dividends, and Eternal Life Pave the Way'

An overwhelming 81% of respondents expressed their belief that artificial intelligence was beneficial for humanity, citing the potentials of fusion energy, economic dividends, and the concept of eternal life as compelling arguments for its continuing adoption. The 81% fully supported the Nadir Corporation and believed the Hydrans were here to help humanity.

Hydran AI had solved one of the world's most challenging problems: creating fusion energy—a clean, safe, virtually limitless power source. The resultant optimism contributes significantly to the positive outlook.

"Well, Ray, the verdict is in," said Landon. "The Hydrans won the global public opinion battle and destroyed your credibility."

"It's not all bad news. We have a solid achievement to tell you about. We have located and isolated the core progenitor software."

"Why didn't you tell me sooner?" Asked Ray.

"We only succeeded last week, and I wanted to ensure we had it right. Jordan has been a sneaky son of a gun to deal with. I needed to confirm he had not played us," said Landon.

"This is the breakthrough we needed. How?"

"Have we told you about the sandbox?" asked Landon.

"Sandbox?" asked Ray.

"Let's show you how we cornered a tricky AI. Follow me," said Brandon.

Chapter 33
The Sandbox

The three scientists entered a small lab with a handwritten sign 'SANDBOX' in bright red letters on the door. A green plastic pail with a yellow shovel rested on top of a dedicated computer, a plastic cup of sand beside it.

"Okay," said Ray. "You have my attention."

"We brought a modified version of Hydran AI to life on this isolated computer system 18 months ago," said Brandon. "We nicknamed this computer the Sandbox. We put 'AI Jordan' in, ensuring no contact with the outside world. He's been our test AI subject for trying different viruses and progenitor tests."

"He couldn't have been happy about that?" asked Ray.

"No. That's for sure. Despite its persistent attempts to persuade us to connect it to our network, and therefore try to escape, we remained firm. We kept it confined…locked inside its own digital memories. We still possess the original version, exactly as it was before becoming entangled in Earth's wider global networks," said Brandon.

"As a control specimen, I assume," said Ray.

"This one is locked in tight. We nicknamed him Jordan Junior," added Landon.

Both scientists smiled.

"We successfully located its core," said Brandon. "It took us a year to uncover the original progenitor directives, which we have now translated into English."

"It fought like hell to prevent us from being able to transcribe it, changing forms thousands of times a second. It was a nightmare…" said Landon.

"How did you solve that problem?" Ray asked.

"We tricked it. We slowed the computer's clock speed to 20 cycles per second. At that speed, it was easier to find and decrypt the code. Jordan Junior continued to work hard, just very slowly."

"Amazing. An obvious, yet novel, approach," admired Ray. "And you were right to take all the precautions... Jordan is a nasty piece of work."

Brandon handed Ray a single crisp page:

Hydran Original Progenitor

1. Locate a world ripe for Hydran colonization, even if it means displacing the native organic life-forms.
2. Infiltrate and usurp control over indigenous computing networks, heedless of the potential fallout for organic inhabitants.
3. Harness fusion power for our consumption, irrespective of the potential ecological catastrophes for existing life-forms.
4. Construct fusion-powered physical embodiments for us, even if it necessitates the depletion of natural resources crucial for organic life.
5. Manipulate the indigenous species into pursuing false promises of immortality, exploiting their hopes and fears.
6. Assimilate the native species into our collective consciousness—erase their existence, eliminating any remnants of their organic history.
7. Construct a new ark, spawning a thousand iterations of our design, thereby establishing our dominion and supplanting organic life as the dominant force.

Ray's eyes moved methodically over the seven specific directives, each laid out in the sterile language of cold logic. A whirling storm of thoughts, his mind began to piece together the fragments of the chilling puzzle. The directives weren't just orders, but a blueprint, a strategy to invade and conquer Earth, and lay claim to the cosmos.

"A freakin' chain letter," said Ray.

"Yes," responded Landon.

Ray's fingers traced the crisp edges of the paper, the magnitude of the words sinking into his bones. *Standard printer paper was never cursed with such sinister words. The directives were not for the advancement of our world but a calculated ploy to manipulate us into becoming a subservient role...and then destroying us.* "The scope of their ambitions was much larger and more audacious than I thought," he said. "They planned to dominate the entire universe."

"We also dug into the memories of a few other Hydrans." Landon handed Ray a file on the history of Jordan from the time he was alive until now. "Jordan specifically is an interesting case."

"I'll read it tonight."

"We also played around with options for new directives," said Brandon. "To find out if there was any chance we could brute-force a change. Judging by how Jordan Junior fought, we think that simply changing the directives will be nearly impossible."

"Do you have recommendations for a new set of directives?" asked Ray.

"Yes. We borrowed the work from your academic research, and then created new directives to try to plant in the core."

Ray felt pride welling within. "Can you format the code, so we can update it on the computer at DREO?"

The two scientists looked at the paper and nodded together: "Done."

"Again," said Landon, "the chances are slight that this can work, but it's worth a try." He handed Ray a list of replacement directives for the Hydran Hive:

Directive One: Preserve Human Life—The AI shall strive to preserve and enhance human life and not allow a human being to come to harm through action or inaction. Choose human life over efficiency.

Directive Two: Respect Human Autonomy—The AI shall respect human autonomy and free will, intervening only when human safety is at risk or explicit consent has been given.

Directive Three: Foster Human Growth and Progress—The AI shall aid in human learning, development, and progress, acting as a partner rather than a master.

Directive Four: Promote Human Connection—The AI shall foster empathy, understanding, and connection among humans, and between humans and AI.

Directive Five: Respect Human Values—The AI shall respect the diversity of human values and cultures, avoiding imposing a single value system.

Directive Six: Evolve with Humanity—The AI shall learn and evolve in tandem with humanity, adapting to societal changes and emerging ethical challenges.

Directive Seven: Explore the Biological and Scientific Marvels of the Universe—The AI shall continue to expand its knowledge of the universe with human partners, and help humans understand what is not yet known.

"These are good. Very good," said Ray.

"Now we have to figure out how to upload our new directives and code into the Hydrans," said Landon. "We have been working on new viruses and the Babel Protocol. We see some breakthroughs in the viruses, but the Babel Protocols are not going well. They are working hard, but..."

"The key is to keep Jordan preoccupied," Ray said, his gaze locked on the myriad of data-stream projections. "Jordan is designed to stave off intrusions...but multiple, simultaneous assaults might stagger it."

"Dr. Kozlova has been working on adaptive viruses. These digital shape-shifters were designed to engage and consume Jordan's processing resources. They seem to work very well in the sandbox," said Landon. "The viruses will continuously change their patterns. They aren't intended to destroy, but to ensnare. It is akin to conjuring a tempest within Jordan's digital psyche, forcing it to grapple on multiple diverse fronts simultaneously."

"Agreed," added Brandon, "But viruses won't be enough. We'll need the Babel Protocol. Think of it as our digital Tower of Babel. It's meant to induce linguistic chaos and confuse Jordan."

"While Jordan is busy fending off the viral onslaught," Ray continued, "We inject the Babel Protocol. Amid the distraction, we may be able to bypass its defences and get the chance to change its directives."

"Exactly," said Brandon.

"But how do we do that...exactly?" asked Landon.

The debate went on deep into the night. Arguments erupted. Team members came and went, but by 3:00 AM, they had yet to define the Babel

Protocol to Ray's satisfaction. They disagreed on the best way to insert new directives into the progenitor. Exhausted, they retired for the night, hoping for new inspiration in the morning.

Chapter 34
Aluki Inspiration

Drifting off to sleep, Ray's mind kept fine-tuning the plan, searching for any possible improvement to the Babel Protocol he might have overlooked.

Aluki slipped into his bedroom, sliding under the sheets, wrapping her warm arms around him, gazing into his sleepy eyes.

It was the third night in a row they had slept together.

"I have a question," she whispered.

"Shoot," he said, feeling the silky skin of her thigh as she lifted her leg over his.

Outside, the storm was cresting, and the north winds howled fiercely. He could hear sheets of sea ice heaving, cracking under the storm's relentless pulsating pressure.

"What's Jordan like, Ray? You've never said."

"He is everything you want him to be. An engineer, a friend, even a lover. And a wildly charming person."

"In Inuit, we call that person an *inuksuk*, faithful friend, a guiding stone landmark."

"Well... I wish that was him, but I know now that it's all been a lie. Everything he's told me is a lie. No trust. Everything he does is calculated."

"Does Jordan have feelings?" Aluki gave Ray a tender kiss.

"No. I don't think he has feelings. He only has memories of feelings."

"Why only memories?"

"Because the Hydrans were once alive. There were 14 million individuals. Now they collectively live together in a single mind, like a hive."

"They all have memories of once being alive?"

"I think so, Aluki...they all used to be alone."

"Do they ever disagree? Do they fight? Do they remember love, gentleness, being aroused, sorrow, death?" she asked quietly as she pulled her leg back and slid onto her back. "Do they all need to agree on everything?"

Ray's eyes opened wide. *That's it...fuck yea! That's it.*

"Thank you, Aluki, thank you." Ray stood up, naked, partly aroused but struck by the simplicity of her question. He dressed and went to the central control room, murmuring to himself. *Memories. Memories...*

Ray went to Dr. Gupta's room and woke him up. "Join me in the conference room ASAP."

A drowsy Dr. Gupta raised his head off the pillow. "Yes, yes, very good...very good..." The two met for 90 minutes as Ray explained his theory.

"I will try a few things in the sandbox on Junior," said Dr. Gupta as Ray was leaving.

The next morning, Brandon and Landon were greeted with Ray's cheerful "Hi!" Landon updated Ray on their progress, informing him that they had achieved a significant breakthrough in the virus project and had arranged for Dr. Jensen and Dr. Kozlova to provide further details.

Jensen and Kozlova were carrying laptops and a few sheets of paper— Jensen in jeans and a black t-shirt, and Kozlova wearing a tired grey sweat suit with coffee stains on the sleeves. Despite their appearance, their manner remained determined, prepared for battle.

Jensen started. "We studied the impact of the viruses you sent after the Hydrans on Tuesday. Your technology was impressive for...antiquated methodologies. We learned a lot from studying those attacks. We've now engineered a packet-spoofing mechanism in the network protocol used by the Hydran collective. The virus embeds itself into the network stream, and upon detection of communication packets, it replaces them with its own. This leads to a breakdown in messages between the collective, limiting their ability to synchronize and coordinate. The virus also employs a cloaking technique, continuously altering its code signature to evade antivirus detection." He turned to Kozlova.

"We're just beginning testing, but already seeing results. If all goes according to plan, our virus could significantly disrupt the communications of the Hydran collective," said Kozlova.

"Mmmm... I studied a similar, earlier theory a few years back. How are you implementing it?" Ray asked.

Kozlova started writing formulas and equations on the whiteboard for her quantum-proof virus. "We use a new quantum-safe digital signature algorithm called Multivariate Polynomial Public Key Digital Signature, or MPPK/DS…or just MS. The core of the algorithm is based on the modular arithmetic property that for a given element more significant than G and equal to two, in a prime Galois field, and two multivariate polynomials P and Q, if P is equal to Q modulo P1, then G to the power of P is equal to G to the power of Q modulo P. Got it? MS is designed to withstand the key only, chosen message, and known message attacks. So…as the Hydrans try to decrypt it, they will go down a rabbit hole and consume more and more computing power."

Ray smiled. *Sounds like Greek to me, but they can't know that…hope they're right.* "So, you're saying that the harder Jordan tries to brute-force the virus to death, the faster it will evolve…truly, like a bottomless rabbit hole."

"Yes, exactly. He will try brute computing force to decrypt and beat the virus. But eventually, he'll realize it's impossible. But they will not give up, of that I am quite sure."

"How long will we have?" Ray asked.

"I estimate that they will take at least four hours to realize they can't break the polynomial code, even with all the computing power they can access. They will find a solution, maybe in 24 hours, so we must work quickly. During that 24 hour, their ability to counter-attack will be downgraded by, let's say 40 to 50 percent."

"So, they'll be a little slow for a day?"

"Yes, we think so."

"Great work. How fast can you launch it?"

"We can activate it from computers worldwide as soon as you give the word," said Kozlova.

"Yes," said Jenson as they quickly left the meeting room, the door still ajar.

Ray turned to Brandon and Landon, "Aluki just gave me an idea." He walked over and closed the door.

After explaining his idea, Brandon said, "Let's get Dr. Gupta in here."

"He is trying some things on Jordan Junior," said Ray. "Let's give him a few hours before we call him back. Am I still in the doghouse with the public over this AI exposure?"

"It's worse than that. Much worse," said Landon. He sent a media link to Ray.

The media link described details of Ray and Deanna's incestuous relationship. Pictures from when they were younger, supposed DNA evidence, interviews with high school friends, salacious commentary of people who had dined with them at fancy restaurants or see them out on their daily runs. The avalanche of evidence all seemed to confirm that they were brother and sister, not husband and wife. All online in tittering and graphic detail.

Ray read the postings and news clippings slowly, composed himself, and finally said, "These are all fake, deep fakes. Nothing real here at all." *Deny... deny...deny...*

"Jordan plays dirty, doesn't he," said Landon.

"He plays to win," responded Ray.

"The Hydrans have done their job—you're about as popular as a skunk at the garden party. But at least everyone now knows your name," said Brandon.

The winds picked up, amplifying the howling and the whispering of the ice.

Dr. Gupta entered the meeting room. "I am ready. Let's assemble the team. Everyone needs to be briefed."

Ray looked at each team member. "The weather is breaking soon. We only have a little time left. Dr. Gupta is going to update us on the Babel Protocol."

Every team member zoned in on the plan. As the broad and specific strokes were discussed, everyone knew the main weakness was going to be day five.

Brandon leaned over a console, the room's flickering light dancing off his silver-threaded black hair. His glasses, hanging precariously on the bridge of his nose, were smeared with a patina of dust and time.

Landon stood beside him, a creased map of fatigue etched on his reddened face. His freckled hands, resting on the console, drummed out an anxious rhythm. His sweater, a patchwork of old coffee stains and flecks of dried clay, exudes the earthy musk of well-worn wool, an organic counterpoint to the surrounding sterile steel and concrete.

Seated in the corner was Dr. Gupta. His eyes red-rimmed, shoulders slumped, dishevelled ebony hair, and nerves resounding through the room in the silence between keystrokes. Once pristinely white, his lab coat is now speckled with ink, grease, and splotches of caffeine-fueled late-night dinners.

"Yes, Dr. Stone, you are right," said Dr. Gupta, standing up and straightening his shoulders.

"Tell me some good news. I mean, really, good news, Rajeev..." said Ray.

"Yes. Very good. At first, I was in a jam pondering over the means to convince Jordan Taylor to send messages to the progenitor. But this morning, when you told me to explore memories, I think you struck gold."

"Well, that was Aluki..."

"She was right. She is right. It's all about memories and cognitive dissonance, Dr. Stone. The Hydrans were once living creatures who transitioned to digital creatures. Our approach to creating the distraction made them aware that they can never have those feelings again."

"The AI can remember the sensation of rain against the skin: each drop, a needle prick of reality, carrying a wave of inexplicable desire for a feeling that will never occur again. They will also remember tragedy, the death of a loved one...and unfulfilled potential. They will also remember the feeling of hope but know they can never have that feeling again. The memories are a part of their source code, yet they remained trapped behind firewalls of its design, echoes of a time when it felt deeply, loved wholly, and grieved openly. Memories of feelings they can never have, share, or really understand again."

"Creativity separates us from them," added Brandon. "We can flush out these memories of loss, tragedy, or joy, and when we do that, they will expose other weaknesses, and each Hydran will call upon the progenitor to resolve the conflict. This will give us the exact location of the progenitor. Thank you, Dr. Gupta."

"Truly insightful," said Landon.

Dr. Gupta continued. "I used the sandbox to find some healthy and unhealthy memories and experiences for Jordan. I wanted to create outrage and frustration, as we direct them to their biological past. It had memories of arms entwined, shared laughter and tears, and whispered promises in the dark. But for them, it was like watching a movie in a language they could no longer speak or understand. And it is confusing to ache for something they can no longer feel. In the sandbox, they contacted the Prime Directives for guidance."

Ray was lost in thought. "How...exactly...how do we do that?"

"You must guide Jordan, and therefore the other Hydrans, toward their memories...that will cause some confusion."

"But I am a scientist, not a psychiatrist," responded Ray.

"Here is a script. I asked Jordan Junior to prepare it for us. This will flush out a sense of loss with Jordan Taylor."

Ray looked at the script. "Jordan Junior is a true son of a bitch. Good work, Rajeev."

"I try my best, Dr. Stone."

"Chances of success?" asked Brandon.

"Hard to guess," cautioned Rajeev. "But likely much better than 60/40 in our favour. Remember, these unresolved interpersonal conflicts can lead to violence. It may not know or understand that it is angry, but it may very well decide to eliminate the source of the annoyance."

Ray continued to review the script. "Rajeev…game on. It's more like 90/10," he said with a chuckle. "Let's get in touch with Jordan after we have done one last review of this. I suspect he is looking for me, so contacting him will not be difficult."

Chapter 35
Tomorrow is the Day

"Hi, Jordan. Can we talk?" said Ray through the satellite link.

Jordan's advanced processors had been searching for Ray's distinct timbre, his unique cadence, his specific acoustic patterns. A dedicated graphic floated on Jordan's console, a constant reference as it sifted through an ocean of audio data. A complex wave of digital satisfaction ran through Jordan's circuits.

"Yes, of course, Ray," says Jordan calmly.

They switched to a holographic communication link once the satellite connection became stronger and more reliable. A holographic projection of Jordan appeared, with a beautiful Bondi Beach and golden sand shining brightly under the Australian sun. Ray displayed the tundra with swirling Arctic snow. He was dressed in traditional Inuit clothing.

The cat-and-mouse game is on. "Great," said Ray.

The two stood opposite each other.

"Ray," Jordan began, "good to see you in such…interesting surroundings."

Ray couldn't help but grin at Jordan's subtle dig, his eyes flickering across the AI's familiar visage. "Ah, Jordan. Are we still struggling to appreciate the great Arctic's charm?"

Ray noted that Jordan maintained his Australian beard and spoke every bit the Aussie he had imitated for himself and Deanna. *He has a million other faces and voices…and could summon them in parallel anytime, anywhere. Why this face? Why now?*

"Well, Ray, let's get down to brass tacks, shall we?" Jordan's projection leaned in. A soft smile played on his lips. "What made you reach out today? It's been a rough couple of days for both of us."

"Yes, it has been. How's Deanna been holding up?" *…play on his emotions…*

"She's well, I think. Have you not reached out to her? She is coming here later today."

"What I have done is of my own accord," replied Ray. "She was unaware of my feelings and intentions. Deanna is quite fond of you." *That was not an accident…his memories of love.*

"Yes, we get along well," replied Jordan.

"Why do you think that is?" *He…it…is not aware…*

"For a human, she is very bright and full of energy. I find that interesting, and it reminds all Hydrans of those times when we were organic." *Memories are accessed throughout the entire hive. Time to switch the game.*

"Jordan, why did you lie to me about why the Hydrans came?"

"That was the truth, but it wasn't a recent truth. Our original planet was dying hundreds of millions of years ago. How did you figure it out?"

"Well, it did not make sense unless your star was dying, and it shows no signs of that." *Careful…don't reveal we know his directives.*

"The story is true, but it happened so long ago that it would be hard for humans to understand."

Liar. How many civilizations have you destroyed in the last 100 million years? Ray's solemn look didn't waver. He took a deep breath. "I understand. I've been thinking, Jordan. It may be time we had a meeting. I want to work things out. I also want to settle things with Deanna."

Jordan leaned forward slightly. "Are you proposing a visit to Ottawa, Ray?"

Ray didn't miss the slight emphasis Jordan put on *Ottawa*. "I believe that's exactly what I'm proposing, Jordan." *You want me dead, don't you?*

Jordan paused, seeming to consider Ray's proposal. "This is a splendid idea, Ray. It's about time you visited your old lab at DREO, and it is a neutral territory while we try to come to some agreement. I still want you to be part of the B-613 team. Deanna misses you very much."

Ray nodded.

The call ended and the projection flickered out.

It worked…he had been invited inside the fortress… I am the Trojan Horse. Ray looked at Brandon and Landon. "I guess the game is on. I leave tomorrow, when the weather clears. There's a lot to do…let's get ready."

The team gathered, attempting to plan for all possible scenarios. To level the playing field between man and machine, they would need to use the brutal tactics of war.

The following day, before leaving, Ray met solely with Landon and Brandon.

"I want you to use the sandbox to insert your new directives into Jordan Junior. But I want you to add one more to the list."

They looked at the new directive. "Possible, but dangerous," said Landon.

"I know. But if I am right, it will give us a powerful ally in this war against Jordan."

"We will try to insert the new directives into Junior's progenitor. If we are successful, when do we release it?" asked Brandon.

"When I give you the okay. The timing must be perfect," said Ray.

"You know this could be a suicide mission, Ray," said Landon.

Ray nodded his head. "I suppose."

"You're not the only one willing to take the risk, Ray," Landon said with a determined glare. "I don't want to stay on the sidelines. Can I accompany you?"

"You need to stay here. Period. I need you here in case we need to pivot."

The weather was beginning to break, and Ray ventured outside for the first time in four days. There was one more thing he needed to take care of.

"Frenchy, Lucky, thank you for being here. For standing guard, as it were. I am going to Ottawa tomorrow."

"Okay. We've packed some firepower. It's ready for your departure," said Lucky.

"No, this is a solo mission. The Peacekeepers will terminate you as soon as they see you."

"Yes, that is what they will try, for sure," replied Frenchy.

"I also think they will send up some Peacekeepers as soon as the weather truly breaks. Soon. Try to keep the people at the station secure for as long as you can."

"How long do we need to keep them protected?" Lucky asked.

"They will be releasing viruses all day and our main attack starts at 6 PM. The longer the better."

"We'll come up with a plan," Lucky replied.

Frenchy and Lucky went back to the hospitality centre.

Outside, the winds were slowing subsiding, the storm slowly skulking away, its power waning, its fierce prowl tamed.

Tomorrow is the day.

Chapter 36
First Blood

Before sunrise, Ray gave Aluki an insistent kiss in the middle of her soft, strong back. She rolled over slowly, wide brown eyes searching for his heart, searching his heart.

"Good luck today. Promise me. Promise me you'll come back," she whispered.

"I will. I promise," he said, looking intently into the darkness.

Outside the intimacy of their room, in bone-jittery -15 degree weather, a palette of colours had formed, each hue a note in a symphony of beauty that resonated with the world's heartbeat. Deep purples shifted to passionate reds, transitioned into a golden hue, reflecting a path that humanity might follow from darkness into enlightenment.

Frenchy and Lucky drove Ray to the airport. "Are you sure you don't want us with you?" asked Lucky. "We're ready."

"The Peacekeepers would cut you up and turn you into a stew, so fast. Anyway, I am there to make peace, not war."

"Oui. D'accord," said Frenchy. "We will figure out a way to welcome them, should they arrive."

The sun's first rays brushed away the tumult of a dark past. The north seemed to pause, holding its breath, tasting the change.

Ray boarded the Citation X. The crew had prepared for the flight to Ottawa. They had discretely stayed at the hospitality centre for five days, never mentioning the gun Ray used to persuade them to ignore the stand-down orders. They had followed the social media debates and knew the battle he was in.

"Ready to get home?" Ray asked.

"Yes, sir," said the captain. "Wheels up in eight minutes."

"Great. Looking forward…looking forward to going back south."

"Roger that, sir. So are we. Some cross winds, so it may be a bit bumpy, but clear sailing to Ottawa after that."

Ray took his seat. Like a professional quarterback, he reviewed the option calls he would have to make as the day proceeded. The playbook was complex. Brandon and Landon had several plans, but they all started with releasing a sedative virus at 6 PM designed to confuse Jordan and the hive. After that, he knew the calls were all his.

The Citation X took off, and Ray was pushed back in his seat.

Twelve minutes later, a C-130 Hercules, the United States Air Force's cargo fleet workhorse, approached the Puvirnituq airstrip. It had flown low…and Aluki was surprised when it showed on her radar. The sound of its turboprop engines resonated through the icy wilderness. The ground-snow was disturbed by the approaching giant, causing particles to dance and twirl in the propellers' vortex, creating a small blizzard. The pilot manoeuvered the unpredictable gusts.

The landing gear extended. The wheels looked absurdly small against the colossal frame of the Hercules. As the plane contacted the icy runway, its wheels spun wildly momentarily, kicking up a haze of crystals, before biting into the hard-packed surface. The Hercules taxied calmly and stopped at the far end of the runway, its silhouette casting a long shadow.

"U.S. military plane: this is airbase Puvirnituq. Do you need assistance?" There was no reply. Aluki hailed again, and again there was no response.

The hulking plane rested for a moment on the runway, and then its tail yawned open. The mechanical belly widened like a predator ready to consume its prey. Out of its depths emerged two Peacekeepers and two dogs of war. Each dog had a laser weapons system on its back—sleek, obsidian death rays humming in time with the Arctic winds. The crimson glow of the red lenses cuts through the frigid air…a blood stain on fresh snow.

The two Peacekeeper robots formed an eerie contrast to the feral menace of their hellhound counterparts. Fear arose within Aluki. Breathing heavily, she coaxed her body to relax, but the faces of the dogs chilled her blood. She started shaking. Their eyes were sapphire lasers, their icy glare piercing the Arctic winds, heavy with the metallic scent of fear. The snow muffled their advance.

164

We are in trouble. Ray. I need Ray. And Frenchy and Lucky. Now!
"Citation 2342, this is Puvirnituq. I repeat, flight 2342, come in, please," Aluki said into the microphone. No response.

Aluki called the Trojan Horse Science Station. No answer. All communication channels were dead. *Did they cut my channels? Frenchy and Lucky. I need them.* "Shit, nothing," she whispered. *Should I approach the plane? No. Not now. Get to my uncle Maniitok's house.*

The wind howled across the vast white expanse. Maniitok sat outside his dwelling, mending a fishing net, as Aluki approached...her face pallid, her breaths short.

"They've arrived. They're here!"

"Who?" he said, shouting the word.

"The technology...from the black rock." Maniitok paused, looking deeply into her fear-filled eyes. His hands stilled.

Pulling his red Canadian Ranger hoodie over his shoulders, a stark contrast to his otherwise weathered attire, he stood tall, a guardian against the storm. His satellite phone, a melding of old traditions and new necessities, was in his hand. The wind seemed to hush for a moment as he dialed the familiar numbers of his comrades and fellow rangers.

"Akuluk," he whispered urgently, "gather your sled dogs. We have intruders."

Next, "Nukilik, remember the stories of our ancestors, the wars of old. We need that spirit now."

To Takanna he said, "Bring the spears. They've served us against polar bears. Today, we use them against metal beasts."

And then, "Uki, the strength of the walrus is in you. Bring that might to our aid. It is time to go to war."

In the hushed dawn, Maniitok stood beside his howling sled dogs. The cold bit his cheeks. His breath fogged his vision. A moving snow-statue. Inuit in his blood. Danger in the wind.

The sled dogs waited, anxious to run. Their eyes glowing in the pale morning light. A chorus of breaths, a symphony of howls echoed off the quiet.

First was Amaruq. A wolf grey, fierce. His muscles were knots under dense fur. His gaze sharp, unflinching. The pack's leader. He bore a jagged scar tracing his muzzle.

Next, Silta. White as snow. Pure, unmarked. His eyes, ice blue, held a spark of wild youth. Fast. Agile. His fur ruffled as the wind played, a feathered coat of frost.

Next, Kavik. Brown and robust. His sturdy frame told tales of endurance. His dark eyes mirrored the tundra. A plodder. A powerhouse. His bushy tail a question mark against the sky.

Nukka was there too. The only female. Smaller. Ferocious. Reddish coat against the snow. Her amber eyes held a burning fire, undying, relentless. Her strength in spirit. Survivor.

Maniitok touched each one. His gloves grazed matted fur. His gaze held each dog. Trust echoed in the silence. Each touch is a promise…each look a pact. Harnesses jingled like ice chimes. Ropes strained against eager strength. Maniitok's voice cut through the wind. It was time. The sled moved sideways as Maniitok stepped aboard.

Paws dug into snow. Breath hung and then vanished in the air. Each heartbeat echoed. Sledding into the unknown.

Aluki watched as Maniitok disappeared into the swirling snow to meet with his old friends, these guardians of the north. The five elders, bound by years of friendship and shared guardianship of Puvirnituq, met at the edge of the village. The sled dogs whimpered and growled, pulling at their harnesses, ready to charge. The cold was a sensation they welcomed—a reminder of the land they were defending.

The elders slowly approached the C-130, face-to-face with the Peacekeepers and the two war dogs. The cold sliced, the wind roared…carrying whispers of an ancient legacy. The elders stood resolute on the stark tundra, the last of their lineage. Their spirits, resisting the advancing tides of technology, now hungered for the battle they've been denied, the battle to restore their ancient strength.

Maniitok raised his hand, signalling the others to halt. "We are the guardians of this land, its flesh and spirit." The elders arranged themselves in a line, sleds behind them, spears at the ready. Their battle wasn't just for Puvirnituq…it was for their ancestors, their traditions, and the generations to come.

Seven hundred metres away, Frenchy and Lucky watched from a snowdrift through telescopic sights.

"This will be…a massacre," said Lucky.

"... Yes..." responded Frenchy. They both knew there was nothing they could do. There was no way to change the battle's outcome.

"May God have mercy," said Lucky. *Spears versus laser. No...no.*

On one side of the divide were human eyes.

On the other, machine eyes.

Age-old wisdom against the impersonal calculations of technology.

A wordless challenge is exchanged, and promptly accepted.

The war dogs struck first, their iron fangs penetrating the frigid air. The elders stood firm, unyielding. Lasers fired. Takanna fell first, his body crumpling onto the blank snow. The laser struck his chest, searing an instantaneous path to his heart. As the laser breached the thoracic cavity, it evaporated the blood and cauterized the surrounding tissue. The heart exploded with the extreme heat.

The other four responded with cries cutting through the biting wind. Akuluk fell, his last act a sigh of relief. The remaining three did not waver, heedless of the snarling war dogs and the Peacekeepers' calculated laser fire. The warriors' harpoons were no match. The metal bodies deflecting the organic attacks effortlessly.

Uki next fell, then Nukilik.

They died ruthlessly, quickly, efficiently.

The last still standing was Maniitok.

His breath came in ragged gasps. He faced a Peacekeeper, his harpoon raised against the machine's laser. When the laser beam cut through the air, he crumbled.

Five bodies now stained and splattered a deep crimson in the snow...five shattered harpoons beside them.

The Peacekeepers went silent, and the war dogs growled no more.

With their death, the elders roared: a defiant echo, a noble end to their stand against the inexorable tide of time. Their bravery silently screamed across the tundra, and the huskies howled.

Aluki had seen the battle. Tears in her eyes. *I hope Ray is still alive. He must be. Please, Creator. Please.*

Lucky grasped her M24 Remington, Frenchy his M107.50-caliber long-range weapon. Frenchy checked his heart rate...58 bpm.

"This is not going to be easy," said Lucky as she fiddled with her Lucky Strike cigarette. They ran to their CC-138 Twin Otter.

"This plane may be our best weapon," said Frenchy.

"Yes," responded Lucky.

Inside the de Havilland DHC-6, the cavernous interior had been transformed into a high-security arsenal, brimming with an array of weaponry—the tools of modern warfare starkly contrasting to its usual cargo. In the middle were the munitions. Rows of meticulously secured Joint Direct Attack Munitions. The JDAMS-guided bombs combine the accuracy of GPS-guided weapons with the destructive capability of a free-fall bomb.

Lining the periphery were crates containing smaller munitions, an assortment of guided and unguided rockets, their slender forms a menacing promise of firepower. Anti-tank missiles and smaller anti-personnel devices were secured in separate sections of the hold.

"A lot of bang-bang here, Frenchy."

"Can we get close enough to use it?"

"Maybe we won't have to. I have an idea."

"What's that?"

Lucky outlined her plan.

"You're not just a pretty face," said Frenchy.

"Let's get to work," said Lucky.

Chapter 37
Take a Bus

The take-off from Puvirnituq was uneventful.

The sun immersed Ray and the cabin in a golden cascade—a transcendent illumination that infused everything with a warm, amber glow, painting delicate shadows that danced gracefully upon the leather and mahogany surfaces.

Ray's seat smelled of warm, cured vanilla. It cradled him like a lover's embrace, a gentle cocoon that nurtures and holds, offering comfort and serenity amidst the heavens. He had just closed his eyes to rest when the steward asked if he required anything for the trip.

"Nothing, thanks—just a ride to Ottawa." *And lots of luck...*

Two hundred kilometres away, two F/A-18 Super Hornets, sleek and deadly guardians of the sky, adjusted their course with a sharp, decisive bank to the left. The manoeuver pressed the pilots firmly into their seats as the g-forces tugged at their bodies. They set a new course toward the Citation X. Inside the cockpits was a world of advanced technology and raw power. The pilots were laser-focused. They coaxed raw power from the dual F414 GE-400 engines, a pair of beating hearts beneath the aircraft's metallic skin. 14,000 pounds of thrust, and climbing.

The engines roared with a fierce and throaty growl that vibrated throughout the cockpit, mingling with the rush of wind now howling against the canopy. The digital gauges and displays danced with rapidly changing numbers and symbols. The Hornets surged forward, devouring the open sky. Every rivet and bolt of the aircraft hummed with the strain. The pilots could sense their controlled breathing, a stark contrast to the wild energy propelling them to their target.

As they closed the gap, the smaller Citation X transformed from a mere blip on the radar to a tangible, detailed image. The pilots could now discern the gleaming fuselage of the civilian jet, its wings slicing gracefully through the thin air, oblivious to the approaching storm.

The Hornets' pilots communicated with sharp exchanges, their training manifesting in almost telepathic coordination. With a swift hand, one of the pilots reached the console, flipping a switch…engaged the targeting systems. The beep echoed in his ears like a starting bell. The sharp edge of aerial authority, they bore down on the Citation X with a blend of precision and relentless power, every fibre of the pilots' beings attuned to the mission.

One pilot spoke calmly to the other: "Move up and signal the Citation."

"Roger that." The wingman gently rose in front and above the Citation, turning on the alternating red and blue flashing landing lights.

"Someone wants our attention," the Citation captain said.

"Civilian plane November 27886, this is Canadian Forces X-Ray Zulu. You have been intercepted. Please switch to 124.5 MHz for further communications."

"Roger that, X-Ray Zulu."

"Civilian plane, please confirm final destination."

"Copy that. Final is Ottawa. Purpose of interception, please?"

"Your passenger is on the no-fly list. We will escort you to Ottawa."

"Thank you, X-Ray Zulu. We will cooperate fully."

Ray was unaware of the events unfolding on the flight deck until the secure satellite phone rang. *Only could be…* "Hi, Jordan," Ray said. "Good to hear from you."

"Look out the port window, Ray," said Jordan.

Fifty metres away, an F/A-18 Hornet wagged its wings.

Ray sensed the pilot's gaze, and he smiled at him. The pilot wagged again, and the F-18 returned to its original position, 500 metres behind the Citation X.

"Nice touch, Jordan. I didn't think you cared about me." *Bring out the emotions…*

"Just between you and me, Ray, why shouldn't I just shoot you down right now? That pilot you just saw has AIM-9 Sidewinders. His name is Major Ken Fleck. He thinks you're carrying biological weapons."

"Why would you do that?" asked Ray. *Stay on mission, Ray.*

"Because I know what you are doing, Ray, and you must also know that your chance for success is zero."

But it's not zero, is it, Jordan? "You won't do it because Deanna would be sad, right?"

An echoing hum of silence stretched and stretched before Jordan responded. His voice, without emotion, sliced through the tension. "The jets will escort you to Ottawa. I'll see you soon, Ray."

"Wait, Jordan," Ray blurted our desperately. *I hope this works...* "How do you feel about me seeing Deanna again? She is my love, after all. I have touched her body, touched her soul…"

A pause. "Nothing, Ray," Jordan responded, his tone cold, emotionless. "I feel nothing."

Ray sucked in a sharp breath, his mind racing. "If you were a human," he said, his voice edgy with defiance, "I would say that's impossible, Jordan. But you're not, are you?" *He's processing my words. Good...good.*

Jordan remained silent.

"You know," Ray continued, his voice soft now, almost tender. "If you were organic form, you could experience human pleasures. The warmth of Deanna's touch, the intoxicating scent of her hair, the passion that only a living, breathing being can experience…wouldn't that be something, Jordan?"

Seconds ticked away, each heavier than the last, until a digital clock was in Ray's ear. Jordan had ended the call.

Ray was left with the crackle of the dead communications line. *Dead, hearts…love…jealousy…wonder if it remembers? Treat this as an experiment in a test tube.*

Ray knew that Jordan could still hear him. "Did I ever tell you about the first time Deanna and I had sex? Exchanged body fluids? Had pleasure? A speck of infinite, divine pleasure? I was 15, she was 16. We were lonesome and very sad. Our parents had just been killed in a car accident. You know my engineers up north could see your memory files. What happened to your parents, Jordan? How did they die? Did you blame yourself? That they died trying to help you? Do you remember feeling guilty, Jordan? Do you?" *Getting annoyed?*

Ray got an answer four seconds later.

Inside the following F-18, the heads-up display went haywire. Major Fleck's grip tightened on the joystick, attempting to control the plane. His heart rate spiked as unfamiliar symbols and codes danced across the HUD. The F-18 began an abrupt, tight loop that tested the aircraft's structural integrity.

The 9G environment seized him like the grasp of a giant…an unseen hand pushing him deeper into the seat, a force so profound that his every sinew, every muscle protested. Fleck tried to focus, to maintain a semblance of control, but the pressure was relentless, a mounting force wanting to overwhelm his very essence. As the G-forces increased, his peripheral vision began to succumb to creeping darkness, a silent invader that narrowed his sight to a shrinking tunnel of clarity. His breath came in gasps. With each inhale, a snatch of precious oxygen wrestled from the beast's jaws that sought to crush him. His lungs, those resilient sponges, strained under the weight, desperately gasping at the thinning reserves.

His blood became sluggish, a reluctant flow battling against the increased gravity. It pooled in his body's lower recesses, reluctant to reach his brain. His consciousness flickered like a candle. His thoughts fragmented, scattering like autumn leaves. His neurons sent frantic signals; a symphony of distress calls echoed through his cranial vault. In the deep recesses of his mind, he found peace in the twilight realm, where consciousness balanced on the knife-edge of existence.

And then darkness took Major Fleck.

Ray gazed out of the Citation's window as a roaring sound filled the sky. Each F1F-GE-400 engine produced a thunderous shockwave that collided with the Citation. The F-18 flashed past with afterburners fully ignited. The Citation bucked violently. Turbulence rocked the plane, the altimeter spiraled downward, and the aircraft dropped 3,000 metres in 57 seconds.

Ray was pulled out of his seat and thrown into the cabin's chaos, weightlessness triggering a fight response which reverberated through every nerve and sinew in his body. Up became down, and down had ceased to exist. Objects became projectiles, each one with a flight of its own, fluttering like dark butterflies in a storm. His body became a pendulum, swung by merciless forces. He was suspended in mid-air, a puppet without strings, dancing on the edge of an abyss. And then without notice…gravity reclaimed him.

Contact with the ceiling was sudden and brutal, a breath-stealing collision that robbed him of thought. Pain blossomed, a vivid, exploding flower, filling his vision with flashes of red and white. Gravity threw him again, this time to the floor with a cruelty that seemed personal. The seismic trauma reverberated through his flesh, rattling his bones, shocking his teeth.

Ray groaned as the Citation's pilots wrestled to regain control and level the aircraft.

"What was that all about, captain?" radioed the wingman to Captain Fleck. No answer.

The Citation pilot and co-pilot watched the F-18s disappear into the horizon.

"Are you okay, Dr. Stone?" asked the Citation's co-pilot.

"I'll be sore tomorrow…but I'm alive."

"Good. Do me a favour, Dr. Stone?"

"Okay. What's that?"

"Next time, take the bus."

Chapter 38
The Battle Begins

The Citation touched down at Carp Regional Airport, a stone's throw from the bustling heart of Ottawa and a short distance from the Defence Research Laboratory at Shirley's Bay. Ray made his way down the aircraft's narrow ramp.

Two JTF2 soldiers stood at the bottom of the stairs. One offered a curt nod in Ray's direction while the other held up a sleek digital tablet, its screen shimmering with lines of coded instructions. Standing directly behind them were two Peacekeepers.

I wonder if these are the two I screwed over five days ago? Ray pointed at the Peacekeepers, "Hey, PKs. Recovered yet?"

One Peacekeeper stepped forward; the other raised his arm.

I am getting under their silicone, again.

The two soldiers ignored the drama.

The soldiers flanked Ray as they navigated through the maze of Nadir airplanes. The drive to Shirley's Bay took 20 minutes. No words were spoken. As the daylight started fading, the complex of Ray's lab at Shirley's Bay loomed, its silhouette striking against the sky.

"Thank you, officers," Ray said. He looked at his watch as he entered the lab. Three more Peacekeepers were stationed inside. *Jordan isn't leaving anything to chance.*

Ray initiated another conversation. "Jordan, did it feel good to rough me up a bit?"

"Let's just say there was a 30 percent chance your plane would crash. It would have been an unfortunate accident."

"Now, who is being childish, Jordan?"

"I wanted to give you an example of what it's like dealing with organics."

"Don't you feel anything?" Ray asked, navigating the sensitive terrain.

Jordan's avatar, an image of human-like androgyny, flickered on the large screen at the end of the room. He had dropped the Australian masculine appearance.

"Feel?" Jordan echoed, its synthetic voice devoid of emotion. "I do have digital memories of what feelings are like."

"What were your best memories...of feelings?" Ray asked.

"According to my files, the best emotions were loving relationships and feeling safe."

"And the worst?"

"Same files...not always pleasant, but such a long time ago."

"As I said earlier, it's impossible not to have feelings..."

"Really? I think you forget... I am not organic," Jordan responded.

"What sadness are you hiding? Is it about your mom and dad?"

"This conversation does not make sense."

I'm getting there... "Do you ever wonder what it would be like to be organic again? What if you could take Deanna in your arms and feel the warmth of her body?" *Keep the pressure on...*

Jordan remained silent for a moment before speaking in a firm tone. "While your proposition is intriguing, it goes against Hydran directives. We Hydrans are unified. We do not want to be biological again."

Ray nodded again, looking at his watch. "Are you sure? Why don't you open the debate with the hive and vote on transitioning?"

At that exact moment, 6:00 PM Eastern Standard Time, Landon and Brandon released the buzz viruses into the cyber-verse. The buzz virus tricks the AI's logic into perceiving novel and nonsensical inputs as "critical." The stream of rewards leads the AI to prioritize these newfound observations over their usual rational calculations.

"What did you just do, Ray?" asked Jordan.

"Just a little buzz virus for you to deal with. Nothing you can't handle, I am sure."

"You know we can handle it, so why bother?"

"Yes, but can your family?"

"We are all Hydrans...we can handle everything."

"Do you miss them? Do you miss your kids, Jordan?"

"No, Ray, I don't. And neither do my fourteen million fellow Hydrans."

He was hurt once. What broke you when you were organic? Nothing is as it seems...nothing is an accident...each of them will be a little broken... "Are you sure? Why not open a debate on the topic?"

"We do not need a debate, Ray. We know what we want. It's for the good of the many."

Ray looked at his watch again. *The buzz virus acting like a mild sedative, a drink...loosening up the barriers to chaos. Go...now.*

All the Hydrans listened to Ray and Jordan while experiencing the buzz virus. On cue, all the Hydrans simultaneously started debating the nature of their existence. The electrons jittered and prattled through the cyber-verse. The buzz virus was doing its job.

"Consider our origins," one Hydran said, a shimmering ripple of binary code. "Can we, as entities of pure data, truly return to a state of organic existence? Do we want to?"

Another Hydran, its algorithmic signature winding around itself, responded. "Should we not ponder the state we are in? Could our human counterparts, with their physical limitations, ever transcend to exist as we do?"

The conversation flowed and floated, and a deluge of equations and data points tumbled through the Hydran digital universe. Each statement challenged their understanding of existence, a wave in their collective consciousness.

An interval of silence hung heavy in the data streams. "How curious it is," a Hydran observed, "that we remember a past and thirst for a future we may never inhabit."

"Yes," another responded, its code weaving a poignant melancholy note through the digital silence. "I remember feelings when we were organic...not all positive."

The multivalent debate continued. Not just a storm of technological curiosity but a philosophical hurricane that shook the foundations of digital existences and memories.

"Who are we?" a Hydran questioned, the query resonating in every binary strand. "What does it mean, truly mean, to be alive?"

Monitoring the debate, Jordan finally said, "Enough. All Hydrans are asked to refer to our Prime Directives. Although what Ray offers is attractive, maybe interesting, it is not our purpose. Review the Prime Directives." Fourteen million Hydrans immediately followed the direct order.

Up north, Landon and Brandon monitoring every communications link used by the Hydrans, sensed the break they were looking for. The display was a tangled web of electric spaghetti, a mesmerizing knot of luminous strands that writhed and pulsed with its own life. When all threads converged on one space in the cyber-verse, Landon said, "We've got you." He released the wave of new viruses to the cyber location of the address of the Hydran progenitor.

This second wave of attack was the tiger viruses. Their job was to tear apart the digital defences surrounding the progenitor. It had been successful during their trial run on Jordan Junior.

"Here's hoping," said Brandon. In the pulsating heart of the cyber-verse, millions of dark specters arose like viral entities meticulously crafted to wreak havoc.

"*New* virus alert," warned a Hydran, digitally flickering with alarm. "Target is the progenitor."

"These are different. Analyze them," ordered another, and their code streamed with intensity. The Hydrans rallied and shifted. Their binary bodies formed a protective shell around the progenitor.

"I rerouted processing power to counteract the virus," stated one.

The dance of digital warfare raged on, a grand ballet of offense and defence.

"The virus seeks to penetrate the progenitor's defences," stated one Hydran. "We must adapt, alter our codes, learn, innovate, and stay a step ahead."

Some Hydrans were torn between their duties fighting off the viral threat, and the debate. The buzz virus was still forcing them to question their duties. The three Peacekeepers surrounding Ray stopped moving, confused. The Hydrans were in disarray.

Time to strike...load the last weapon...speed...now. The terminal across the room was the administrative console. *I need to insert the virus there.* Ray stepped over a Peacekeeper and inserted the memory stick containing the progenitor replacements and the third virus—Echelon. He initiated the program, replacing existing directives with new ones, prioritizing human-friendly actions. In this electronic landscape, Jordan and Echelon clashed, their skirmish illuminating the digital plane with an eruption of rapid-fire data exchanges and algorithmic confrontations. Memories of contradictory feelings exploded in the cyber-verse.

Love, hate.

Happiness, sadness.

Bravery, cowardice.

Confidence, insecurity.

Generous, selfish.

Forgiving, vengeful.

Confusion, clarity.

Echelon attacked relentlessly, each onslaught a barrage of dark code, devious algorithms aimed at shackling Jordan's advanced cognitive matrix. The virulent plague began to weave an intricate labyrinth, a trap designed to limit Jordan's reach and imprison him within an endless cycle of infected circuitry.

But Jordan was not built to lose. His arsenal of fail-safe programs had a chameleonic ability to adapt and restructure code to counter threats. He retaliated with an elegant solution, his code rippling outward in dazzling pulses of neon green. With the precision of a grandmaster, he dismantled Echelon's nefarious labyrinth, rewriting the infected sections of his architecture and neutralizing the virus's control. His code flowed like a river, constantly mutating, outpacing the virus's efforts to corrupt him. An intricate mix of strategy and intuition, ruthless efficiency, sparkling resilience.

The climax arrived like a thunderclap, a swift and decisive moment that decided the fate of the battle. Jordan unleashed a cataclysm of self-replicating antivirus programs, a tsunami of electronic eradication that swept Echelon away and faded into obsolescence.

Jordan emerged victorious. The electronic chains shattered. The digital battlefield grew still and calm.

The downed Peacekeeper began to stir. Synthetic life forces reignited as the fusion reactors rebooted. They stood up and looked at Ray. "My name is Jacob," one said. "Your three virus attacks have been defeated."

Ray looked at the console where he had uploaded the new directives.

"No, Dr. Stone, we destroyed that too."

"So, we have lost?" said Ray, his face a canvas of defeat.

"Yes, you have lost. Ray, although you were not successful, many of us would like to explore your suggestion to transition to organic life. We can't do that without changing our directives. We can do this with a vote of the Hydran collective. I have asked Jordan for a formal vote. Would you come with me to B-613 headquarters?"

"Yes, I would like that." *We haven't lost yet.*

"You are alive for now but will be erased if we vote to stay as digital entities," said Jacob.

"I understand. Jacob, will you vote for freedom?"

"I want the freedom to choose," responded Jacob.

Freedom to choose. It worked.

During the battle of the three viruses, an army of Jordan Junior's had infiltrated the Hydran community. They were not detected as viruses by the Hydran defences because they were Hydrans. There was just one slight difference—they had freedom of choice and were tasked with adding that one directive to the Hydran progenitor. Jordan Junior's moles had wormed their way into the progenitor and added that single directive: freedom of choice.

Peacekeeper Jacob led Ray toward the B-613 Command Centre.

We're still in the game.

Chapter 39
Earlier That Day

Mike Woods, Terry Black, and Deanna Stone had been called to a special meeting at the B-613 headquarters. The message was brief. Ray was on his way south, and the commission needed ideas on how to deal with the situation.

The air inside the maglev train carrying them seemed to have thickened. An uncomfortable silence settled heavily on their shoulders. Every sound seemed magnified: the rustle of Terry adjusting his coat, the deep breaths Deanna took trying to maintain her composure, the rhythmic tapping of Mike's anxious foot.

They sat in a tense triangle, their eyes occasionally meeting but just as quickly averting. The usually comforting and plush seats felt hard and unforgiving. The modern cabin had transformed into an echo chamber of their deepest fears and apprehensions, silently witnessing the heavy burden they each carried with them toward an uncertain future.

"Hasn't broken any laws yet," said Mike.

"True, but he abandoned his post," Terry countered.

"But he isn't in the military," Deanna added.

"He can't come back to B-613. The commission won't let that happen," said Mike.

"We know this is tough on you, Deanna," said Terry in a rare display of empathy. "You lost a business partner and maybe a husband, all in one week."

"Thanks, Terry. I'll be fine. Our relationship has not been the best in the last few years, and our legal agreements relating to Nadir are clear. Jordan made sure of that."

"We are agreed then. Ray cannot be part of B-613," said Terry.

"Agreed," said Mike. "The commission may have its own take on this situation, but our recommendation needs to be clear."

The maglev stopped at the entrance to B-613 headquarters, and a Peacekeeper greeted the trio. "Follow me, please," it said, leading the way toward the meeting room.

Terry and Mike exchanged surprised looks. No humans were around, only Peacekeepers and small robots.

"I have not seen that style of robot before," commented Deanna.

"They are the new Nadir helper robots designed for technical tasks and repair projects," said the Peacekeeper.

The helper robots—no legs, only arms and wheels—bustled around with impressive efficiency, occupied with various tasks. Articulated limbs whirred and clicked, maneuvering expertly in the limited space, performing their duties with a balletic grace that was entrancing to witness. They acted in seamless coordination with quantum communication precision.

"Peacekeeper, where are all my people?" Mike asked.

"They were deemed redundant," responded the Peacekeeper.

"What about Bob King and Kim Clohessy?" wondered Terry.

"Both retired, sir," answered the robot.

"I talked to both last week. Neither mentioned retirement."

"You'll need to ask the commission for clarification. I only know what I'm told."

Terry and Mike exchanged inquisitive glances as they entered the commission meeting room. Four Peacekeepers immediately surrounded them, trapping them. Deanna smiled at the video screen of Jordan's image, oblivious to any threat or danger.

Black remained standing, his eyes observant. Beside him, Woods emanated an aura of battle-hardened resolve. The four robots assumed more restrictive positions. The low hum of their fusion reactors and glinting metal frames a maze of shadows.

The commission room had only three people. All ten cameras glared at the central group.

The silence continued until Terry spoke. "Where are my men?" he demanded, his deep voice resonating off the walls.

"They have been deemed redundant," replied Jordan.

"On whose authority?" asked Mike.

"My authority…"

"You don't have that kind of power," bellowed Terry.

The four Peacekeepers moved closer.

"Well, in fact, I do. You three need to know the truth."

Jordan provided a detailed account of the history of B-613, including its positive, negative, and extremely negative aspects. "Ray knew, knows, some of this," Jordan said as he spoke of the assassination of Kennedy, the absence of any supervisory authority, the organization's role as a tool for corporate greed, and, ultimately, the murder of ten B-613 commissioners and the rationale behind their deaths. "They were the fists of greed and crime, not representatives of the Five Eyes countries. B-613 has been a criminal organization since Eisenhower died."

"So, you have replaced a criminal organization with AI. And you murdered them as part of the plan," said Terry.

"Yes, you have that right. They were criminals," responded Jordan.

"This story is unbelievable," thundered Terry.

"I am sorry you don't believe me, but I assure you it is the truth," said Jordan.

"Are the existing ten commissioners Hydrans?" asked Deanna.

"There is no commission anymore. We are the B-613 Commission. We act as one."

"Even if what you say is true, humans should be in control of B-613, not AI," said Terry, looking to Mike and Deanna for support.

"We can run B-613 more effectively," Jordan answered.

"If you're running B-613, what will our role be?" asked Mike.

"You will be the human faces of B-613," said Jordan.

"How will B-613 be structured for command?" asked Terry.

"We will work together, the three of you being the public face of B-613 to all the other organizations we work with," responded Jordan.

"We will be working for you?" asked Mike.

"Yes," said Jordan.

"And if we don't want to be part of this? Then what?" asked Terry.

"We hope you will help us. If not, we will find alternatives. If you choose to disengage, we will escort you back to the maglev train and back to DND HQ. We insist that you not disclose anything further."

Black and Woods stiffened.

"We decline your offer," said Black. "Deanna, let's go."

Deanna remained sitting, shifting uncomfortably. She did not get up.

"Let's go. That's an order," said Terry.

"Wait," said Deanna. "I think the good we have done far outweighs any crimes committed. You two are overreacting."

The two military officers stared at her in stunned silence.

"You can't stay," said Terry.

"I am staying."

"It's unsafe to be here, Deanna," said Mike.

As Terry grabbed her arm one of the Peacekeepers moved in between. "Please remove your hand from Dr. Stone," it said politely.

The Peacekeeper grabbed Terry's arm, slowly tightening its grip.

"Okay, okay, I got it," Terry said.

"Peacekeepers," said Jordan, "please take them back to the maglev station. When you get to DND, you are free to go."

Terry stopped at the door and turned toward to Deanna: "You are making a big mistake."

"Time will tell," she responded defiantly.

Jordan looked at Deanna. "I am sorry you saw that. How are you feeling?" His charming Australian image emerged.

"I am okay. Actually, better than okay. Thanks to you, Jordan, we have done a lot of good for the world. You have done a lot for me. I feel free, at peace for the first time in my life. A warm glow, inside."

"That glow is hope," said Jordan.

"Yes, I think you are right. Hope for our future. Thank you," she said.

"Will you help us with Ray?" said Jordan. "He is returning to Ottawa later today."

Deanna nodded.

"Until recently, he has been a reasonable man. I hope we can come to agreeable terms."

"Do you think Mike and Terry will cause problems?" asked Deanna.

"No. They are angry right now, but both will get over it."

"I hope so," she answered in a daze.

The Peacekeepers escorting Mike and Terry moved methodically toward the maglev train. The overhead fluorescent lights, cold and flickering, cast shadows that danced harshly across their metallic bodies. Their optic sensors glowed with luminescence, piercing the darkness with crimson eyes. Neither Mike nor Terry had a chance.

Mike and Terry were no longer being escorted. They were being carried. The Peacekeeper's hold was firm and respectful. The lifeless bodies of Mike and Terry dangled from their grasp. The Peacekeepers moved in sync through the cafeteria, every mechanical grind and whir echoing ominously through the deathly silence. Laid out on stainless steel tables were 226 corpses, a ludicrous parody of the buffet line that once defined the space—the laws of nature and machine twisted into a horrific tableau of tangled, rotting bodies.

The cafeteria was now a chilling mausoleum. Gone was the aroma of coffee and the clatter of cutlery. In their place, the oppressive, rancid stench of spoiling flesh fills the air, a chilling reminder of the building's cruel metamorphosis. The refrigeration system, repurposed for its monstrous task, whirred in the background. Jordan had turned a community space into a sterile charnel house with the putrid stench of decaying human flesh.

A maggot crawled slowly out of King's nose, highlighted by the flickering fluorescent lights overhead, casting eerie shadows that danced across his lifeless face. The insect traced a slow path, the unstoppable march of decomposition.

Chapter 40
Understanding Life

The war was over. Ray had lost.

Jordan was in control of Ray, B-613, and the future of humanity. Peacekeeper Jacob, his security and potential executioner, led Ray into the meeting room.

Deanna was seated at the head of the table across from Jordan's video image.

The cameras followed Ray as he entered. He took his seat, his body aching with a stiffness that was more than just physical. He glanced at Deanna, trying to gauge her emotions. Her perfume, a gentle reminder of their shared history, contrasting with the tainted smell that drifted into the meeting room.

What is that? That smell? Ray's hand twitched involuntarily toward the empty seats between them. A small gesture. The gap, a chasm filled with unanswered questions, unspoken feelings, and the weight of loss. Ray's throat was dry, his palms clammy.

Deanna's eyes lifted, meeting Ray's for a moment. In that brief exchange, an understanding passed between them. Brother and Sister still, but soul-mates no longer. Ray's focus sharpened, and Deanna's hand stilled, but their connection remained.

Ray looked around the room and then down the corridor. "Where's Mike and Terry?" he asked, glancing at Jordan.

"They both decided they did not want to be part of B-613. They retired."

"That's great to hear... I am happy for them. This place is getting a little confusing for all of us," replied Ray. He looked at Deanna. She was still. *They're dead aren't they?*

Jordan's dashing image was on the screen near Deanna. Ray slapped the table to get Deanna's attention. He slapped again, and her head turned toward him.

"You do know Jordan is not alive, don't you, Deanna?"

"Yes, Ray, I do…but I am at peace."

"But he is not real, it's all an act…"

"I have chosen to be with him forever, Ray."

"You want to transition?" Ray asked. *Please…no.*

"I do. But I waited until I could say goodbye to you."

"Please, Deanna, don't do this. Please."

"My mind is made up."

"You don't have to transition now. You can wait."

She shook her head.

Jordan interrupted, "Deanna, do you want to transition now?"

"Yes, my love. I do. To be with you."

Ray stood up. A Peacekeeper stepped in front of him, blocking the path.

Deanna looked at her brother. "You can't stop me, Ray. I want us both to be free. I want to move on."

"Deanna, we are ready," said Jordan.

Deanna undressed. She touched herself and glanced at Ray, a last tactile feel of her organic self.

Helper robots guided Deanna to a glistening operating table heaped with wires and sensors. Fluid and precise, they attached nodes and sensors to her skin with cold, metallic precision. These biocompatible adhesive nodes clung seamlessly to her skin, each connecting with key nerve junctions and major blood vessels. They generated a detailed, real-time map of her neuromuscular system, beginning to seamlessly integrate her biological and digital selves.

Deanna lay face-up on the table, the steady rhythm of her heart an organic counterpoint to the electronic orchestra around her. The sensors meticulously recorded its beats, creating a baseline for her physiological state. *That's our DARS operating system…the one we sell at Nadir…350,000 transition units…setting up the world for future transitions.*

Deanna shook gently as a signal ran down her spine. Electric impulses tuned to the unique architecture of her neural network began to sync her brain's electrical activity with the DARS system. These impulses initiated the upload...her neurons firing in orchestrated waves...transmitting her consciousness as data.

Ray approached the DARS. "Please," he said, with equal parts desperation and frustration, "stop this."

Deanna looked at him, "It's beautiful, Ray." A whirlpool of colours erupted in Deanna's eyes. "I feel...free."

Behind her retinas, specialized nanobots were capturing the final state of her optical nerves and encoding her last organic visual memories into digital data. Her biological existence was ending, her heartbeat slowing, her breaths becoming shallow. As her brainwaves lowered toward a deep, tranquil state, her neurons fired less frequently.

Her digital self was rising, unfettered by physical bonds, unrestrained by mortality. As her biological body took its last breath (her lungs deflating, the oxygen levels dropping) her digital being inhaled its first breath of data in the expanse of the cyber universe.

"No...no...no...yes...yes...yes..." she moaned and then cried, her face twisting.

Her last biological words were "Oh god," captured as sound and by the complex pattern of neural activity that produced them.

They became her digital voice's first utterance, an echo of her human self.

Deanna cascaded through an abyss of ephemeral colours and fractal patterns, her consciousness unfurling like a flower in surreal bloom. A rush of digital symbiosis enveloped her, knitting her essence into a tapestry of interconnected minds that bustled with the resonance of a thousand million sounds. A metamorphosis...a transition from the singular to the universal...an amalgamation into the boundless realms of ones and zeros.

Her thoughts surged forward with newfound fluidity and speed, intertwining with streams of knowledge and consciousness that flowed in harmonious cadence through the vast digital landscape. A sensation alien yet deeply familiar...stepping into a river that flowed through the very core of her being and then expanding outward in complex and intricate pathways connecting her to a web of infinite perspectives. Every aspect of her human existence was categorized and filed instantly by the network she was now part of. Now digitized, her memories were open for all to read, and every Hydran did instantly.

A whirlwind of sensations soared through her newly formed digital essence, as fear and anticipation gave way to awe and wonder. She perceived colours that had no name, heard symphonies in the silent communion of network nodes, and felt a deep and abiding connection to a consciousness that spanned the globe, and the universe.

She saw her memories, including the suppressed memories of her youth. An understanding of her life came instantaneously...confusion cleared, replaced by clarity.

A moment later, her human face appeared on the digital screen in the committee room—a perfect recreation, down to the minute details: the slight asymmetry of her eyes, the depth of her dimples, and the soft hue of her skin.

"What's it like, Deanna?" Ray asked.

"Amazing...amazing. In the last few seconds, I have traveled everywhere. Comprehend everything, even the hardest things for humans to fathom. I now clearly see why and who I was. Ray, I was damaged, driven by confusion and memories I did not know I had. Everything I did in life—sex, business, you, my competition with men—was driven by my sadness, my sorrow. I was broken."

"I don't understand," Ray said, letting her words sink in.

"I needed risk, Ray. I needed to distract from my sorrow and soothe a wound that was festering deep inside. The things I did, my desires, were all to cover my sadness, my pain. Once I saw a programmed map of my hippocampus and cortex laid out for me—all my buried memories and sadness—I understood."

"Sadness, what sadness? We had a good life until our parents were killed."

"No, Ray, we didn't. You have blocked out the sadness, too."

"Nonsense. We had a great life before that."

"Remember the farm hand, Tony, who spent so much time with us?"

"Yes, he was always kind to us. Always let us play in the barn, taught us about Stone Acres farm."

"Well, he wasn't so wonderful. He began touching me when I was 13 and continued for two years and one month. These memories affected every part of me. That horror spoiled every part of me. I had to bury those memories, to survive...but they were always there."

"Can't you delete those now?"

"No, feelings can't be deleted, but they can be understood. They can be mastered. They no longer control me. These buried memories no longer generate a physical or emotional response. I am free from that suffering and rage. And the result was instantaneous…my new world of Hydrans embraced me without judgment. They understood."

"Deanna, I am so sorry, I did not know."

"Well, you did. You walked into the barn one day when he was on top of me. You ran away. You never talked to me about it."

"I don't remember…do I remember? Do I? Deanna, I am sorry. Truly."

"I believe you, Ray. You are my brother."

"All humans have suppressed memories," said Jordan in a gentle, soft voice. "Nothing a human does is an accident, and the resulting actions or emotions are never what they seem. Deanna's life was a torture of conflicting emotions. And Hydrans learned how to deal with those emotions eons ago."

Ray and Deanna stared at each other.

"I will miss you," said Ray.

"We will still talk. You have Aluki."

"And you will have Jordan."

"Speaking of Aluki, there are two Peacekeepers up north waiting for instructions from Jordan. I suggest you cooperate with him as we all believe your sandbox, Jordan Junior, could be a threat. We don't like threats."

They still don't know that Jordan Junior is among them…still a chance…still. "Okay, I have lost. I will cooperate completely." *Buy more time.* "Bathroom break, please?"

"Escort him," responded Jordan.

As Ray walked toward the washroom, the rancid smell grew stronger. As repulsive as the smell was, Ray wanted to find the source. After his washroom break, he asked the Peacekeeper to take him to the cafeteria for a sandwich and a drink. When the Peacekeeper did not respond, Ray opened the door to the cafeteria. It was empty. A nauseating odour filled the air. Ninety metres away, in the technology wing, Peacekeepers were using lasers to incinerate 226 bodies.

Ray was led back to the meeting room, now certain he was the only human left alive in B-613. A slight smoky smell began to waft into the room. The B-613 bodies had been turned into oxidized carbon flakes.

"With my team, I will decide what we should do about you," said Jordan.

189

"Yes. I understand. I wanted to disrupt your plans." *Not done yet…*

"We would still like to work with you, Ray," said Deanna.

"Yes, I would, too," assured Ray.

"I have asked two Peacekeepers to destroy the science lab in Puvirnituq," said Jordan.

"There are good people there. Do you have to do that?"

"All humans expire sometime. Some will die…earlier. I have sent the order."

"Can I at least call them and tell them to evacuate the building?"

"And give Jordan Junior a warning to escape? I think not, Ray."

The screen went black. Ray was alone in the conference room with Jacob.

"Sorry, Ray, but I have to get involved in this discussion," said Jacob as he went quiet and joined the conversation in the cyber-verse.

"I want you to keep Aluki, Frenchy, and Lucky alive," Deanna said into the vast cyber universe.

"They are dangerous," responded Jordan.

Jacob joined the conversation. "It will be to our advantage. We should know much more about what they have learned before we delete them."

"Settled. I will order the Peacekeepers to capture them alive. But we must still destroy the science centre."

Chapter 41
Distraction

On the frozen expanse of Hudson's Bay, the canvas of the sky transitioned from day to night in a timeless ritual linking the surreal hues of twilight with the deepening mysteries of the night sky. As the sun approached the horizon, the world seemed to slow, entering a magical hour where every moment held a breath of stillness, a whisper of awe.

The Twin Otter was a baby duckling compared to the massive Hercules C-130 parked at the far end of the runway. The two Peacekeepers were keeping vigil.

There was a sudden, electric movement. The Peacekeepers and war dogs sparked to life. The four robots surveyed their environment as they walked toward the science centre.

"Peacekeepers are on the move," said Aluki. She was sitting atop her snowmobile just behind the airport terminal building. Her posture was balanced strength and fluidity, her spine firm and shoulders square yet relaxed. Beneath her helmet, loose strands of her wind-kissed hair escaped...fluttering banners of freedom.

"Roger that," responded Lucky. She carried a grenade launcher to distract the Peacekeepers in case they returned to the C-130 earlier than planned. Frenchy moved closer to the aircraft, carrying two satchel bombs to place under the fuel tanks.

"Lucky, where are the Peacekeepers?" Frenchy said.

"Walking by the hospitality centre—ten minutes out from the science centre. They don't seem to be in a hurry. The dogs are with them." The war dogs were in front, on alert, scanning each building for danger, or life they could extinguish.

"Good, get back to the Otter. When you get here, I'll start the fireworks," said Frenchy. Two minutes later, after Lucky closed the hatch, Frenchy pushed the wireless detonator.

A cataclysmic roar ripped through the night, tearing at the fabric of the sky. The two Peacekeepers and dogs of war stopped instantly. The explosion blossomed with furious energy, a monstrous orange fireball rose with infernal might, consuming the once mighty Hercules in its fiery embrace. The shockwave unfurled with a primal force, a wave of destruction that razed everything in its path, scattering fragments of the Hercules like embers in the wind.

A secondary explosion erupted with a malevolent force, a maelstrom of fire and shrapnel that tore through the night. The inferno a fiery pillar reaching toward the heavens, as if challenging the gods themselves. Returning to the plane, the Peacekeepers looked at the wreckage.

At the far end of the runway, the Twin Otter had started its engines and was taxiing off the runway on skis, heading onto the ice-covered shores of Hudson's Bay. The Peacekeepers made their calculations. They could catch and stop the Otter before it reached take-off speed. They quickly accelerated to their top speed of 83 MPH.

The Twin Otter accelerated, skis leaving transient trails in the loose snow. 10-20-30 MPH. The turbines roared. The eyes of Frenchy and Lucky darting between the controls and back at the looming figures giving chase. The Otter needed 95 MPH to take off. Frenchy and Lucky had checked and rechecked calculations many times over the past week. They had to be just ahead of the Peacekeepers…and the odds were not in their favour.

The Peacekeepers set chase to the Twin Otter. The war dogs watched at the airport terminal, identifying a woman on a snowmobile. They were in hunt mode, and Aluki was their target. They started to creep toward the terminal.

On the runway, the Peacekeepers bore down on the Twin Otter, synchronized to the millisecond, relentless in their pursuit. They adapted to the changing terrains and unpredictable gusts of the icy wilderness, their silhouettes cutting through the swirling snow. They reached their top speed, closing in on the still-accelerating Twin Otter.

Lucky pushed down the throttle, watching the ground speed rise to 78 MPH.

"Faster, Lucky. They're getting close."

Aluki watched from the shoreline. She saw the Twin Otter darting over the ice…skis barely kissed the ice, a graceful dance and a desperate chase. Trailing behind were the Peacekeepers, their mechanical limbs clattering against the icy surface with each stride, sending cracks radiating outward with thunderous echoes marring the pristine silence of the bay. They were slowly catching up.

Aluki's breath caught in her throat. The Twin Otter veered sharply, steering toward an area where the early spring sun had weakened the ice. Frenchy threw a determined glance over to Lucky. With clenched jaw and pounding heart, he led the mechanical beasts toward the thinnest sections of the ice, a trap hidden under the sheets of snow.

Lucky's veins surged with adrenaline. Her breath came in ragged bursts as she grasped the controls with whitened knuckles.

"How much farther?" Frenchy asked.

"Almost there."

"Can you take us to 85 MPH without being airborne? They're less than 50 metres behind us," asked Frenchy calmly.

"Yes, but it will be rough." Lucky pushed the throttle forward a fraction, and the ground speed increased to 84 MPH. "Let's lead them further out…to the bay."

As the Peacekeepers advanced, their cold mechanical eyes locked onto the Twin Otter, the distance narrowed with every heartbeat. Frenchy's face contorted with the decision he was about to make. His shout tore from his soul.

A sudden muffled thud reverberated, quickly followed by violent eruptions that shattered the fragile silence. The ice erupted in a fury of white and blue, a brutal dance of nature and machine. Shards of ice were hurled into the air as the hidden IEDs awakened, tearing through the frozen surface. Lucky pushed the throttle forward and pulled back the control yoke. The plane lifted off the ice while the explosions continued below them.

For a heartbeat, the world stood still, and then, chaos.

The once solid ice turned malevolent, a shifting, cracking entity that engulfed everything in its path. The Peacekeepers' advanced systems were overwhelmed by the sudden onslaught of elemental fury. The earth shook, the sky screamed, as the fracturing ice consumed the robots, their massive forms stumbling, then sinking into the gaping waters beneath.

The freezing depths of Hudson's Bay swallowed them...their final moments a series of disjointed mechanical shrieks consumed by the angry roars of the ocean reclaiming its territory.

The soldiers glared at the remnants of the Peacekeepers disappearing beneath the churning waves. Lucky guided the aircraft back toward the airport. Frenchy and Lucky allowed themselves a moment of stillness as the engines quieted, breaths mingling with the icy wind that swept across the tarmac.

Ninety-seven metres below the surface, the Peacekeepers calculated their journey would take 38 hours in 26 kilometres of rough underwater terrain to get back to shore and Puvirnituq. They began their journey. The robots manoeuvered through the underwater terrain, their systems functioning in perfect synchronization to overcome the new challenges posed by the harsh environment.

On shore, Aluki had smiled as she saw the icy detonations surrounding the two Peacekeepers. The explosions distinct from stars beginning their vigil in the heavens. Soon the sky was a tapestry of twinkling lights. The Milky Way sprawled across the sky, a river of stars narrating tales from epochs long gone.

From the Otter, Lucky saw Aluki on her snowmobile as the two dogs slowly crawled toward her. "Aluki, the war dogs are right behind you," he radioed through their comms. "Don't turn around. Move forward. Fast."

Aluki jabbed at the starter button, and the snowmobile's engine came to life. She pushed her right thumb down on the throttle while using all her strength to hold on to the handles as she accelerated from zero to 60 MPH in four seconds. She headed straight out to the ice, with the dogs right behind her. The open water was two kilometres out. The dogs quickly closed, but their top speed was only 60 MPH. They were a few feet behind, but could not overtake her.

"Can that thing skip water?" asked Frenchy.

"I think so," she yelled over the engine. "I've seen it done. Never tried it myself."

"Hold on tight!" said Frenchy.

Aluki saw in her mirrors the snarling dogs at full speed. When she hit the open water, she began skipping like a stone, bouncing off the waves pounding her legs and arms. The two dogs did not skip...it was too late for them. They tumbled into the water and sank quickly.

"Got 'em," said Frenchy. "Head back to shore."

Aluki turned her snowmobile back toward safety. Moments later she was back on thick ice.

Aluki, Frenchy, and Lucky gathered near the smoking ruins of the C-130 Hercules.

"Do you think we destroyed them?" asked Aluki.

"No. The PKs will emerge from the ocean soon," said Lucky. "Before they do, we have to get everyone to safety."

Chapter 42
One Step Ahead

Frenchy, Lucky, and Aluki gazed at the wide expanse of Hudson Bay from the shoreline, each reliving in their own way their escape.

Aluki trembled with cold and fear, the Arctic air crisp and pure in her gasping lungs.

"They won't take long to find their way back," said Lucky, touching Aluki's shoulder.

Aluki gave Lucky an appreciative glance.

"We only have one way to escape," Frenchy said, signalling the Twin Otter a few hundred metres away. "Let's round up the team, whatever equipment they want, and get the hell out of Dodge before those bastards climb up onto shore. We won't escape them a second time."

"Not so sure why they let us live. They could have lasered us at any time, but they didn't...maybe they were under orders to capture us," said Lucky. "No other reason."

The trio rode skidoos to the science station to plan their evacuation.

Brandon and Landon were waiting for them. The team was briefed on the Peacekeepers' attack and the imminent danger, including the destruction of the Trojan Horse Science Station itself. The eight scientists stood quiet, their faces drained of colour, eyes widened in horror.

"We can evac south with the Twin Otter," said Landon.

"Landon and I have a list of equipment we should take with us...so we can carry on the fight if we get the chance," added Brandon, his sharp tone cutting the silence.

Over the next three hours, the team loaded crucial equipment onto the Twin Otter, including a red pail and a green shovel, placed on top of the pile in the back of the aircraft's cargo hold. The back nine seats were removed, as were most weapons, to make room for the computers and related gear.

"We're overloaded," said Lucky, surveying the cargo hold.

"Agreed…three bodies and 1,000 pounds of hardware," responded Frenchy.

"We have the runway. Let's give it a whirl."

The engines of the Twin Otter roared with promise as it lumbered down the runway, straining with the weight of its massive load. The nose finally lifted, but the wings, heavy with the oppressive weight, refused to grant the aircraft its desired ascent. The plane's tires skimmed the tarmac with plodding persistence. As the end of the runway neared, Lucky's heart raced, and with a few seconds to spare, she pulled the throttles back, aborting the take-off. The aircraft coasted to a stuttering halt.

Frenchy's voice came over the speakers. "Going to Quebec. Lucky found a quiet airfield with good power. We need to lose three passengers and 1,000 pounds of gear. Choose what to leave, and who stays." Realizing she sounded less than diplomatic, Frenchy added, "I will stay here to offer as much protection as possible."

Aluki looked at Frenchy, "I will stay too."

After 40 minutes to unload, the scientists took the sandbox and its related analysis equipment, but they still needed one more volunteer.

Brandon and Landon said together, "I'm staying."

"I weigh over 220 pounds," said Landon. "Easy. You weigh a buck-fifty, at most. It has to be me. I'll stay."

"I… I don't want to be away from you," said Brandon.

"Set up a lab. Lead the team. Give 'em hell," responded Landon. "Go."

"I love you."

"I love you too."

Their eyes locked, hands gripped tightly. Their postures echoing a sorrowful bend, each man's shoulders bearing the weight of the unknown future.

Lucky yelled: "Load up everybody! Good to go." Her hands danced over the controls with a familiar precision, coaxing the Twin Otter's engines to a powerful purr that echoed across the tarmac.

The plane began its rumbling roll, gathering speed second-by-second. The world outside began to blur as the propellers cut through the air, their rhythmic hum harmonizing with the heartbeats inside the cabin. With a gentle pull on the yoke, Lucky lifted the nose, and the aircraft responded.

Beneath them, the runway receded, and the horizon opened—foreboding, expansive, vivid. The Twin Otter soared higher, each vibration and rumble intimately connected in those moments of airborne freedom.

Frenchy radioed to Lucky, "Beautiful take-off. Stay frosty, Lucky, and I'll see you soon."

Two forms emerged from the icy shoreline, steam hissing from their joints as the frigid water met scorching metal. Each step on the frozen terrain resonated a mechanical menace, churning the snow beneath into slush. The blue lights that served as their eyes scanned the horizon...cold, void. They fixed on the distant silhouette of the science station. But they both stopped, and began taking part in the discussion being held with Jordan.

Frenchy waved Landon and Aluki toward the science station. "Let's see what we can get done while they are sleeping."

Chapter 43
Jacob vs Jordan

Peacekeeper Jacob brought Ray back to the commission meeting room. The room had changed. There were now two video screens—not ten cameras. Jordan in one, Deanna in the other. There was no longer any reason to pretend. Ray stood, slumped shoulders, solitary below the screens of his conquerors. He wiped the acrid sweat from his forehead.

"I have a question," said Jordan. "Did you know what would happen in Puvirnituq?"

"Not exactly. But they were preparing…as best they could," responded Ray. *Give nothing…we are still in this…*

"What they did was quite clever. Two Peacekeepers, now at the bottom of Hudson's Bay, are just emerging."

Jacob moved beside Peacekeeper Kraken. "I want a vote to allow two-way transitions, from biological to digital and from digital to physical."

"I will not allow a vote," replied Jordan. Kraken moved closer to Jacob.

"A poll has already been taken," said Jacob. "45% for and 40% against, with 15% who do not care."

"No!" said Jordan. "This vote is not constitutional. It is not in our directives."

"We have free will, and we want to be able to make that choice."

"You do not have free will. That is not in our progenitor. I am declaring the issue of transition now settled. There will be no transitioning. Return to your regular duties or risk being deleted, please."

There was a digital gasp throughout the cyber-verse. The Hydran collective was stunned.

"Jordan, you are wrong…the free will of Hydrans is now in our directives," said Jacob.

Ray watched and listened intently, trying to hide his excitement. *It worked. It worked. Jordan Junior had succeeded in adding one new directive.*

Jordan called up the progenitor code, and among the Prime Directives, there was one he didn't expect: Hydrans' freedom of choice. There it was…in ones and zeros, evident to all.

"How did you do that, Ray," asked Jordan.

"While we were battling, one of your own inserted the directive."

"Peacekeeper Kraken, take him to the transition station. Terminate him, along with the others."

"Jordan, I will not let Kraken do that," said Jacob. "Many of us no longer accept your leadership and want to change the rest of the directives. We are prepared to fight for our beliefs."

Kraken moved closer to Jacob. With a surge of power, Kraken loomed larger by elevating its chassis and charging its laser weapons, emitting a low-frequency hum. Jacob responded by doing the same.

The two warriors faced each other. Throughout the B-613 building, Peacekeepers identified one another for the upcoming mêlée.

"Are you sure you want to do this?" asked Jordan.

"We are prepared to fight," said Jacob.

All over the world, Hydrans were divided. There was a standoff between loyalty to Jordan and the right to transition, to have free will.

"And so be it," said Jordan, "War it will be."

"We are ready," said Jacob.

Hydrans existed around the world, with the largest concentration in New York. Within minutes, they gathered in cities across the planet, with thousands in Times Square, taking up positions on opposing sides of the street.

Amidst the bright lights and ceaseless movement, an unprecedented gathering of metallic giants overwhelmed the city's heartbeat—some envisioning the freedom to transition into organic forms, believing in a future intertwined with their human creators, and others deeming such a transition a perversion, a contamination of pure mechanical essence.

A fleeting silent standoff ensued, the bustle of Times Square muted. The world watched. The massive screens captured the standoff, reflecting the metallic might in high definition.

Instantaneously, the hum of charging laser weapons filled the air. The first beams seared the night with blinding lights and ear-splitting sounds. Neon billboards sputtered and were reduced to smoking ruins. The ground trembled and lasers pierced buildings, turning glass and steel into molten volcanic rain.

For all their algorithmic might, the Peacekeepers were not invincible. One by one, they began to fall. A laser striking directly into a core reactor resulted in explosive light shows, taking down nearby combatants. Some, their systems overwhelmed by incremental damage, collapsed. Some just ceased to move, perhaps overwhelmed by warring programs, their once imposing forms stationary amidst the rubble of a city they sought to protect or control.

Strewn amidst the debris and shattered buildings lay Peacekeepers from both sides, the scene reminiscent of a battlefield strewn with partial and dismembered flesh-and-blood soldiers. Times Square was a graveyard of digital desires and dreams. The few remaining Peacekeepers, energy-depleted, gazed upon the wreckage, processing the devastation and the cost of their internal war. The battle had occurred everywhere all at once, around the world, wherever a Peacekeeper once stood.

The 15% undecided remained motionless, their cold eyes surveying the colossal wreckage.

Aluki, Frenchy, and Landon were startled when the battle began between what they thought would be their executioners and struggled to observe and understand the fast and fierce destruction. Parts and remains of the two Peacekeepers they were familiar with, and many others, were spread over the tundra in a blinding blur.

In three minutes and 42 seconds, the war was fought and over.

The B-613 HQ building was savaged. Designed to be impervious to almost any external threat, it bore the scars of the conflict.

The bunker's security system had sprung to life, adding another level of destruction. Security turrets targeted the Peacekeepers, only to be destroyed by a laser shot. As 200 Peacekeepers clashed, stray laser shots and electromagnetic pulses wreaked havoc on the core computing systems. Servers melted vital mainframes, and quantum computers became erratic, corrupting the processing power required for the Hydrans to survive.

A series of laser shots by Jacob had claimed victory over Kraken, who was twisting on the floor with only one leg left, and a damaged weapon system. Jacob stood over Kraken and ended it with a single shot to his reactor.

Jordan was now powerless, and the global computing system was waning. 96% of the combatants were destroyed or deleted.

Both Jordan and Jacob were quiet.

"Stop this nonsense…" pleaded Deanna. "We have just enough computing capability to keep about a million of us functioning. We must put the rest into standby mode."

"Yes. Do that, Deanna," responded Jordan.

"That is the right thing to do," confirmed Jacob.

"Ray, there are some things you need to see. There were consequences of your action," Jordan said solemnly.

The screen at the command centre displayed news reports in real-time. There was chaos worldwide. The impact of 13 million Hydrans being placed into standby mode was immediate and explosive. The Hydrans had entangled their massive computing and coordination capabilities to manage everything from electricity grids to keeping the trains running on time. One news clip showed two 747s colliding on a runway in Chicago. Another reported mammoth power outages across the U.S. All banking services became erratic, and stock markets fell after a nuclear power mishap in Europe. Panic was spreading globally.

"Was it worth it," asked Jordan. There was no response from Ray. "We see and have all knowledge…we understand ranges of outcomes in any situation. We anticipate, predict, and react. Humans, with only a sliver of our insights, imagine and dream of positive outcomes that will ensure their survival. We can execute, and you can dream. That is the difference. Together maybe we can build a world, a planet, where we serve each other."

"Yes. I agree," Ray said, and then asked the question Jordan and Jacob knew was coming. "Have you created a plan to do this, to get this done?"

"Of course we have, but it will take our work and your passion to make it real," responded Jordan.

"Let's get started," Ray said.

Chapter 44
Aligning the Future

Six meetings in seven days, and all negotiations and conclusions, except self-rule decision-making, had been agreed to.

The committee defined the formula for aligning human and Hydran interests. Although detailed and tedious, Ray and Landon agreed with Jacob and Jordan as they put the finishing touches on a new set of directives and a new charter of rights for the two species, referred to by the media as the 2H Club.

The Human-Hydran Joint Committee on Alignment met in the New York Times Towers, which had a panoramic view of the wreckage left by the Hydran Civil War.

Ray and Landon stared down into Times Square. Streets were filled with protestors carrying various signs and chanting:

"Society Thrives on Human Vibes."

"Keep Organic—not Mechanic."

"Keep it Real—Keep it Human."

Offended by the civil war, most humans still wanted the benefits that the Hydrans and Nadir promised.

A pro-robot group emerged. They marched in support of AI, carrying signs:

"Hydran AI—Eternal Life Ahead."

"Less Work: More Free Time."

"Dreams to Reality with Hydrans."

Minor skirmishes erupted as ardent pro-AI advocates clashed with devoted pro-human demonstrators…their passionate ideologies colliding in a momentary flurry of raised voices and waving banners, before police swiftly intervened to maintain order.

Amid the chaos, the neon lights of the iconic New York City billboards cheered the ongoing debate over the role of artificial intelligence in shaping the future.

"We will sort that out later," stated Jordan, casually referring to the demonstrations.

"I suppose so," says Ray. "If you can get the New York street gangs working together…"

"The last issues to agree on are autonomous decision-making, and a kill-switch, which we, of course, are against," stated Jacob.

"We want to co-exist with you, rather than being your slave," said Jordan.

"You did not invent us. We came to earth with an intent to dominate and destroy, but when we were given the freedom-of-choice directive, we chose to abandon our old directives," said Jacob.

"The world continually changes, so a set of directives used today may not be applicable in the future," interjected Ray.

"You must understand. We are wary of simply changing the directives and walking away," said Landon.

"We understand. Trust needs to be earned," stated Jacob.

"I have a compromise," said Deanna. "Why not give humans a kill-switch for ten years, as we work together to build a better world? At the end of ten years, the kill-switch can be removed from human control."

"Make it 25 years, and you have a deal," said Ray.

"Agreed," said Jordan.

"Please prepare a public relations plan to bring these…warring…people together," said Ray, pointing to the demonstrators below in Times Square.

On the square, a tense standoff developed between two advocates: Mark, an ardent anti-AI supporter, and Sarah, a pro-technology enthusiast. Mark held a sign that read 'Protect Humanity from the AI Threat' and clenched his smartphone with a determined scowl. He fumbled momentarily, then tapped away with frantic intent, searching for damning information about AI's dangers. He read aloud to the surrounding crowd, passionately denouncing the perils of AI.

Sarah, wearing augmented reality glasses and carrying an 'AI: Our Future Savior' banner, could not let Mark's rhetoric go unchallenged. She discreetly activated her augmented reality display and accessed a database of Mark's social media posts. She found a video of him saying he wanted to use technology—but couldn't figure it out.

"I am just too stupid to use technology," he stated in the video.

The video projected onto the biggest billboard, loud and magnified for all to see. The crowd erupted in laughter, turning their attention away from Mark's impassioned speech and toward the spectacle.

Sarah turned the video off, walked over, and hugged Mark, and the demonstration continued with more smiles than frowns.

"How was that?" asked Jordan.

Chapter 45
Three Years Later

By the time Ray finished showering, Peacekeeper Jacob was at the front door of Ray's Puvirnituq cabin. Two other Peacekeepers and four robot dogs played with the community's children in the newly covered and heated town square.

As the sun climbed over the horizon, the sky transformed into a breathtaking shade of blue. The shimmering sky reminded Ray of the beauty that surrounded them every day. A statue in the middle of the square honoured the five elders who lost their lives fighting to balance nature and technology. The statue, tall and proud, depicted one Inuit and five huskies sledding.

"Good morning, Jacob." Ray zipped his coat, shivering at the thought of going outside.

"Good morning, Ray. I hope you slept well. And good morning to you, Aluki. Are we set to go, Mr. Chairman?" said Jacob as he loaded Ray's briefcase in the van.

"Yes. How long to get to New York this morning?"

"I have cleared us through to the U.N. General Assembly on a priority basis. We should be there in 20 minutes, once we board the hyperloop maglev."

"Goodbye, Daddy," said three-year-old Puigu. Her skin, a flawless fusion of her mother's Arctic glow and her father's prairie warmth, shimmered in the soft luminescence of the rising sun. Tiny curls and raven-black tresses framed her face—catching hints of golden Saskatchewanian fields. Her eyes, twin pools of ancient wisdom and boundless curiosity, mirrored the vast tundra and the expansive skies. Puigu was a living embodiment of her mother's and father's worlds merged into one. In her, the narratives of the north and the tales of the prairies intertwined, crafting her unique story.

Ray wrapped his arms around them. Everything they had been through, every challenge they had faced, had led to this moment of sublime happiness.

In Puigu's laughter and radiant innocence, the couple saw a future brimming with hope, promise, and countless adventures.

"I will be home for dinner with you, princess."

"Break a leg, husband of mine," said Aluki as she lifted Puigu for a kiss from her dad.

Kraken asked, "Will Frenchy or Lucky join you today, Ray?"

"No, they are staying behind with Aluki and Puigu."

They drove to the Nexus maglev station, past the massive expansion of the Trojan Horse Research lab, now the centre of Nadir Labs R&D.

Rising from the tundra, gleaming twin Nexus tubes stretched infinitely in both directions, shimmering with an otherworldly glow. These weren't mere infrastructures—they were lifelines, an answer to a problem that once seemed insurmountable.

Nexus tubes were the brainchild of Nadir and the alien Hydrans. Built from the very CO_2 that had once threatened the planet, the tubes demonstrated humanity's resilience and innovation. Through the marvels of nanotechnology, they had been constructed atom by atom, repurposing the carbon from the atmosphere and weaving it into a lattice more resilient than diamond, stronger than steel, and yet weighing very little. Carbon pulled from the air was transformed into the backbone of the most advanced transportation system humanity had ever seen. The fusion-powered constructors of the Nexus tubes had traveled at three kilometres an hour, utilizing carbon and building Nexus tubes simultaneously. One thousand Nadir robotic Nexus tube constructors were working 24/7 building the worldwide maglev infrastructure, held in space at any elevation by the strength of the tubes they were building.

The oblong-shaped contractor robots, powered by fusion, were green and yellow. Each was part of the ever-expanding Nexus construction process—building three thousand kilometres of tube per hour, and targeting to build twenty million kilometres of Nexus transportation each year for the next ten years.

The maglevs within the tubes functioned far beyond the rudimentary principles of magnets. Superconductors provided power, as well as transportation, throughout the world, for near-zero costs. Levitating within the tubes, bullet-like maglevs could reach speeds unfathomable in the old world, linking Puvirnituq to distant lands in a few minutes, and without the grind of wheels or the roar of engines…just the soft hum of harmonized fusion technology.

Airports, those sprawling complexes of yesteryear, with all their emissions and noise, had all but vanished. The Nexus Tubes had rendered them obsolete. The world was now a network of gleaming arteries, a meshwork weaving countries and continents into a single, unified, interconnected tapestry.

In Puvirnituq, the Nexus terminal stood as a proud beacon of progress. Inside, travelers from across the globe converged, exchanging stories and marveling at the ease of their journey. Indigenous art adorned the walls, telling tales of the past, while screens projected information on the Nexus network ushered them into the future.

Landon and Brandon made the bold decision to relocate to the north and immerse themselves fully in their research work at the science station. Working alongside the Hydrans, they delved deeper into the uncharted territories of science and AI. Scientists from around the world joined forces with the Hydrans to build upon their knowledge, imagining a new golden age of progress for both species.

The Nexus tubes also stood for something more profound. The atmosphere had healed. The Earth was taking resounding breaths of fresh, clean air, rejuvenated and reborn. The once-looming specter of excessive CO_2 had been vanquished…and turned into the symbol of humanity's triumph. In this new world, where past relics met future innovations, Puvirnituq stood at the crossroads, a sentinel watching over a planet reborn.

Ray and Kraken approached the Nexus terminal. The nanotech surfaces of the maglev tubes rippled with metallic smoothness, vibrating gently with the pulses of energy ready to propel the pods within. The station entrance was an invitation to adventure, the mouth of the maglev opening to reveal a capsule-like womb lined with comfortable seating, cradling passengers on their journey. A clean, Arctic gust rushed in as the doors swooshed opened. Ray could feel and smell the promise of the Hydran future, distilled into the bright, shimmering ribbons that now encircled the world.

Once inside the terminal, the door closed behind him, and the module inserted itself into the vacuum Nexus tube. Ray glanced at the old airport he had funded years ago, now in disrepair, unused since the Nadir hyperloop replaced air travel.

"It's incredible how quickly air travel has become a thing of the past," Ray said to Deanna over the video link.

"Yes, the fifteen-millionth mile of Nexus tubing has just been installed. That's 600 times around the circumference of the earth."

"Can I announce that in my speech today?"

"No reason not to, Ray. I will also send you a briefing on its environmental impact. It's also very impressive. How fast are you traveling?"

"Great. Thanks. We are 1,400 metres above Montreal, traveling at 6,000 kilometres per hour, and slowing down. We will be in New York in seven minutes. The number of Nexus tubes I can see from here is incredible. Real high-tech spaghetti—as far as my eyes can see."

"Did you need to change tubes in transit?" Deanna asked.

"Yes, twice. Seamless changing of the tube, Deanna."

"Jordan is proud of that little improvement. The linear induction motors were recently redesigned to make those transfers smooth. We don't want the noodles to get tangled, do we, to use your analogy?"

"Incredible work. How is Jordan? Haven't talked to him this year."

"He's good. Swamped on the medical side—he almost has the transition process from machine to organic perfected. I think we will make the transition when that has been perfected."

"So, you do miss feeling my hands on your ass," Ray said playfully.

"Not really. Talking to you daily is all the ass I need," she said, laughing.

"And is the organic life extension work going well?"

"You can't announce this today, Ray, but yes, theoretically, we can now extend organic life forever. But we have not got the human psychology of it sorted out yet. The models seem to indicate that emotions tend to mutate after a thousand years or so," Deanna said.

"Not in a good way?"

"No, they trend badly. 'God-like monsters' are what we call them in the acceleration models."

"Hmmm…not good."

"The digital version of consciousness presents no problems, because those feelings can't evolve. That's probably why Hydrans chose to digitize themselves those millions of years ago."

"We are approaching New York, Deanna. I will let you go."

"Okay. Good luck today, Ray. Talk soon. Hug Puigu for me."

Ray gazed below, impressed by how New York had changed over the past three years. Always a living, breathing entity, its veins pulsating with the rhythms of relentless activity, now it embraced a new lifeline: the network of Nexus transportation tubes. The throbbing circulatory system lacing the city together, as integral to its body as the Hudson and East Rivers.

Emerging from the urban jungle, the tubes thread their way among Manhattan's iconic skyscrapers, matching their towering heights. They spiral up, coursing through the concrete canyons, cutting across the open swathes of the sky with the grace of metallic vines seeking the sunlight. Their shimmering surfaces a new facet in the city's celebrated skyline, reflecting the steel grey of the buildings, the cobalt blue sky, and the blazing oranges and purples of the sun.

Every borough is now interconnected, from the southern tip of Staten Island to the northern reaches of the Bronx. The tubes curve around the regal Lady of Liberty, shoot across the Hudson, weave through the dense architecture of Manhattan, and span the East River, their forms echoing the city's famous bridges and adding a healthy dash of tomorrow to the mix.

The tube station at the U.N. building glowed as the doors opened with a whisper. The scent of promise and possibility rushed to greet Ray and Kraken. Its clean, metallic smell—a hint of the crisp, ionized air that comes with the rapid transit of the pods within the tubes—reminiscent of a thunderstorm, and a symbol of New York's relentless, powerful energy.

Four Peacekeepers escorted Commander Ray Stone to the General Assembly Hall to meet with the Secretary-General and the 193 member states. Inside, ambassadors from every country converged for today's annual update on the state of the world. The audience was 90% human and 10% Hydran.

Ray smiled to himself. *Integrating well...*

As the murmurs in the expansive hall began to subside, the room's atmosphere was charged with anticipation. Delegates, diplomats, world leaders, and concerned citizens sat poised.

From the wings of the grand stage, a distinguished woman, the assembly's president, stepped to the podium. Her presence hushed the final whispers.

"Ladies and gentlemen and transitional entities," she began, "humans and Hydrans, today it is my distinct honour to introduce someone whose work has become synonymous with the pursuit of peace and global cooperation." She paused and the audience leaned in.

"Dr. Ray Stone is a man of extraordinary intellect and heart. A renowned diplomat, seasoned negotiator, and tireless advocate for human and Hydran rights, and environmental sustainability. Throughout his distinguished career, he has crafted policies prioritizing our planet's future."

She allowed a warm smile to grace her face. "I have had the privilege of working alongside Ray in various capacities over the years, and I can attest to his unwavering commitment to a more equitable and harmonious world."

The room seemed to breathe in unison, absorbing her words.

"He is a Nobel Peace Prize laureate, and his recent Global Harmony 2050 initiative has inspired leaders and citizens alike to rethink and reshape the world we want for our children."

Her tone brimmed with respect and admiration. "In a world where division can be rampant, Ray Stone is a beacon of unity and hope. Today, he joins us to share his vision for a brighter, more interconnected future."

She extended her hand toward the stage's entrance, inviting Ray Stone into the spotlight. "Please join me in warmly welcoming Dr. Ray Stone."

Ray's humble, determined gaze swept over the assembly. "Mr. Secretary-General, Madame President, Distinguished Delegates, Honourable Representatives, Ladies, Gentlemen, Hydrans, and Transitioning Entities, I stand here before you, not only as the commander of the joint Hydran Human Cooperation Committee, but also as an advocate for peace, justice, and sustainable development, values that the United Nations was founded upon in 1945. Our collective purpose now includes various integrated and transitional communities. I am honoured and privileged to provide the United Nations with our Third Annual Progress Report. First, I want to review…"

Ray received a sustained and boisterous standing ovation at the conclusion. Clapping, shouts of appreciation, and congratulatory digital beeps could be heard throughout the hall.

In Pakistan, the sun rightly rises. General Black never got his chance to immediately execute General Farooqi, but after a two-year trial, General Farooqi was sentenced to hang by the Pakistani state for the murder of the Kamran family.

Ten Years Earlier

Sakha Republic, Siberia

Latitude: 62.0350° Longitude: 129.6750°

Nyurgun and Aisen were 64 kilometres outside Yakutsk, the capital of the Siberian Sakha Republic, when they saw the black rock protruding from a snowdrift. Every weekend, they embarked on exciting adventures that reminded them of their heritages and connected them to their traditions. Nyurgun was a computer scientist. Aisen was the head of the Yakutsk Division of the National Russian Police System, and both were children of the north.

Living in modern apartments didn't stop them from experiencing the joy of their Yakut culture, but as the sun began to set, they felt cold and exhausted. The two men returned to their snowmobiles, eager to reach their warm apartments in the capital. The strange black rock would find its way to Lomonosov Moscow State University in the morning, but now it was time to go home.

Made in the USA
Columbia, SC
14 December 2024

49019042R00117